NEW ORLEANS STORIES

GREAT WRITERS ON THE CITY

Edited By **JOHN MILLER**
AND **GENEVIEVE ANDERSON**

Introduction by Andrei Codrescu

CHRONICLE BOOKS
SAN FRANCISCO

Special thanks to Susannah Clark, Tom Morgan, and the New Orleans Public Library

ISBN: 0-8118-4494-3

The Library of Congress has cataloged the previous edition as follows:

New Orleans stories : great writers on the city / edited by John Miller
   and Genevieve Anderson.
   p.   cm.
   ISBN 0-8118-0059-8 (pbk.)
   1. American literature—Louisiana—New Orleans. 2. New Orleans
(La.)—Literary collections. 3. American literature. I. Miller,
John II. Anderson, Genevieve.
PS559.N4N43   1992
810.8'03276335—dc20   91-26303
                                                               CIP

Manufactured in the United States of America

Editing: John Miller and Genevieve Anderson
Book design: Linda Herman + Company
Cover design: Kimberly Glyder
Cover photo: Tim Bieber/GETTY
Composition: TBH Typecast

Distributed in Canada by Raincoast Books
9050 Shaughnessy Street
Vancouver, British Columbia V6P 6E5

10 9 8 7 6 5 4 3 2 1

Chronicle Books LLC
85 Second Street
San Francisco, CA 94105
www.chroniclebooks.com

TABLE OF CONTENTS

Introduction by ANDREI CODRESCU   iv

ANONYMOUS: *The Exploration of Louisiana*   3

WALKER PERCY: *The Moviegoer*   9

LOUIS ARMSTRONG: *Growing Up in New Orleans*   23

ANNE RICE: *The Feast of All Saints*   39

ZORA NEALE HURSTON: *Hoodoo*   57

LAFCADIO HEARN: *A Creole Mystery*   67

JOHN KENNEDY TOOLE: *A Confederacy of Dunces*   70

JOHN JAMES AUDUBON: *New Orleans Journal*   82

TENNESSEE WILLIAMS: *A Streetcar Named Desire*   86

TRUMAN CAPOTE: *Dazzle*   105

WILLIAM THACKERAY: *A Mississippi Bubble*   116

M. DUMONT: *Indian Troubles and Hangmen*   119

ISHMAEL REED: *Mumbo Jumbo*   123

WILLIAM FAULKNER: *Absalom, Absalom!*   127

ELLEN GILCHRIST: *Rich*   134

MARK TWAIN: *Southern Sports*   155

CARL SANDBURG: *A Scar for Abraham Lincoln*   163

KATE CHOPIN: *Cavanelle*   167

JOHN DOS PASSOS: *Funiculi Funicula*   173

WALT WHITMAN: *Three New Orleans Sketches*   181

ROBERT PENN WARREN: *Mason City*   190

LYLE SAXON: *Gumbo Ya Ya Superstitions*   199

Author Biographies   213

INTRODUCTION

Andrei Codrescu

There are certain cities and certain areas of certain cities where the official language is dreams. Venice is one. And Paris. North Beach in San Francisco. Wenceslaus Square in Prague. And New Orleans, the city that dreams stories. Writers come and eavesdrop and take some of those stories with them, but these are just a few drops from a Mississippi River of stories. The Mississippi brings all its stories here from the rest of the country and can barely contain itself from bursting when New Orleans adds its own stories. (The greatest story of them all is in fact the tragic love of the old man Mississippi for the considerably younger and swifter Atchafalaya River, a love that the Army Corps of Engineers has been doing its darndest to prevent with locks and keys and cement . . . all in vain, according to most river watchers. In time, old man river will join his love.)

Ghosts and pirates, the subjects of some of the stories in this book, are thick as the morning fog on certain days in New Orleans. You open your notebook at some outdoor café in the Vieux Carré and find yourself holding instead intense congress with the shadows between the huge leaves of the palm or the fig above you. On certain afternoons light filters its arabesques through the grille work of the balconies and you dream without touching your coffee. The dead pass casually by: Buddy Bolden, the creator of Jazz; young Louis Armstrong; Marie Laveau, voodoo queen on whose grave at St. Louis Cemetery there are fresh offerings every night; Jean Lafitte, the pirate, whose treasure is still buried in the fireplace of the Old Blacksmith Shop on Bourbon Street; beautiful and sad Creole mistresses of French and Spanish aristocrats; old carnival krewes; and mobs of others, slaves, sailors, adventurers, writers.

Near where I live, there is the Lafayette Cemetery on Prytania Street. Anne Rice's Vampire Lestat lives in one of the tombs. F. Scott Fitzgerald wrote *This Side of Paradise*, his first novel, in an apartment overlooking the cemetery. He was 23 years old. A few decades later, a young poet,

Everette Maddox, moved to New Orleans and rented Fitzgerald's apartment. It's still available, cheap, like everything else in New Orleans. There is no memorial plaque. If New Orleans went into the memorial plaque business for all the writers who ever lived here they would have to brass-plate the whole town. There is a plaque on Pirate's Alley on the house Faulkner lived in but there isn't any on Audubon's house.

When writers come here they walk about smelling everything because New Orleans is, above all, a town where the heady scent of jasmine or sweet olive mingles with the cloying stink of sugar refineries and the musky mud smell of the Mississippi. It's an intoxicating brew of rotting and generating, a feeling of death and life simultaneously occurring and inextricably linked. It's a feeling only the rich music seeping all night out of the cracks of homes and rickety clubs can give you, a feeling that the mysteries of night could go on forever and that there is little difference between life and death except for poetry and song. Rarely do writers come here to meet other writers. The life about them suffices. I saw Richard Ford at a party here and asked him what he was doing. "Been living here for two years," he said. I had no idea. Now and then I hear of other writers moving quietly in. You meet them occasionally, but you're just about as likely to run into Walt Whitman, drinking café au lait and eating beignets at Café du Monde.

The other day, passing the ornate façade of the old United Fruit Company building (the company made famous by the great poet Pablo Neruda's curse on it) I had the fleeting thought that everyone, dead or alive, returns to New Orleans. If people can't come back in their lifetimes they come back when they are dead. And everyone who ever lived here, the costumed Spanish and French dandies, the Victorian ladies of Kate Chopin's age, the whores and ruffians, and the poets, are all still here. In a city like New Orleans, built for human beings in the age before cars, it's possible to move about the streets with ease and there is plenty of room for everyone.

New Orleans is a small city but it seems spacious because it is always full of people . . . like a crowded barroom at night. At dawn, a deserted barroom seems small beyond belief: how did all those people fit? The answer is that space and time are subjective no matter what the merciless clock of late-twentieth-century America tells us. And there is more subjective time and space here in New Orleans than almost anywhere else in

the United States. Which is not to say that the sad ironies of dehuman-
ized commerce and violence do not touch us here: they do, as Walker
Percy's *Moviegoer* or John Kennedy Toole's Ignatius Reilly amply prove.
But the city puts up a fight, a funny, sad fight composed sometimes of
sly stupidities and Third World inefficiency. The city can drive a sober-
minded person insane, but it feeds the dreamer. It feeds the dreamer
stories, music, and food. Really great food.

NEW ORLEANS STORIES

STORIES

GREAT WRITERS ON THE CITY

Anonymous

The Exploration of Louisiana

On MONDAY, March 2nd, 1699 [nearly five months after the expedition, consisting of four ships and around five hundred men, set sail from Brest], we sighted the mainland [of Louisiana] and coasted along the whole distance in our long-boats. A few of our company were in bark canoes. The seas ran so high that we were obliged to fix up tarred canvas on the gunwales about a foot in height to prevent the water from breaking into the boats. We drew nearer the land for fear of missing the river. We sailed closer to the wind and took in our large sail to avoid being driven ashore. After beating about in the seas for two hours, and fearing the waves would fill the bark canoes, M. d'Iberville, our commander, made us run before the wind. At this moment we perceived a pass between two banks, which appeared like islands. We saw that the color of the water had changed. We tasted it and found it fresh, a circumstance that gave us great consolation in that moment of consternation. Soon after we beheld the thick, muddy water. As we advanced, we saw the passes of the river, three in number. The current of the stream was such that we could not ascend it without difficulty, although the wind was fair and favorable. The entrance of the Mississippi runs southeast and west by northwest, and may be about a quarter of a league wide at its estuary.

The coast consists of nothing more than two narrow strips of land, about a musket shot in width, having the sea on both sides of the river, which flows between these two strips of land, and frequently overflows them. At four o'clock, after having ascended the river one league and a half, we landed in a thick cane-brake, which grows so tall and thick on both banks of the river, that it is difficult to see across, and is impossible to pass through without cutting it down. Beyond the canes are impenetrable marshes. The banks are also bordered by trees of prodigious heights, which the current of the river draws down to the sea, with their roots and branches.

We found twelve feet of water at the pass, and within from twelve to fifteen fathoms. On Tuesday, the 3d, mass was performed, and a *Te Deum* sung in gratitude for our discovery of the entrance of the Mississippi river;* after which we made a light breakfast, wishing to be sparing of our provisions, which consisted of two casks of biscuit, a small quantity of peas, and a quarter of flour for each long-boat. We set sail with a northeast wind. At a quarter of a league from our encampment we found a large arm of water, which broke over everywhere. At nine o'clock, we were dismasted in a squall. We landed as soon as possible to adjust our masts, and found an abundance of blackberries, nearly ripe, and a few trees, of middle height. The banks of the river ran west by northwest. At five leagues from the mouth, it is not more than musket-shot wide. There are bushes on each side, but as you ascend the banks appear more and more submerged, the land being scarcely visible. We saw a great quantity of wild game, such as ducks, geese, snipe, teal, bustards, and other birds.

Between five and six o'clock we landed and encamped in fine country. Some of our men went hunting and found a variety of animals, such as stags, deer, and buffaloes. The wind continued moderately fresh and somewhat cold. We must have been ten leagues from the entrance of the river. On the 4th, which was Ash Wednesday, religious ceremonies were attended by everyone. Mass was said and a cross was planted. After that we breakfasted and, at seven, embarked again. The wind having calmed, we took to the oars and rowed about two leagues. We saw some small canoes, each made from three bundles of cane, bound with thin wooden straps.

The Indians make use of these in the chase and in crossing from one side of the river to the other. At six o'clock we landed and encamped. On ascending a tree we could sight the sea at a distance of about a league and a half from us. At this point we found the rapidity of the current stronger than usual. One of our bark canoes, which had remained behind with three hunters, reported they saw

---

* This discovery took place seventeen years after La Salle had explored the Mississippi to its mouth. The Mississippi had been discovered in 1542, by Hernando de Soto, 140 years before La Salle's exploit.

three crocodiles [alligators] on the bank of the river. This day we made eight leagues, assisted by the sails. The forest trees began to assume larger dimensions, but not very close together, for we could see across the country, which was very marshy. We had made, altogether, some eighteen or nineteen leagues in the river.

On Thursday, the 5th, three of our men went hunting at daylight; they saw many tracks and heard the howlings of wild beasts. We planted a cross and made several marks upon the trees, and fired off one of our swivels to give notice to the savages. We breakfasted, as usual, with a soup made of flour, water, and lard, for we always reserved the lard for breakfast. Saw a large crocodile on the river banks, sunning himself. Some of our men fired at him, when he immediately threw himself into the water. At eleven o'clock we saw smoke arising from the burning grass, to which the Indians had set fire, either to drive out the game or obtain easier access to fire upon us. At noon we landed to dine, as the wind was contrary. At three o'clock, in going up the river, saw a canoe which had been hollowed out by burning from the trunk of a large tree. We would have taken it if it had not been too much broken. Between five and six o'clock landed on a small point where we encamped and cooked as usual; this day we made six leagues and must have been about twenty-four leagues in the river.

On Friday, the 6th, we distributed two baskets of bread among our twenty-six men with a quantity of meat, after which we fired a swivel. At seven o'clock we embarked in a fog so thick we could scarcely see. At sundown we landed and camped. We sent a man up a tree-top to look out; but he could not see anything. Two of our men, who were in a bark canoe, told us they had seen three crocodiles, one of which was a monster. At seven o'clock a buffalo was killed; we were then thirty leagues up the river.*

On Saturday, the 7th, we embarked, after having erected a cross, and marked some trees. Weather calm. At nine o'clock, in ranging along the river we saw three buffaloes lying down on the bank. We landed five men to go in pursuit of them, which they could not do, as

---

* They had now reached the present site of New Orleans, which was laid out and settled twenty-three years later. The first white men to view the place were Luis Moscoso and the survivors of de Soto's expedition, who sailed down the river in 1543.

they soon got lost in the thick forest and cane-brakes. A short time after, in turning a point, we saw a canoe manned by two Indians, who took to land the moment they saw us and concealed themselves in the woods. A little farther on we saw five more who executed the same manoeuvre, with the exception of one, who waited for us at the brink of the river. We made signs to him. M. d'Iberville gave him a knife, some beads and other trinkets. In exchange he gave us some dried bear's meat. M. d'Iberville commanded all of our men to go on board the long-boats for fear of intimidating him, and made signs to him to recall his comrades. They came singing their song of peace, extending their hands towards the sun and rubbing their stomachs, as a sign of admiration and joy. After joining us they placed their hands upon their breasts and extended their arms over our heads as a mark of friendship. M. d'Iberville asked them, by signs, if their village was far off. They told him it was five days' journey hence.

What troubled us most was that our provisions were falling short. M. d'Iberville gave them some beads, knives and looking-glasses; in return they gave us dried bear's meat, which they had in their canoes. Our men also trafficked with them for some trifling objects. One good old man extended his meat upon the ground, after the same manner our butchers do in our markets of Europe, and sat down beside it. Two of our men went to him, and each one gave him a knife and took the whole of the meat, consisting of at least one hundred pounds. All seemed satisfied with their bargain. M. d'Iberville asked them if they would show him their village. They gave him to understand they were going on a hunt, and could not accompany him. But having offered a hatchet to one of them, who seemed very desirous to possess it, he agreed to go. We asked them if they had heard the sound of the swivel; they said they had heard it twice. We fired it again before them, at which they were greatly astonished, for it was the first time they had ever heard it so near them. We passed two hours among them. One of them came on board of our boats. We made him a present of a shirt; the others did not appear jealous of the gift, so indifferent are they.

The following is a description of the manners, habits, and customs of these savages [as observed a few days later when the members of the expedition visited an Indian village]. The Chief of the Mongoulachas was clothed with a blue cloak after the fashion of the Canadians, with stockings of the same color, a cravat of a villainous red stuff that had formerly served as a flag; all of which had been presented to him by M. de Tonty, at the time of his descent in search of M. de la Salle.* The chief possessed an inconceivable haughtiness; he smiled, and looked at our men with a fixed gaze. As to the others, they were dressed with the skin of bear or deer, which covered them from the shoulders down to the knees, according to the size of the hide. The greater portion of them, however, go naked, without anything about them except a flap. The women are either clothed with a bear's skin or a flap fastened by a girdle which extends to the knees, leaving naked the breast and loins. The hair of the men is all cut or pulled out, except a small cluster on the crown of the head, which they let grow long, and to which they attach the feathers of birds of various colors. They also attach ornaments about their thighs, these ornaments having the appearance of horse tails, to which they fix small copper bells, which, when dancing, create a noise like that made on the road by Spanish mules. They wear upon their arms copper bracelets, and besmear their faces blue and black, and paint their eyebrows with a color like vermilion mixed with black. They sometimes pierce the nose and ears, in which they suspend pieces of coral, or ornaments, and wood of a peculiar quality and shape. As to their food, it consists principally of Indian corn, with very little meat, which they only eat when they are hunting, or at a distance from their villages.

The chiefs have their hunting-grounds bounded, and when another tribe intrudes beyond its own limits, it gives rise to war. During the evening, we fired off the swivel, which threw them into consternation. They repeated "*afferro, afferro,*" which signifies in their language, "I am astonished." One morning we went to visit the chief and carry him presents, which consisted of a scarlet coat with gold facings, red stockings, two shirts, axes, knives, beads and mirrors. They seated us upon mats and gave us pipes to smoke; afterwards they

---

* De Tonty went down the Mississippi in 1686 in search of La Salle, but found no trace of him.

brought us dried buffalo and bear's meat and bread, of which we partook, and then went out to visit the village temple, in which they keep a fire continually burning. In the interior of the temple were figures of animals, marks of their sacrifices, and scalps of their enemies hung up as trophies. Very soon after there came a crowd of Indians bringing corn in the ear and grain, which they afterwards pounded and made into bread, which pleased us very much, for we were short of provisions, and knew not where to obtain fresh supplies. Some of our men afterwards went back to the village to traffic for bear's skins and deer's skins, in exchange for beads, knives and trinkets. I noticed about the middle of their village, in an open space, what appeared to be a depot of arms. Before the door of the temple were two large posts, about forty feet in height, upon which two scalps were placed. The village contained some four or five hundred persons of both sexes, large and small.

They sleep on mats resting upon stakes, about three feet from the ground. When the weather is very cold, they kindle a fire under these mats, as they have nothing but some skins with which to cover themselves. The fields where they cultivate their millet are near their village. They break up the ground with buffalo bones. Much of their time is spent in amusing themselves with a round stone ball which they strike with sticks. When any of them die, the body is carried about fifty paces from the village, where it is placed upon a platform raised upon four posts, and covered with mats. Afterwards they throw up a bed of earth near by, several feet thick, upon which they place victuals for the deceased to eat.

1699

Walker Percy

The Moviegoer

THIS MORNING I got a note from my aunt asking me to come for lunch. I know what this means. Since I go there every Sunday for dinner and today is Wednesday, it can mean only one thing: she wants to have one of her serious talks. It will be extremely grave, either a piece of bad news about her stepdaughter Kate or else a serious talk about me, and the future and what I ought to do. It is enough to scare the wits out of anyone, yet I confess I do not find the prospect altogether unpleasant.

I remember when my older brother Scott died of pneumonia. I was eight years old. My aunt had charge of me and she took me for a walk behind the hospital. It was an interesting street. On one side were the power plant and blowers and incinerator of the hospital, all humming and blowing out a hot meaty smell. On the other side was a row of Negro houses. Children and old folks and dogs sat on the porches watching us. I noticed with pleasure that Aunt Emily seemed to have all the time in the world and was willing to talk about anything I wanted to talk about. Something extraordinary had happened all right. We walked slowly in step. "Jack," she said, squeezing me tight and smiling at the Negro shacks, "you and I have always been good buddies, haven't we?" "Yes ma'am." My heart gave a big pump and the back of my neck prickled like a dog's. "I've got bad news for you, son." She squeezed me tighter than ever. "Scotty is dead. Now it's all up to you. It's going to be difficult for you but I know you're going to act like a soldier." This was true. I could easily act like a soldier. Was that all I had to do?

It reminds me of a movie I saw last month out by Lake Pontchartrain. Linda and I went out to a theater in a new suburb. It was evident somebody had miscalculated, for the suburb had quit growing and here was the theater, a pink stucco cube, sitting out in a field all by itself. A strong wind whipped the waves against the seawall; even inside you could hear the racket. The movie was about a man who lost his memory in an accident and as a result lost everything: his family, his friends, his money. He found himself a stranger in a strange city. Here he had to make a fresh start, find a new place to live, a new job, a new girl. It was supposed to be a tragedy, his losing all this, and he seemed to suffer a great deal. On the other hand, things were not so bad after all. In no time he found a very picturesque place to live, a houseboat on the river, and a very handsome girl, the local librarian.

After the movie Linda and I stood under the marquee and talked to the manager, or rather listened to him tell his troubles: the theater was almost empty, which was pleasant for me but not for him. It was a fine night and I felt very good. Overhead was the blackest sky I ever saw; a black wind pushed the lake toward us. The waves jumped over the seawall and spattered the street. The manager had to yell to be heard while from the sidewalk speaker directly over his head came the twittering conversation of the amnesiac and the librarian. It was the part where they are going through the newspaper files in search of some clue to his identity (he has a vague recollection of an accident). Linda stood by unhappily. She was unhappy for the same reason I was happy—because here we were at a neighborhood theater out in the sticks and without a car (I have a car but I prefer to ride buses and streetcars). Her idea of happiness is to drive downtown and have supper at the Blue Room of the Roosevelt Hotel. This I am obliged to do from time to time. It is worth it, however. On these occasions Linda becomes as exalted as I am now. Her eyes glow, her lips become moist, and when we dance she brushes her fine long legs against mine. She actually loves me at these times—and not as a reward for being taken to the Blue Room. She loves me because she feels exalted in this romantic place and not in a movie out in the sticks.

But all this is history. Linda and I have parted company. I have a new secretary, a girl named Sharon Kincaid.

For the past four years now I have been living uneventfully in Gentilly, a middle-class suburb of New Orleans. Except for the banana plants in the patios and the curlicues of iron on the Walgreen drugstore one would never guess it was part of New Orleans. Most of the houses are either old-style California bungalows or new-style Daytona cottages. But this is what I like about it. I can't stand the old-world atmosphere of the French Quarter or the genteel charm of the Garden District. I lived in the Quarter for two years, but in the end I got tired of Birmingham businessmen smirking around Bourbon Street and the homosexuals and patio connoisseurs on Royal Street. My uncle and aunt live in a gracious house in the Garden District and are very kind to me. But whenever I try to live there, I find myself first in a rage during which I develop strong opinions on a variety of subjects and write letters to editors, then in a depression during which I lie rigid as a stick for hours staring straight up at the plaster medallion in the ceiling of my bedroom.

Life in Gentilly is very peaceful. I manage a small branch office of my uncle's brokerage firm. My home is the basement apartment of a raised bungalow belonging to Mrs Schexnaydre, the widow of a fireman. I am a model tenant and a model citizen and take pleasure in doing all that is expected of me. My wallet is full of identity cards, library cards, credit cards. Last year I purchased a flat olive-drab strongbox, very smooth and heavily built with double walls for fire protection, in which I placed my birth certificate, college diploma, honorable discharge, G.I. insurance, a few stock certificates, and my inheritance: a deed to ten acres of a defunct duck club down in St Bernard Parish, the only relic of my father's many enthusiasms. It is a pleasure to carry out the duties of a citizen and to receive in return a receipt or a neat styrene card with one's name on it certifying, so to speak, one's right to exist. What satisfaction I take in appearing the first day to get my auto tag and brake sticker! I subscribe to *Consumer Reports* and as a consequence I own a first-class television set, an all but silent air conditioner and a very long lasting deodorant. My armpits never stink. I pay attention to all spot announcements on the radio about mental health, the seven signs of cancer, and safe driving—though, as I say, I usually prefer to ride the bus. Yesterday a favorite of mine, William Holden, delivered a radio announcement on litterbugs. "Let's face it," said Holden. "Nobody can do anything about it—but you and me." This is true. I have been careful ever since.

In the evenings I usually watch television or go to the movies.

Weekends I often spend on the Gulf Coast. Our neighborhood theater in Gentilly has permanent lettering on the front of the marquee reading: Where Happiness Costs So Little. The fact is I am quite happy in a movie, even a bad movie. Other people, so I have read, treasure memorable moments in their lives: the time one climbed the Parthenon at sunrise, the summer night one met a lonely girl in Central Park and achieved with her a sweet and natural relationship, as they say in books. I too once met a girl in Central Park, but it is not much to remember. What I remember is the time John Wayne killed three men with a carbine as he was falling to the dusty street in *Stagecoach,* and the time the kitten found Orson Welles in the doorway in *The Third Man.*

My companion on these evening outings and week-end trips is usually my secretary. I have had three secretaries, girls named Marcia, Linda, and now Sharon. Twenty years ago, practically every other girl born in Gentilly must have been named Marcia. A year or so later it was Linda. Then Sharon. In recent years I have noticed that the name Stephanie has come into fashion. Three of my acquaintances in Gentilly have daughters named Stephanie. Last night I saw a TV play about a nuclear test explosion. Keenan Wynn played a troubled physicist who had many a bad moment with his conscience. He took solitary walks in the desert. But you could tell that in his heart of hearts he was having a very good time with his soul-searching. "What right have we to do what we are doing?" he could ask his colleagues in a bitter voice. "It's my four-year-old daughter I'm really thinking of," he told another colleague and took out a snapshot. "What kind of future are we building for her?" "What is your daughter's name?" asked the colleague, looking at the picture. "Stephanie," said Keenan Wynn in a gruff voice. Hearing the name produced a sharp tingling sensation on the back of my neck. Twenty years from now I shall perhaps have a rosy young Stephanie perched at my typewriter.

Naturally I would like to say that I had made conquests of these splendid girls, my secretaries, casting them off one after the other like old gloves, but it would not be strictly true. They could be called love affairs, I suppose. They started off as love affairs anyway, fine careless raptures in which Marcia or Linda (but not yet Sharon) and I would go spinning along the Gulf Coast, lie embracing in a deserted cove of

Ship Island, and hardly believe our good fortune, hardly believe that the world could contain such happiness. Yet in the case of Marcia and Linda the affair ended just when I thought our relationship was coming into its best phase. The air in the office would begin to grow thick with silent reproaches. It would become impossible to exchange a single word or glance that was not freighted with a thousand hidden meanings. Telephone conversations would take place at all hours of the night, conversations made up mostly of long silences during which I would rack my brain for something to say while on the other end you could hear little else but breathing and sighs. When these long telephone silences come, it is a sure sign that love is over. No, they were not conquests. For in the end my Lindas and I were so sick of each other that we were delighted to say good-by.

I am a stock and bond broker. It is true that my family was somewhat disappointed in my choice of a profession. Once I thought of going into law or medicine or even pure science. I even dreamed of doing something great. But there is much to be said for giving up such grand ambitions and living the most ordinary life imaginable, a life without the old longings; selling stocks and bonds and mutual funds; quitting work at five o'clock like everyone else; having a girl and perhaps one day settling down and raising a flock of Marcias and Sandras and Lindas of my own. Nor is the brokerage business as uninteresting as you might think. It is not a bad life at all.

We live, Mrs Schexnaydre and I, on Elysian Fields, the main thoroughfare of Faubourg Marigny. Though it was planned to be, like its namesake, the grandest boulevard of the city, something went amiss, and now it runs an undistinguished course from river to lake through shopping centers and blocks of duplexes and bungalows and raised cottages. But it is very spacious and airy and seems truly to stretch out like a field under the sky. Next door to Mrs Schexnaydre is a brand new school. It is my custom on summer evenings after work to take a shower, put on shirt and pants and stroll over to the deserted playground and there sit on the ocean wave, spread out the movie page of the *Times-Picayune* on one side, phone book on the other, and a city map in my lap. After I have made my choice, plotted a route— often to some remote neighborhood like Algiers or St Bernard—I stroll around the schoolyard in the last golden light of day and admire the building. Everything is so spick-and-span: the aluminum sashes fitted into the brick wall and gilded in the sunset, the pretty terrazzo floors and the desks molded like wings. Suspended by wires above the door is a schematic sort of bird, the Holy Ghost I suppose. It gives me a pleasant sense of the goodness of creation to think of the brick and the glass and the aluminum being extracted from common dirt— though no doubt it is less a religious sentiment than a financial one, since I own a few shares of Alcoa. How smooth and well-fitted and thrifty the aluminum feels!

But things have suddenly changed. My peaceful existence in Gentilly has been complicated. This morning, for the first time in years, there occurred to me the possibility of a search. I dreamed of the war, no, not quite dreamed but woke with the taste of it in my mouth, the queasy-quince taste of 1951 and the Orient. I remembered the first time the search occurred to me. I came to myself under a chindolea bush. Everything is upside-down for me, as I shall explain later. What are generally considered to be the best times are for me the worst times, and that worst of times was one of the best. My shoulder didn't hurt but it was pressed hard against the ground as if somebody sat on me. Six inches from my nose a dung beetle was scratching around under the leaves. As I watched, there awoke in me an immense curiosity. I was onto something. I vowed that if I ever got out of this fix, I would pursue the search. Naturally, as soon as I recovered and got home, I forgot all about it. But this morning when I got up, I dressed as usual and began as usual to put my belongings into my pockets: wallet, notebook (for writing down occasional thoughts), pencil, keys, handkerchief, pocket slide rule (for calculating percentage returns on principal). They looked both unfamiliar and at the same time full of clues. I stood in the center of the room and gazed at the little pile, sighting through a hole made by thumb and forefinger. What was unfamiliar about them was that I could see them. They might have belonged to someone else. A man can look at this little pile on his bureau for thirty years and never once see it. It is as invisible as his own hand. Once I saw it, however, the search became possible. I bathed, shaved, dressed carefully, and sat at my desk and poked through the little pile in search of a clue just as the detective on television pokes through the dead man's possessions, using his pencil as a poker.

The idea of a search comes to me again as I am on my way to my aunt's house, riding the Gentilly bus down Elysian Fields. The truth is I dislike cars. Whenever I drive a car, I have the feeling I have become invisible. People on the street cannot see you; they only watch your rear fender until it is out of their way. Elysian Fields is not the shortest route to my aunt's house. But I have my reasons for going through the Quarter. William Holden, I read in the paper this morning, is in New Orleans shooting a few scenes in the Place d'Armes. It would be interesting to catch a glimpse of him.

It is a gloomy March day. The swamps are still burning at Chef Menteur and the sky over Gentilly is the color of ashes. The bus is crowded with shoppers, nearly all women. The windows are steamed. I sit on the lengthwise seat in front. Women sit beside me and stand above me. On the long back seat are five Negresses so black that the whole rear of the bus seems darkened. Directly next to me, on the first cross seat, is a very fine-looking girl. She is a strapping girl but by no means too big, done up head to toe in cellophane, the hood pushed back to show a helmet of glossy black hair. She is magnificent with her split tooth and her Prince Val bangs split on her forehead. Gray eyes and wide black brows, a good arm and a fine swell of calf above her cellophane boot. One of those solitary Amazons one sees on Fifty-seventh Street in New York or in Neiman Marcus in Dallas. Our eyes meet. Am I mistaken or does the corner of her mouth tuck in ever so slightly and the petal of her lower lip curl out ever so richly? She is smiling—at me! My mind hits upon half a dozen schemes to circumvent the terrible moment of separation. No doubt she is a Texan. They are nearly always bad judges of men, these splendid Amazons. Most men are afraid of them and so they fall victim to the first little Mickey Rooney that comes along. In a better world I should be able to speak to her: come, darling, you can see that I love you. If you are planning to meet some little Mickey, think better of it. What a tragedy it is that I do not know her, will probably never see her again. What good times we could have! This very afternoon we could go spinning along the Gulf Coast. What consideration and tenderness

I could show her! If it were a movie, I would have only to wait. The bus would get lost or the city would be bombed and she and I would tend the wounded. As it is, I may as well stop thinking about her.

Then it is that the idea of the search occurs to me. I become absorbed and for a minute or so forget about the girl.

What is the nature of the search? you ask.

Really it is very simple, at least for a fellow like me; so simple that it is easily overlooked.

The search is what anyone would undertake if he were not sunk in the everydayness of his own life. This morning, for example, I felt as if I had come to myself on a strange island. And what does such a castaway do? Why, he pokes around the neighborhood and he doesn't miss a trick.

To become aware of the possibility of the search is to be onto something. Not to be onto something is to be in despair.

The movies are onto the search, but they screw it up. The search always ends in despair. They like to show a fellow coming to himself in a strange place—but what does he do? He takes up with the local librarian, sets about proving to the local children what a nice fellow he is, and settles down with a vengeance. In two weeks' time he is so sunk in everydayness that he might just as well be dead.

What do you seek—God? you ask with a smile.

I hesitate to answer, since all other Americans have settled the matter for themselves and to give such an answer would amount to setting myself a goal which everyone else has reached—and therefore raising a question in which no one has the slightest interest. Who wants to be dead last among one hundred and eighty million Americans? For, as everyone knows, the polls report that 98% of Americans believe in God and the remaining 2% are atheists and agnostics—which leaves not a single percentage point for a seeker. For myself, I enjoy answering polls as much as anyone and take pleasure in giving intelligent replies to all questions.

Truthfully, it is the fear of exposing my own ignorance which constrains me from mentioning the object of my search. For, to begin with, I cannot even answer this, the simplest and most basic of all questions: Am I, in my search, a hundred miles ahead of my fellow Americans or a hundred miles behind them? That is to say: Have 98%

of Americans already found what I seek or are they so sunk in everydayness that not even the possibility of a search has occurred to them?

On my honor, I do not know the answer.

As the bus ascends the overpass, a concrete hill which affords a fine view of New Orleans, I discover that I am frowning and gazing at a noble young calf clad in gun-metal nylon. Now beyond question she is aware of me: she gives her raincoat a sharp tug and gives me a look of annoyance—or do I imagine this? I must make sure, so I lift my hat and smile at her as much as to say that we might still become friends. But it is no use. I have lost her forever. She flounces out of the bus in a loud rustle of cellophane.

I alight at Esplanade in a smell of roasting coffee and creosote and walk up Royal Street. The lower Quarter is the best part. The ironwork on the balconies sags like rotten lace. Little French cottages hide behind high walls. Through deep sweating carriageways one catches glimpses of courtyards gone to jungle.

Today I am in luck. Who should come out of Pirate's Alley half a block ahead of me but William Holden!

Holden crosses Royal and turns toward Canal. As yet he is unnoticed. The tourists are either browsing along antique shops or snapping pictures of balconies. No doubt he is on his way to Galatoire's for lunch. He is an attractive fellow with his ordinary good looks, very suntanned, walking along hands in pockets, raincoat slung over one shoulder. Presently he passes a young couple, who are now between me and him. Now we go along, the four of us, not twenty feet apart. It takes two seconds to size up the couple. They are twenty, twenty-one, and on their honeymoon. Not Southern. Probably Northeast. He wears a jacket with leather elbow patches, pipestem pants, dirty white shoes, and affects the kind of rolling seafaring gait you see in Northern college boys. Both are plain. He has thick lips, cropped reddish hair and skin to match. She is mousy. They are not really happy. He is afraid their honeymoon is too conventional, that they are just another honeymoon couple. No doubt he figured it would be fun to drive down the Shenandoah Valley to New Orleans and escape the honeymooners at Niagara Falls and Saratoga. Now fifteen hundred miles from home they find themselves surrounded by couples from Memphis and Chicago. He is anxious; he is threatened from every side. Each stranger he passes is a reproach to him, every doorway a threat. What is wrong? he wonders. She is unhappy but for a different reason, because he is unhappy and she knows it but doesn't know why.

Now they spot Holden. The girl nudges her companion. The boy perks up for a second, but seeing Holden doesn't really help him. On the contrary. He can only contrast Holden's resplendent reality with his own shadowy and precarious existence. Obviously he is more miserable than ever. What a deal, he must be thinking, trailing along behind a movie star—we might just as well be rubbernecking in Hollywood.

Holden slaps his pockets for a match. He has stopped behind some ladies looking at iron furniture on the sidewalk. They look like housewives from Hattiesburg come down for a day of shopping. He asks for a match; they shake their heads and then recognize him. There follows much blushing and confusion. But nobody can find a match for Holden. By now the couple have caught up with him. The boy holds out a light, nods briefly to Holden's thanks, then passes on without a flicker of recognition. Holden walks along between them for a second; he and the boy talk briefly, look up at the sky, shake their heads. Holden gives them a pat on the shoulder and moves on ahead.

The boy has done it! He has won title to his own existence, as plenary an existence now as Holden's, by refusing to be stampeded like the ladies from Hattiesburg. He is a citizen like Holden; two men of the world they are. All at once the world is open to him. Nobody threatens from patio and alley. His girl is open to him too. He puts his arm around her neck, noodles her head. She feels the difference too. She had not known what was wrong nor how it was righted but she knows now that all is well.

Holden has turned down Toulouse shedding light as he goes. An aura of heightened reality moves with him and all who fall within it feel it. Now everyone is aware of him. He creates a regular eddy among the tourists and barkeeps and B-girls who come running to the doors of the joints.

I am attracted to movie stars but not for the usual reasons. I have no desire to speak to Holden or get his autograph. It is their peculiar reality which astounds me. The Yankee boy is well aware of it, even though he pretends to ignore Holden. Clearly he would like nothing better than to take Holden over to his fraternity house in the most casual way. "Bill, I want you to meet Phil. Phil, Bill Holden," he would say and go sauntering off in the best seafaring style.

It is lunch hour on Canal Street. A parade is passing, but no one pays much attention. It is still a week before Mardi Gras and this is a new parade, a women's krewe from Gentilly. A krewe is a group of people who get together at carnival time and put on a parade and a ball. Anyone can form a krewe. Of course there are the famous old krewes like Comus and Rex and Twelfth Night, but there are also dozens of others. The other day a group of Syrians from Algiers formed a krewe named Isis. This krewe today, this must be Linda's krewe. I promised to come to see her. Red tractors pulled the floats along; scaffoldings creak, paper and canvas tremble. Linda, I think, is one of half a dozen shepherdesses dressed in short pleated skirts and mercury sandals with thongs crisscrossed up bare calves. But they are masked and I can't be sure. If she is, her legs are not so fine after all. All twelve legs are shivery and goosepimpled. A few businessmen stop to watch the girls and catch trinkets.

A warm wind springs up from the south piling up the clouds and bearing with it a far-off rumble, the first thunderstorm of the year. The street looks tremendous. People on the far side seem tiny and archaic, dwarfed by the great sky and the windy clouds like pedestrians in old prints. Am I mistaken or has a fog of uneasiness, a thin gas of malaise, settled on the street? The businessmen hurry back to their offices, the shoppers to their cars, the tourists to their hotels. Ah, William Holden, we already need you again. Already the fabric is wearing thin without you.

The mystery deepens. For ten minutes I stand talking to Eddie Lovell and at the end of it, when we shake hands and part, it seems to me that I cannot answer the simplest question about what has taken place. As I listen to Eddie speak plausibly and at length of one thing and another—business, his wife Nell, the old house they are redecorating—the fabric pulls together into one bright texture of investments, family projects, lovely old houses, little theater readings and such. It comes over me: this is how one lives! My exile in Gentilly has been the worst kind of self-deception.

Yes! Look at him. As he talks, he slaps a folded newspaper against his pants leg and his eye watches me and at the same time sweeps the terrain behind me, taking note of the slightest movement. A green truck turns down Bourbon Street; the eye sizes it up, flags it down, demands credentials, waves it on. A businessman turns in at the Maison Blanche building; the eye knows him, even knows what he is up to. And all the while he talks very well. His lips move muscularly, molding words into pleasing shapes, marshalling arguments, and during the slight pauses are held poised, attractively everted in a Charles Boyer pout—while a little web of saliva gathers in a corner like the clear oil of a good machine. Now he jingles the coins deep in his pocket. No mystery here!—he is as cogent as a bird dog quartering a field. He understands everything out there and everything out there is something to be understood.

Eddie watches the last float, a doubtful affair with a squashed cornucopia.

"We'd better do better than that."

"We will."

"Are you riding Neptune?"

"No."

I offer Eddie my four call-outs for the Neptune ball. There is always the problem of out-of-town clients, usually Texans, and especially their wives. Eddie thanks me for this and for something else.

"I want to thank you for sending Mr Quieulle to me. I really appreciate it."

"Who?"

"Old man Quieulle."

"Yes, I remember." Eddie has sunk mysteriously into himself, eyes twinkling from the depths. "Don't tell me—"

Eddie nods.

"—that he has already set up his trust and up and died?"

Eddie nods, still sunk into himself. He watches me carefully, hanging fire until I catch up with him.

"In Mrs Quieulle's name?"

Again a nod; his jaw is shot out.

"How big?"

The same dancing look, now almost malignant. "Just short of nine hundred and fifty thou." His tongue curves around and seeks the hollow of his cheek.

"A fine old man," I say absently, noticing that Eddie has become as solemn as a bishop.

"I'll tell you one thing, Binx. I count it a great privilege to have known him. I've never known anyone, young or old, who possessed a greater fund of knowledge. That man spoke to me for two hours about the history of the crystallization of sugar and it was pure romance. I was fascinated."

Eddie tells me how much he admires my aunt and my cousin Kate. Several years ago Kate was engaged to marry Eddie's brother Lyell. On the very eve of the wedding Lyell was killed in an accident, the same accident which Kate survived. Now Eddie comes around to face me, his cottony hair flying up in the breeze. "I have never told anybody what I really think of that woman—" Eddie says "woman" as a deliberate liberty to be set right by the compliment to follow. "I think more of Miss Emily—and Kate—than anyone else in the world except my own mother—and wife. The good that woman has done."

"That's mighty nice, Eddie."

He murmurs something about how beautiful Kate is, that next to Nell etc.—and this is a surprise because my cousin Nell Lovell is a plain horsy old girl. "Will you please give them both my love?"

"I certainly will."

The parade is gone. All that is left is the throb of a drum.

"What do you do with yourself?" asks Eddie and slaps his paper against his pants leg.

"Nothing much," I say, noticing that Eddie is not listening.

"Come see us, fellah! I want you to see what Nell has done." Nell has taste. The two of them are forever buying shotgun cottages in rundown neighborhoods and fixing them up with shutterblinds in the bathroom, saloon doors for the kitchen, old bricks and a sugar kettle for the back yard, and selling in a few months for a big profit.

The cloud is turning blue and pressing down upon us. Now the street seems closeted; the bricks of the buildings glow with a yellow stored-up light. I look at my watch: one is not late at my aunt's house. In an instant Eddie's hand is out.

"Give the bride and groom my best."

"I will."

"Walter is a wonderful fellow."

"He is."

Before letting me go, Eddie comes one inch closer and asks in a special voice about Kate.

"She seems fine now, Eddie. Quite happy and secure."

"I'm so damn glad. Fellah!" A final shake from side to side, like a tiller. "Come see us!"

"I will."

1960

Louis Armstrong

Growing Up in New Orleans

I'M ALWAYS wondering if it would have been best in my life if I'd stayed like I was in New Orleans, having a ball. I was very much contented just to be around and play with the old timers. And the money I made I lived off of it. I wonder if I would have enjoyed that better than all this big mucky-muck traveling all over the world — which is nice, meeting all those people, being high on the horse, all *grandioso*. All this life I have now — I didn't suggest it. I would say it was all wished on me. Over the years you find you can't stay no longer where you are, you must go on a little higher now — and that's the way it all come about. I couldn't get away from what's happened to me.

But man I sure had a ball there growing up in New Orleans as a kid. We were poor and everything like that, but music was all around you. Music kept you rolling.

When I was about 4 or 5, still wearing dresses, I lived with my mother in Jane's Alley in a place called Brick Row — a lot of cement, rented rooms sort of like a motel. And right in the middle of that on Perdido Street was the Funky Butt Hall — old, beat up, big cracks in the wall. On Saturday nights, Mama couldn't find us 'cause we wanted to hear that music. Before the dance the band would play out front about a half hour. And us little kids would all do little dances. If I ever heard Buddy Bolden play the cornet, I figure that's when.

Then we'd go look through the big cracks in the wall of the Funky Butt. It wasn't no classyfied place, just a big old room with a bandstand. And to a tune like *The Bucket's Got a Hole in It,* some of them chicks would get way down, shake everything, slapping themselves on the cheek of their behind. Yeah! At the end of the night, they'd do the quadrille, beautiful to see, where everybody lined up, crossed over — if no fights hadn't started before that. Cats'd have to take their razors in with them, because they might have to scratch somebody before they left there. If any of them cats want to show respect for their chick—which they seldom did—they'd crook their left elbow out when they danced and lay their hat on it—a John B. Stetson they'd probably saved for six months to buy. When the dance was over, fellow would walk up and say, "Did you touch my hat, partner?" and if the cat say "yes"—Wop!—he hit him right in the chops.

Once a year, on a certain day, all the social clubs—the Broadway Swells, the Bulls, the Turtles—would have a parade. I eventually joined the Tammany Social Club. One was called the Moneywasters. They used to carry a big cabbage with cigars and paper dollars sticking out of it. And oh it was beautiful in the parades—you know? Everybody with silk shirts, white hats, black pants, streamers across their chests with the club's name, everybody shined up, the Grand Marshal always sharp and strutting, and some guys on horses. They always had stops where they go to different members' houses, open a keg of beer, and they liable to end up at a big picnic at the fairgrounds.

And if they have a member that died, they all turn out. It'd be a beautiful thing. Night before a funeral they have a wake, everybody sitting all night around the body singing. You come in there, lead off a hymn and go right back in the kitchen and get cheese, crackers, whisky, beer. Boy, they shouting! Brother's rocking in that coffin. I know a guy who went to all wakes. He didn't care who it was, but he's right on time.

And in those early days, before embalming, some bodies used to come back to life. The body would raise up and sit there on that slab, and goddam, imagine all them people trying all at once to get out of one little bitty door.

Next morning at the funeral the musicians have to stand around outside waiting for the ceremonial to be over. The Catholics, their funerals were quick, but the Baptists, my God, look like they going to never come out of there. We had to do something. There was always a barroom on the corner. Ooooooh, boy!

After the sermon's over, they'd take the body to the cemetery with the band playing the funeral marches—maybe *Nearer My God to Thee.*

Them oldtime drummers, they just put a handkerchief under the snare on their drum and it go *tunk-a, tunk-a,* like a tom-tom effect.

And when that body's in the ground, man, tighten up on them snares and he rolls that drum and everybody gets together and they march back to their hall playing *When the Saints* or *Didn't He Ramble*. They usually have a keg of beer back there and they rejoice, you know, for the dead.

Marching back, the funeral's going along one side of the street, and on the other side is the "second line"—guys just following the parade, one suspender down, all raggedy, no coat, enjoying the music. Course they had their little flasks, but when the parade stop to get a taste in a bar, the second line hold the horses or the instruments for the band and when the guys come back out, they give them their drinks.

In those days in New Orleans, there was always something that was nice and always with music. They used to advertise with them big long wagons they used during the week for hauling furniture. Be a big sign on the side of the wagon advertising a dance or boxing fight— Gunboat Smith was a big name down there. The band would sit in the wagon on chairs, with the trombone and bass at the end where the tailgate lets down. They'd stop at a corner and the band would play. People would come from all the neighborhood and be around the wagon. And here come another wagon and pull up too and that's where that bucking contest used to come—each band playing different tunes trying to outplay each other. King Oliver and Kid Ory used to cut them all. And devilish guys—them old hustlers and pimps—used to chain the wheels of those wagons together so they would have to stay there and play.

Joe Oliver in the Onward Brass Band fascinated me—he was the nearest thing to Buddy Bolden to me. When he went into a bar to yackety with the guys—he didn't drink—or when he'd be parading and not blowing, I'd hold his horn so all he had to do was wipe his brow and walk.

In the evening, people colored and white, used to give parties on the lawns in front of their houses—set up with lemonade and sandwiches and fried chicken and gumbo and the band sit down in front of the door on the porch and play. And people dance. And the musicians always have their uniforms on—a little music lyre on the collar around their neck, and the band's name on the hat. The bands wanted to be stipulated, you know—like the Crescent City Band, Robichaud's Band—

Yeah, music all around you. The pie man and the waffle man, they all had a little hustle to attract the people. Pie man used to swing something on the bugle and the waffle man rang a big triangle. The junk man had one of them long tin horns they celebrate with at Christmas—could play the blues and everything on it. Called him Lonzo. I used to work with him and we'd go in all the rich neighborhoods and buy a lot of old clothes. And I'd be yelling "Old rags and bones, lady! Old rags and bones!" The banana man, he'd be hollering "Yellow ripe bananas, lady, 15 cents a bunch! Yellow ripe bananas!" Oh, yeah, always had music all around me of some kind.

I worked on a coal wagon and, hell, I was singing selling coal. "Stone coal, lady! Nickel a water bucket! Stone coal, nickel a water bucket!" The bottoms of those buckets was all pounded up so maybe three or four big lumps would fill it. We was selling all through the red-light district—it was called Storyville. The women would be standing there in the doorways to their cribs wearing their "teddies"—that was a famous uniform they had, all silk, like baby bloomers only transparent. One of them would call, "Commere boy, Bring me three buckets." And it was fun for me to go in them cribs and for a quarter extra start them fires. And I'd take my little quick peek, you know, scared she'd catch me, slap me and shove me out of there. But they didn't pay me no mind. Just a stone-coal boy— breathing like a bitch, man.

Storyville was just for white people. Most of the whores were white or light creoles or mulattoes. Lulu White had the biggest house. All those rich men used to come there from all around. Only Negro who played there was Jelly Roll Morton on the piano. That's how he got that gold tooth with a diamond in it. I don't think they had colored maids in Lulu White's. But she was colored. It was a crazy deal.

Only way I got to see Storyville then, when I was real little, was on that coal cart. If you was under age, a policeman—the Corporal— he carried a big stick and he'd break your leg. But on Gravier Street, round where I grew up, was just like the red-light district, but cheaper scales. From Franklin to Liberty nobody had no decent home there, but the front doors were always busy—those colored girls sitting on the front steps, all pretty and painted up. You'd walk by and they'd say, "Hello, Daddy. Want to do a little business?"

When I was real little, us kids would pound up a bucket of red brick dust and sell it to the prostitutes on Saturday mornings, make maybe 50 or 70 cents. Every Saturday they'd scrub their steps down with pee and then they'd throw the brick dust on the sidewalk in front, and that brought them luck Saturday night. That was their superstition.

Later on, when I was about 12, four of us made up a little quartet. We used to hear the old timers sing around a bucket of beer—them beautiful chords—and we dug it. We was Little Mack, Big Nose Sidney, myself and Georgie Grey. Red Head Happy was in and out. He was a bulldozer, a bad character, used to come in and take the money. And he got bolder and wanted to pimp, so he put us down 'cause we were squares.

We went all over and would put on long pants and go up to the district, and all the old gammies and pimps, they'd call for us to sing. I used to sing tenor, had a real light voice, and played a little slide whistle, like a trombone. I could feel the positions so beautiful. Our theme song went: *My Brazilian Beauty down on The Amazon/that's where my baby's/gone, gone, gone* (we had a guy who could bass that). Every night I'm dreaming of "my Brazilian beauty down on the Amazon." At that time I didn't even know there was a place called Brazil. And years later, when I went to Brazil on tour—then it dawned on me.

After we'd sung, we'd pass the hat—get six bits, maybe even a dollar each for a night. My mother, Mary Ann—we called her Mayann—used to wash clothes out back in a white family's yard on Canal Street in a big tin tub over a little coal furnace. Made about a dollar a day. In 1915, nice money. My father left home when I was real little. He used to take care of the boilers out to a turpentine factory. He died in 1933.

One New Year's Eve I was out singing with my quartet. That night everybody shoot off their pistols, shotguns, firecrackers, roman candles, all that stuff—all things you ain't allowed to do. Well, I'd been looking at my stepfather's .38 all week in the trunk. And this night I loaded it up with blanks and put it in my belt. We were going up

Rampart Street singing *My Brazilian Beauty,* and a little old cat across the street pulls out a kid's cap pistol and shot it at us—*Dy! Dy! Dy! Dy! Dy! Dy!* The cats in my quartet say, "Get him Dipper!" (they used to call me Dippermouth) and so I shot—*Zoom, Zoom!* and all of the sudden two white arms hugged me, and I looked up and there was a big tall policeman. Boy, I thought the world was coming to an end. And I was crying "Oh Mister, let me alone!—Don't take the pistol! I won't do it no more!" And then they took me to juvenile court and sent me to the Waifs' Home. I got out there just about meal time. I could see that looong table, with that pan coming down it full of beans. I was so sad and homesick I wouldn't eat for four days.

They said I had a bad stamp, that I was a bad boy running around with bad kids. But the bandmaster, Mister Peter Davis, he watched me all that time. And he come up to me and said, "Would you like to play in the band?" I said, "I don't know how to play nothing." I'd been around to the parades and things, but singing was my life.

He kept insisting and give me a tambourine. So I fool with that for a while. Then he give me a snare drum. I used to see them guys play that in the parades and us little kids used to take the rungs off chairs and beat on the steps and I broke it up with that drum doing *At the Animals' Ball.* Then they give me an alto horn. You know, it goes *umpah, umpah* all night. Then I got the bugle and just picked it up and started playing—blew reveille, mess call, taps every day. Finally the little cornet player went home and Mr. Davis taught me how to play *Home Sweet Home* on that.

Pretty soon I was the leader of the band—20 kids and we played pretty good—of course, not like Joe Oliver and Manuel Perez in that Onward band. But we'd hire out to those big social clubs. You know, "Go get those kids." We used to play in that hot sun and had to parade for miles and miles and we'd be *so* tired, and our little lips were sore for a week. But we was glad just to be out in the streets around people. In my neighborhood all the people remember Mayann's kid and they say, "Can we give little Louis some money?" and they give us hats full of money and I turned it over to the orphanage to buy instruments.

I stayed in the Waifs' Home about a year and a half, till my mother and my father got some people who could get me out. I never did go back to school—I was in about the fifth grade—and I regret that to a hell of an extent. But I had to take care of Mama and I was the only one to put a little taste in the pot. And at that time I didn't need the schooling. I had the horn.

I started playing right away. Any time a cat would lay off, they'd say, "Run get little Louis"—I was a little bitty fellow—and I got to play with them good musicians. But I couldn't get enough money together to even talk about a horn of my own—used to rent one for each gig. Then I found a little nickel-plate cornet for $10 in Uncle Jake's pawn shop—all bent up, holes knocked in the bell. It was a Tonk Brothers—ain't never heard of them. Charlie—he was the ofay fellow supplied me with papers when I was a newsboy around there—he lent me the money. I cleaned that little horn out, soalded it good. It was all right. Made a little living with it.

Later, when I was playing in Henry Matranga's honky-tonk, Joe Oliver used to come around after Pete Lala's closed down in the district, and he'd say, "I'm sick of looking at that beat-up cornet. I'm going to give you a horn." So one night he gave me an old York he'd had. Oh, my! I drooled all over the place. "Thanks, Papa Joe, thank you Mister Joe." I always knew, if I'm going to get a little break in this game, it was going to be through Papa Joe, nobody else. He used to have me to his house to eat red beans and rice—which I *loved*. He gave me lessons out of an exercise book—then we'd run down little duets together.

When I got my first job in New Orleans playing in a honky-tonk—Matranga's at Franklin and Perdido—I was 17, and it was same as Carnegie Hall to me. Yeah. Night I made my debut, I thought I was somebody. I took 15 cents home and I give it to my mother, and my sister woke up out of a sound sleep, say, "Huh, blowing your brains out for 15 cents." I wanted to kill her. Finally I got raised up to $1.25 a night—top money, man.

I played with a piano and a drum, two guys I only knew as Boogus and Garbee. We'd play from about 8 to daybreak, take little intermissions and go have a beer with some of the gamblers. And Mama would make a lunch—cabbage and rice, or something—to eat at the honky-tonk around midnight. I'd get a couple of hours sleep at home, then I had a job at the coal yard loading carts. I was getting 15 cents a load and made five loads a day. That shovel was a big as a table.

Then I had to deliver that coal maybe across the city, and you make a little extra taste if you put the coal in the bin, maybe 40 cents and a sandwich. They call that "cakes throwed in."

Then I'd come home, put the mule up and sum up my coal money—75 cents. By the end of the week you get about $5.00. And I was young, full of fire, even with the shovel. So I try to get me an old lady on the money, too—and got to give her a couple little dollars.

When I wasn't down at the coal yard, I was unloading banana boats. And them bunches touch you on the shoulder and they both hanging to the ground. A big snake, big rat, anything might run out of them. I don't see why I got any strength left at all. But at that time I was enjoying it, being around the cats I wanted to be with, and as a kid I didn't know no better. I had to help Mama and sister. My stepfathers—you know stepfathers—they just going to do so much. Had to eat.

Once I was promised $50—more money than I'd ever seen all at once—for a tune I wrote I called *Get Off Katie's Head*. I sold it to a A. J. Piron and Clarence Williams to publish. Weren't no contracts or nothing. They wrote some words and called it, *I Wish I Could Shimmy Like My Sister Kate*. They never did pay me for it, never even put my name on it. I didn't bother about it. You can't get everything that's coming to you in this life.

Every corner in my neighborhood had a honky-tonk. There was Spano's and Kid Brown's and Matranga's and Henry Ponce. The first room in a honky-tonk was the saloon, and there'd be two rooms in back. Just throw everybody back there and they have a ball. One was for gambling, playing cotch. You deal three cards from the bottom of the deck and the highest cards win. I never did play much. I was too glad when I got a good hand so that everybody could tell.

The other room was for dancing—doing that slow drag, close together, humping up one shoulder—maybe throw a little wiggle into it. Had a little bandstand catty-cornered, benches around the walls. Drinks were cheap—and strong. Used to get beer in tin lard buckets and it was *cold*—liked to see that sweat on the outside—and you could get as high on that as regular whisky now. Whisky then was 100 proof and raw, too. Real rough. Us kids couldn't take it.

Around four or five in the morning, that's when all them whores would come in to the tonk—big stockings full of dollars—and give us a tip to play the blues. I was just a little fellow and they used to sit me on their knees behind their bottle of beer. And all the gals had their little perfume. They'd get a little box of powdered chalk, buy 15 cents worth of perfume, pour it over the chalk and powder themselves with it. It was pink chalk. Couldn't stand white chalk—looked like you scratch your leg in wintertime. So everybody was smelling. And they'd wear their little calico dresses, show them cute shapes. I'll tell you one thing, they was attractive and very encouraging to look at. There wasn't no problem for them to do business. I thought the women in those days looked a lot more inviting than chicks today wearing all those damn tight-butted pants.

These gals in the tonk would take their trick to a room and the pimp would go hang around to see how long she stayed with the trick—and if she was a little too happy there, she gets a whipping after. And some of them was bad whores—knife in their stockings, down their bosom. Those big bylow knives. Oh, yeah. Ann Cook and Mary Jack the Bear who lived in my neighborhood was the most promising ones. One time a nice girl named Alberta come stay in the neighborhood, just come out of school, and it's bad. Ooooh! Mary Jack the Bear find out that her man, her pimp, was crazy about this young gal and he was taking the money she done hustled and giving it to Alberta. Quite naturally when Mary Jack met this girl right in front of Gravier and Franklin, they stood right out in the street and there it was; I ain't never seen so much knife walling. Toe to toe. One take a slice there, the other take a slice here. Man! Mary Jack died of it.

One of the greatest characters I ever know was Black Benny. He was going with one of those bad whores and he whipped her up in a honky-tonk one night and she shot him. He lived for a whole week with a bullet in his heart. He was good with his dukes, always had a pistol, but the church people liked him, everybody liked him. He was devilish. There was an old raggedy cat, did nothing but hang around and hustle drinks, and they named him Jesus. Black Benny filled his big .45 with blanks, and right in front of the church on New Year's Even, with everybody coming out, he shot right at Jesus. *Boom, Boom,*

Boom. And Jesus fell out for dead. And when the church sisters and everybody was screaming, "Oh, Lord, he killed him, he killed him!" – Jesus got up and run.

And then Benny'd go in another neighborhood, and any cat that pull out a pistol, Benny would put .45 in his side, saying "I'll take this one." And he took guns all night and come around and sell them for 50 cents, a dollar – white handled, fur handled. He was wonderful. And if you chip in to buy a bucket of beer, don't give it to Black Benny first 'cause you'll never get none. That beer go down – "glug, glug, glug" – and he's emptied the bucket – "Ahhhhh" – foam all around his mouth.

All the bands wanted Benny to play the bass drum in the parades. Any time anybody give us kids trouble, Benny'd hit 'em over the head with the drum mallets. And any time he went to jail, the bands would ask the warden to let him out to play at a funeral.

I loved to stay around on the corner and hear the old timers talk, and one day Benny was sitting on a beer box, telling lots of gags and things. This old policeman come up and say, "Benny, got to take you down to the station house." Benny told him, "Well, I played cards last night and I won enough to get this suit out of pawn. Ain't been dressed up for a year."

He was a tall handsome black boy, pink shirt, had the cuffs of his box-back shirt turned up like we used to, them pointed high-button shoes – man, if you paid $26 for a pair of Edwin Clapps, you really had a pair of shoes. So anyway, Benny told him, "Now you can suit yourself, I ain't going to jail today." So the cop reach in the back of Benny's pants, under his coat, you know how they do when they're going to take you to jail, and Benny jumped up, and he's always vivacious and a track runner – and he drug that cop all through that muddy street for over a half a block – then walked away. He was devilish and everybody loved him.

All them bad characters came in to gamble where I was playing in the honky-tonk. They didn't bother with kids like us – but I knew Red Cornelius, carried anything he could get to cut you or shoot you. George Bo'hog another one. There was Dirty Dog, Brother Ford and Steel Arm Johnny, Aaron Harris and Black Benny – always in trouble. That's all they live for, was gambling and that pistol and the gals. Cats used to come in from all the little old towns–Little Woods, Slidell, Bogalusa–on Saturday night. They'd be wearing their overall jackets, all pressed to look sharp, and the more you washed them, the prettier blue they look–and a big .45 under the jacket. They'd just been paid off at the saw mill–cutting sugar cane, cotton, whatever, railroad-section gangs–and some of these cats'd lose, try to raid the cotch table. There'd be a shooting. And I used to see some of them–no money, no place to go, no sleep for days–trying to sleep standing up in a corner of the honky-tonk.

One tonk I worked the manager was named Slippers–good with his dukes and don't fear nobody. So he put a guy out–and the guy turns around and starts shooting his way back in. Well, Slippers got a pistol too, hit him in the belly or somewheres right quick. And every Saturday night the patrol wagon was busy, you could hear that bell– dang, dang, dang–wagon pulling up.

Our bandstand was right by the door, and if somebody start shooting, I don't see how I didn't get hit. Just wasn't my time to die, man. They used to raid the honky-tonks all the time and we'd be locked up maybe nineteen days or so. Had to sweep out the markets. But I was a youngster, knew I was going to get out–it was just fun. Finally the owner, he'd come down, pay the fine or whatever.

All this time I was living with Mama and we always poured our troubles into each other. She was a stocky woman–dark, lovely expression and a beautiful soul. And she instilled in me the idea that what you can't get–to hell with it. Don't worry what the other fellow has. Everybody loved her for that, because if you lived next door and you got the world, that's all right. Just don't mess with her little world. I think I had a *great* mother. She didn't have much power, but she did all she could for me–grabbing little knickknacks here and there and everything, and we put it all together.

Big event for me then was buying a wind-up victrola. Most of my records were the Original Dixieland Jazz Band–Larry Shields and his bunch. They were the first to record the music I played. I had Caruso records too, and Henry Burr, Galli-Curci, Tettrazini–they were all my favorites. Then there was the Irish tenor, McCormack–beautiful phrasing.

When I was 18, I got married to my first wife, Daisy, and left home. Everybody wanted to know, was Mama satisfied that her son's marrying a prostitute 21 years old. She say, "I can't live his life. He's my boy and if that's what he wants to do, that's that." But Daisy had an awful temper, was awful jealous. One time she saw me with another gal, and I saw her coming. She was getting ready to cut me with that razor, and I jumped that ditch and my hat fell off. So she picked it up and started cutting it all up. It was a John B. Stetson and I'd saved a long time to get that hat. Hurt me to my heart, man. Rather lose her than that hat.

In 1917 they closed down the district and all the honky-tonks and in 1918, when Joe Oliver left New Orleans with Jimmy Noone to play in Chicago, they put me in his place in Kid Ory's band playing at Tom Anderson's restaurant. That was a place the horse race crowd hung out, and when those big steaks, half eaten, would go back to the kitchen past the bandstand, we'd tell the waiter– "That's us." And what with all the cats dying and having funerals, I did all right.

A year later, when I was 19, I was hired to play summers with Fate Marable's band on the riverboat *Sidney*, with the big wheel in back. That was supposed to be getting somewhere, you know–up with the best musicians. We did night excursions up the river, leave about 8:30, come back about 12. The next year we operated out of St. Louis on the *J.S.* and the *St. Paul*, with wheels at the side, in the morning moseying down past Alton, Ill, and swing back up again. Take all day. Leaving from the dock, Fate Marable, the piano man, used to go up and play the calliope as the people came aboard. Then we'd start the band and people danced. They brought baskets of food, sometimes have a big orchestra, organizations would come.

Between trips on the boat I'd go up on the top deck with the mellophone player, David Jones, and he'd teach me about reading music–how to divide, like two four time, six eight time, had me count different exercises. Course I'd always had that voody voody there to play the jazz. We'd just go to a department store and get one of them copies. The man who could read take the lead, and we had it from there.

Each spring we used to go to Davenport, Iowa, where they kept the boats in chutes all winter. That's where I first met Bix Beiderbecke.

That was his home. At the time he was just a nice ofay kid the young musicians wanted to introduce to me. Never heard him play till I got his record *Singing the Blues*. Later on in Chicago when I was playing at the Sunset Cafe, he'd make a beeline for there when he finished playing at the Chicago Theater with Paul Whiteman. At 4 o'clock after the doors were closed, we'd all sit around and play a couple of hours. I was thrilled to death with whatever Bix did. He and I never had no contests. He knocked me out. He had such beautiful tone, those beautiful phrases, fingers fast. Yeah, he was my man. Choice man, too. Quiet. Never satisfied with his solos, and people raving. Always figured he had one better.

After Beiderbecke got popular, the boys grab him, keep him on Broadway—and go, cat. Couldn't touch him then. They had him booked for three, four jobs a night. Very important man, see. So we lost him.

The time of those riverboats, we'd just put in to New Orleans and on the levee was a cat name Jack Teagarden wanting to meet me—but I'd never heard of him. And then when he joined my band years later, it was like a holiday—we understood each other so wonderful. There ain't going to be another Jack Teagarden. Never was loud. He loved mechanical things, electronics. Go into his room, you liable to get shocked on wires. He was from Texas, but it was always, "You a spade, and I'm an ofay. We got the same soul. Let's blow"—and that's the way it was. He kept all his sad moments, his grievances to himself. But I could tell his whole heart, his life coming out of that horn. And it was all good.

I played summers on the riverboats for three years and then, in 1922, Joe Oliver sent me a telegram in New Orleans saying, "I want you to come up and join me." I'd just finished playing a funeral with the Tuxedo brass band, and they all come to the station to get my ticket. I used to see so many kids leave New Orleans, and they'd be gone a long time, and then you look around and they have to hobo their way back home. Wasn't nobody going to get *me* to leave New Orleans but King Oliver. All my life was wrapped around Joe Oliver. I lived for Papa Joe. So his calling for me was the biggest feeling I ever had musically.

Just before I left, old Slippers, the bouncer at the honky-tonk where I played, came up to me and said, "I sure like the way you blow that quail (he didn't know it was called a cornet) and you going up North now." And then he said, "Always keep a white man behind you that'll put his hand on you and say, 'That's my nigger.'" Years later I told that to Joe Glaser, my ofay manager and he said, "You're nuts."

For the train ride up to Chicago Mayann fixed me a big trout sandwich. And I had on my long underwear 'cause she didn't want me to catch cold. I had me a little suitcase—didn't have but a few clothes—and a little case for my cornet. I traveled in style, you know, in my way.

When I got to the station in Chicago, I couldn't see Joe Oliver anywhere. I saw a million people, but not Mister Joe, and I didn't give a damn who else was there. I'd never seen a city that big. All those tall buildings. I thought they were universities. I said, no, this is the wrong city. I was just fixing to take the next train back home—standing there in my box-back suit, padded shoulders, doublebreasted, wide-leg pants—when a redcap Joe had left word with came up to me. He took me to the Lincoln Gardens and when I got to the door there and heard Joe and his band wailing so good, I said to myself, "No, I ain't supposed to be in *this* band. They're too good." And then Joe came out and said, "You little fool, come on in here." I said, "OK, Dad." I was home then.

The next night I just went to work. And it was better than all the moments I'd ever had. Didn't get but $52 a week, but that was more than I got in New Orleans.

In those days the bands sat on chairs and Joe, with his big wad of chewing tobacco in his cheek, would go *pa-chooo* into a brass cuspidor, then he'd start beating his foot on top of that cuspidor, setting that tempo, and *blow!* And whatever Mister Joe played, I just put notes to it trying to make it sound as pretty as I could. I never blew my horn over Joe Oliver at no time unless he said, "Take it!" Never. Papa Joe was a creator—always some little idea—and he exercised them beautifully. I hear them phrases of his in big arrangements and everything right now. And sitting by him every night, I *had* to pick up a lot of little tactics he made—phrases, first endings, flairs. I'll never run out of ideas. All I have to do is think about Joe and always have something to play off of.

While the rest of the band was playing, Oliver'd lean over to me and move the valves on his cornet in the notes he would play in the next breaks or a riff he'd use. So I'd play second to it. Pretty fast kid I was, in those days—and I admired him so and dug him so wonderful. A lot of guys would come down and pick up on that, write the notes down on their cuffs.

I was very happy. The band was all fine fellows. Johnny Dodds had a $4,000 diamond ring on his finger as he played the clarinet, and he and I used to buy a newspaper together every day. All Johnny wanted was the baseball scores, and I got the rest of the paper. He was a quiet fellow, but he had his own mind. Saved his money and bought a big flatiron building—and he used to work awful hard on it keeping it in shape. On the piano was Lil Hardin, who was a full-fledged musician, graduated from Fisk University—been playing with all the greats, knew everybody. Later on we got married.

Joe Oliver was a big, tall man, loved his home, and I used to have my meals with him and his wife, Stella. He loved water with lots and lots of sugar in it—could eat a whole loaf of bread with it. He loved baseball, crazy about the White Sox, went to the game every day. And he was a good pool player. Didn't drink or smoke. Had a cataract eye. But it didn't hinder him from reading those music cards in the street parades—or from seeing those horse piles in the streets. He beat the world stepping over them sons-of-bitches. Ain't never scooted in one yet. Oh, God, he was a great boy!

One night playing there in the Lincoln Gardens I suddenly see my mother coming across the dance floor right toward the bandstand, a couple of big paper bundles under the arms. She looked right at me and said, "I come to get you." Seems some cat told her I was stranded in Chicago, and that when he asked me why I didn't go home, I just held my head down and cried. . . . I told her, "Aw, don't believe that."

I rented an apartment and we lived together, and I bought her a lot of fine clothes and everything. They were so nice, she just had to go back home to New Orleans to show all her church women her new clothes. Then she came back up. I married Lil Hardin, and Mayann lived with us. I used to take Mama cabareting, and we'd get soused together. Used to have a very nice time. Yeah, I miss old Mayann. Her funeral in Chicago is probably the only time I ever cried—when they put that cover over her face.

I was making money and she had a beautiful funeral. Thank God for that. Didn't have to put the saucer on her. I've seen that happen to many of 'em don't have no insurance or belong to no club. While you laying out there in the wake, they put a saucer on your chest and everybody who comes in drops a nickel or a dime or quarter to try to make up for the undertaker.

1966

Anne Rice

The Feast of All Saints

O N E M O R N I N G in New Orleans, in that part of the Rue Ste. Anne before it crosses Condé and becomes the lower boundary of the Place d'Armes, a young boy who had been running full tilt down the middle of the street stopped suddenly, his chest heaving, and began to deliberately and obviously follow a tall woman.

This was the street in which he lived, though he was blocks from home, and the woman lived in it also. So a number of people on the way to market—or lounging in the doors of their shops to garner a little breeze—knew the pair of them and thought as they glanced at the boy, that is Marcel Ste. Marie, Cecile's son, and what is he doing now?

These were the riverfront streets of the 1840s, packed with immigrants, where the worlds met over the back fence, and gallery to gallery; yet despite the throng, and the wilderness of masts above the levee markets, the French Quarter was then as forever a small town. And the woman was famous in it.

But all were used to her occasional meandering, a senselessly disheveled figure with beauty and money enough to make her a public offense. It was Marcel they worried about when they saw them together (the woman didn't know they were together). And dozens of others stared at him, too, not knowing him, just for the sake of staring because he was a striking figure.

That he was part African, a quadroon most likely, anyone could figure, and the white and the black blood in him had combined in an unusual way that was extremely handsome and clearly undesirable. For though his skin was lighter than honey, indeed lighter than that of many white people who were forever studying him, he had large vivid blue eyes which made it dusky. And his blond hair, tightly kinked and hugging his round head like a cap, was distinctly African. He had ridgeless eyebrows which were high and gave his expression an appealing openness, a delicate nose with small flared nostrils, and a full mouth like a child's even to the pale rose color. Later it might be sensual, but now, in his fourteenth year, it was a Cupid's bow without a single hard line to it, and the down on his upper lip was smoky as was the bit of curling hair that made up his sideburns.

In short, his was an appearance of contrasts, but everyone knew darker men could pass for white while Marcel would never, and those bound to believe him deprived of a coveted asset were disturbed at times to find themselves so drawn to looking at him, unable to anatomize him in a glance. And women thought him positively exquisite.

The yellow skin on the backs of his hands appeared silky and translucent, and he tended to grasp things that interested him, suddenly, with long fingers that appeared reverent. And sometimes if he turned to look up at you abruptly from a glass display case under a lamp, the light would make his close-cropped hair a halo around his head, and he stared with the serious radiance of those roundfaced Byzantine saints who are rapt with the Beatific Vision.

In fact, this expression was fast becoming habitual with him. He had it now as he hurried across the Rue Condé after the woman, his hands unconsciously formed into fists, his mouth slack. He saw only what was ahead of him, or his own thoughts, you couldn't always tell which, but he never seemed to see himself in the eyes of others, to sense the power of the impression he made.

And it was indeed a powerful impression. For though such dreaminess might have been past all patience in a poor man, or some drifting nuisance for whom things had endlessly to be repeated, it was perfectly fine in Marcel because he was by no means poor, as everyone knew, and was invariably well dressed.

For years he'd been the gentleman in miniature in the streets, on errands or carrying his missal to Mass, his frock coats too perfectly fitted as if he weren't sure to outgrow them in half a year, linen immaculate, waistcoats so smooth over his narrow chest that they hadn't the slightest bulge or wrinkle. On Sundays, he wore a small jeweled stickpin in his silk tie, and had lately been carrying a gold pocket watch which he sometimes stopped dead in the streets to study, teeth pressed to his lower lip, his blond eyebrows knit in a sharp look of distress that strained the taut skin of his forehead. His boots were always new.

In short, slaves of the same color knew at once he was free, and white men thought him at a glance a "fine boy," but when all that is put aside, which is only the beginning, his preoccupation seemed the absence of pride, he was no snob, but possessed a genuine and precocious gentility.

You couldn't imagine him climbing a tree, or playing stick ball, or wetting his hands except to wash them. The books he carried eternally were ancient and tattered, leather covers bound with ribbon or string; but even this was elegant. And he had about him often the subtle scent of a cologne seldom lavished on boys.

Of course Marcel was the son of a white planter, Philippe Ferronaire, Creole gentleman to his fingertips, and in debt on the next crop to the hilt, his white children crowding the family box at the opera every season. And though no one would have thought of calling the man "Marcel's father," that is what he was, and the sight of his carriage listing in the narrow Rue Ste. Anne before the Ste. Marie cottage was somewhat regular.

So people thinking Marcel splendid and rich forgave him his slight peculiarity, and merely smiled when he ran smack into them on the banquette, or leaning forward, snapped their fingers, hissing gently "Hey Marcel!" And he would wake to the solid and familiar to go on being unfailingly polite.

He paid his mother's bills promptly, tipped generously for the slightest service, and on his own brought her flowers from the florist which everyone thought powerfully romantic; and often in the past, though seldom lately, had escorted about his sister, Marie, with an affection and obvious pride in her uncommon in a brother so young. Marie at thirteen was an ivory beauty, ripening beneath a child's lace and pearl buttons.

But people if they knew Marcel at all, had begun to worry about him. He seemed in the last six months bound to ruin himself, for with his fourteenth birthday in the last fall, he had been transformed from the innocent to the mysterious without apparent explanation.

It was a gradual thing, however, and fourteen is a difficult age.

Besides it wasn't ordinary mischief. It had a curious flair.

He was seen all around the French quarter at odd hours, roaming for the sake of roaming, and several times recently he had appeared in the rear pew of the Cathedral, staring at every detail of the statues and paintings as if he were a baffled immigrant off the ship and not a boy who'd been baptized there and made his Communion in the same place only a year before.

He bought tobacco he wasn't supposed to smoke, read a folded newspaper while walking, watched with fascination the butchers under the eaves of the French Market hacking bloody sides of beef into parcels, and wandered astonished along the levee the day that the H.M.S. *Catherine* docked, her load of starving Irish the scandal of the summer. Wraiths too weak to walk, they were carted to the Charity Hospital and some of them right to the Bayou Cemetery, where Marcel stood watching the burials, and all this when he must have seen it so many times in the past with yellow fever coming on every summer and the stench from the cemeteries so thick in the steaming streets that it became the breath of life. Death was everywhere in New Orleans, what of it? Why go stare at it?

In a cabaret, he was served absinthe before the owner recognized him and sent him home. So he took to worse places, waterfront bistros where in the smoke-filled shadows he would pull out a morocco-bound book in which to write, and sometimes with the same book, wander into the Place d'Armes, fall on a bit of grass under a tree as if he were a derelict and there commence the same scribbling or what might have a been the drawing of pictures as he squinted at the birds, the trees, the sky. This was ridiculous.

And yet he didn't seem to know it.

And worse was the sight of his sister, Marie, on tiptoe at the doors of the dram shops, shuffled in such a crowd, her hair down to her waist, her childish dresses hardly concealing the fullness of her figure, beckoning for him to come out.

Mother and daughter came alone to Sunday Mass where there had always been three.

But who knew much about Cecile Ste. Marie, Marcel's mother, except that she was a stunning lady, laced so tight beneath her taffeta that her heart seemed forever fighting for breath beneath the frill at her throat. Her black hair parted in the middle and pulled back over the tips of her ears, she would stand proudly with arms folded at the back door, fighting with butcher and fishmonger before pointing their merchandise to the kitchen. Hers was a French face, petite, sharp of feature, with no trace of the African, except of course for her beautifully textured and very dark skin. She seldom went out, occasionally clipped roses in her garden and confided to no one.

The Ste. Marie cottage gleamed with respectability beyond its short fence and dense banana trees, a sprawl of magnolia limbs over its pitched roof. And one could only speculate, was she worried about her son, Marcel? And what did she say to the white man, Monsieur Philippe, Marcel's father, when he came, if she said anything at all? But neighbors said there was occasional shouting behind the lace curtains and even the slamming of doors.

And what would she think now if she saw her son following this woman, the infamous Juliet Mercier? Should he come too close Juliet might just strike him with her market basket, or scratch his face. She was mad.

And any speculation on her made Marcel at once the paragon. He was, after all, just a boy, and a good one at that. He'd straighten up. He was high in the small private academy of Monsieur De Latte, which cost a fortune, and would undoubtedly come to his senses.

But Juliet was shameful, she had "no excuse," people shunned her, he ought to shun her, certainly shouldn't be following her, she had become the object of absolute scorn. How dare she retreat in her listing mansion on the corner of Ste. Anne and Dauphine and nail boards over the windows that fronted the street, vanishing so totally from life that neighbors thought her dead and beat down the gate? And then to come racing toward them with an ax, her hair streaming like an Ophelia, a gaggle of hens in a swirl of feathers screeching at her wake? So let her be shut up with chickens and flies. Let the cats roam the top of her sagging courtyard walls. One and all banged their shutters shut on her as if she hadn't already bolted her own.

She was not old by any means, had the slender figure of a girl at forty, hair of gleaming black with skin so light she might have passed to the untutored eye, and rings on her fingers when she chose. It was outrageous, this waste of prime and property . . . but worst of all, worst of all . . . it was the matter of her son, Christophe.

He was the one whose name was on everyone's lips these days, a star in this constellation where he had not been for a decade. Because gone to Paris years before, he was now a famous man. For three years his essays and stories had appeared in the Paris press, along with colorful accounts of his Eastern travels, reviews of the theater, art, music. And his novel, *Nuits de Charlotte*, had taken the city by storm. He was a dandy in dress, veritably lived in the cafés of the Rue Saint Jacques, surrounded eternally by exotic and scribbling friends. Children abroad sent home his articles, his stories in the *Revue des Deux Mondes*, copies of his novel and the reviews which sang his praises as a "master of the language," or a "new and unbridled imagination, Shakespearean in power, Byronic in tone." And even those who understood not a particle of the ravings of his bizarre characters nodded with respect at the mention of him and among many he was no longer Christophe Mercier, but merely Christophe, as if he had become familiar and a friend to all those who admired him.

Even the white planters' sons carried his novel in their pockets when they got off the boat and told stories of having seen him emerge from a cabriolet before the Porte-Saint-Martin Theatre, a white actress on his sleeve. And slaves overhearing these stories at table brought them to town.

But among the colored community there was more than a special pride. Many could remember the boy he had been when the dreary house in the Rue Dauphine had blazed with lights, and handsome men were forever at the gate to take the hand of his mother. And most concurred he might have buried his past had he chosen, there was light skin enough and money, and the warm embrace of fame. But he did not. Over and over in this or that notice or bit of article, there appeared the fact that he was a native of this city, that he was a man of color, and that he had a mother residing here still.

Of course, he was in Paris. When you die . . . you go to Paris.

He drank champagne with Victor Hugo, dined with Louis Philippe in the Hall of Mirrors, and danced at the Tuileries. White women were seen occasionally to draw back the curtains from his high windows on the Ile St. Louis and look over the quay toward Notre Dame. He sent home trunks brought in cabs from the customhouse to vanish through his mother's gate. And she, the wretch, unkempt, distracted, wandered to market with her black cat, in the rich and ragged costume of a beggar at the opera.

Marcel was familiar with these tales. He had been at his front gate the day she swung the ax in the dirt corner where their streets met. And knew the letters for "Christophe" that his friends put through the gate were beaten white of ink on the garden path by the falling rain.

What he really didn't know was how things had been before. Though one evening at home, Monsieur Philippe in his blue robe, lounging at table the way Marcel would never have thought to do in his own house even if no one were there, said idly through his aura of cigar smoke, "Perhaps that boy, Christophe, was destined for great things."

"How so?" asked Cecile politely. It was that hour when she sat across from him, her face softened and serene in the light of the candles, enthralled as Philippe unwound his lustrous chatter, and Marcel pretended to read at the open *secrétaire*.

What had the boy, Christophe, been like?

The picture dazzled.

Of how the little one was forever falling asleep in his mother's box at the opera when his legs weren't long enough yet to reach the floor, or at midnight suppers was left to doze on a settee against the folded coat of a gentleman caller, or a visiting ship's captain who had brought with him a parrot in a cage. Men of all hues and shades took their turns at the late night soirees while restaurants of any reputation sooner or later sent steaming trays up the wooden stairs.

And it was the waiters often enough who, having gathered the stained linen and the silver dollars, put the child to bed, removing his shoes.

They said he drew on the walls, collected the feathers of birds, and played in his mother's dresses, acting Henry IV on the dining-room table.

What a figure! Marcel had let his book close. He shut his eyes, thought of those times when this heroic presence had reigned at the very corner of the block. What friends they might have been! And what was there now in his world but well-behaved children! If only he could have spoken directly to Monsieur Philippe, the questions he might have asked.

But the subject made Cecile nervous, it was clear, Marcel could tell. She didn't remember those times, no, she shook her head, as if the world ended at her front gate.

But the story took its turn. Monsieur Philippe loved the sound of his own voice.

And when Christophe was thirteen, a final guest arrived who stayed, though forever shrouded in mystery, a black veteran of the Haitian wars.

"You remember him, that old man." Monsieur Philippe bit off the tip of his cigar and spat it in the grate. Marcel knew those subtle sounds by heart. Like the chink of the neck of the bottle hitting the rim of the glass, and that soft breath of satisfaction after each drink. "Of course we were suspicious of him, who needs these rebel slaves from Haiti . . . Haiti! It was Saint-Domingue when my great-uncle owned the biggest plantation on the Plaine du Nord. Ah, but the point is, the man was abroad so long, money in Paris, New York, Charleston . . . banks here, uptown. Hardly the one to set fire to every sugar plantation on the coast and lead a band of ragged blacks to cut our throats."

In the mirror, Marcel saw his mother shudder; she rubbed the backs of her arms, her head to one side, eyes on the lace tablecloth. Ragged army of blacks to cut our throats, the words struck some sudden excitement in Marcel, what was Monsieur Philippe talking about? But it was Christophe that interested him, not that mysterious history of Haiti of which Marcel got bits and pieces at odd moments, never enough to make a picture of anything except rebel slaves and blood.

And he was old besides, this black Haitian, and crippled. And soon sick of seeing Christophe feast on chocolates and white wine, accustomed to sleep in his mother's bed when he chose, and permitted to lie on the sloped roof at night, three stories above the street to study the stars, he sent the boy abroad.

Christophe was fourteen when he left, and people argued about the rest. It was uncertain, some saying he boarded in England for a while, others that no, he went to Paris, having *in loco parentis* the white family of a hotelkeeper who kept him in a veritable closet under the stairs, without even a candle let alone heat on winter nights. He was beaten there some insisted, others that, spoiled as always, he had had his own way, lashing out at these poor bourgeoisie any time they tried to restrain him.

But one thing was sure, that at sixteen he had run away to Egypt, wandered through Greece and returned to Paris in the company of a wealthy Englishman, white of course, to become an artist. He'd written of these exotic lands, Monsieur Philippe had an article somewhere sent home by his young brother-in-law, Vincent, where was it (what Marcel wouldn't have given to lay hands on it). But back to those times when he was wandering, and slaves over the back fence said the old Haitian, now bedridden, had disowned him. What claim had he over that beautiful Juliet, who could imagine? She with that pale golden skin and delicate face . . . but Philippe merely touched on that lightly, she had died on the vine. Cecile nodded.

And they said she drank sherry and fell to merely watching the rain.

And that she was mean to the old Haitian in the last year of his life, yes, Cecile had heard that too, when paralyzed he had to lie there to be fed softboiled egg with a spoon. The blinds were shut forever. Children of five and six thought the house haunted and loved to run past it squealing. Ah, look at it now, a jungle behind those cracked brick walls, and a peeling hulk on the busy corner.

But at just this time, across the sea, Christophe's star rose.

Marcel could remember the rest.

And long after Monsieur Philippe had let the tale drop, he traced the thread in his own memory—how people had gathered to watch the old man's casket come out because of the son's fame. And only when it was all over, and a ghastly, worn Juliet walked back from the cemetery in the scorching sun, did people begin to whisper the truth. It was on the tombstone. The old Haitian had been her father!

So didn't he have some rights over the boy, his own grandson?

But what would she do now, take lovers? Get new servants for those sold off or dead, patch the walls, bring the drapers and painters up the steps? No one doubted she could do it. She was so-o-o-o lovely still, Marcel at twelve was mad to get a glimpse of her. He didn't really understand about Christophe then. He was "in love" with something or someone else. It did not come to him as having meaning yet that a famous man had lived there, walked there, breathed there.

And she did nothing. Her windows crusted with dirt, her garden wall became a menace. The vines that pushed it out miraculously held it up. She did not answer notes or knocks, and soon the hatred commenced. It was unfair! Christophe's *Nuits de Charlotte* stood open in the windows of the booksellers. Stupid, silly . . . but most of all unfair.

How wonderful it would have been, after all, to "receive" her and hear about the young man firsthand, be her friend. But she became a witch in time, her lone-ness not only absurd but unfathomable. How, after all, could she endure it? The last of her slaves was put to rest in the Old St. Louis. The house was empty save for the cats.

Pity went fast, however, for she was too vicious if you spoke to her on the street, turning away at once, her head bowed, her cat in the basket on her arm. And with her son's fame, increased the hatred.

But the boys Marcel's age were now on fire for Christophe. They worshiped him, and sternly forbidden to go near his mother they nevertheless lingered at her gate, hoping to put but one question, and always in vain. If she came out at all, they scattered. She looked too dreadful with her diamond rings in the noonday sun, an inch of petticoat beneath her hem. The mailman brought her letters from France, they got that out of him, but did she even pick them up from the gravel path? Straining to see through a chink in the wood, they had the worst fears.

But she was Christophe's mother after all. They couldn't despise her out of loyalty, and they had other things on their minds. Like writing stories in his "style," making scrapbooks of clippings sent home by older brothers, uncles, cousins. And lounging about in each others' parlors on afternoons when the adults were out, they dreamed aloud with pilfered brandy of the day they would make the fabled pilgrimage to Paris, might knock on his black lacquered door on the Ile St. Louis and reverently, politely, gently, unimposingly, hand him their sheaf of manuscript pages.

Occasionally there was an uncle or a brother home who had, in fact, drunk with him in some crowded café, and then the rumors went wild.

He smoked hashish, talked in riddles, could be seen quarreling in the streets, and staying drunk for twenty-four hours at a stretch, he talked to himself, and sometimes fell into a stupor at a café table. And there would appear that Englishman, "white of course," who would pick him up, slap his face gently with a few drops of water, and slinging Christophe's arm over his shoulder, carry him home.

But he was kind to his countrymen always. He never read stories shoved at him across tables, but gave gentle general advice, and when a tactful introduction here or there could be effected, did that with grace. He showed no shame of race, clasped dark hands, asked about New Orleans, and certainly seemed to listen. But he was quick to be bored, to grow silent and then be gone. You clanged his bell in vain after that. He knew when he had done all he could and you had nothing to offer.

Ah, admire him if you will, but imitate him never, said the parents to the enamored children. Marcel worshiped him, and those who watched his recent wanderings wondered if it were some mad emulating of the famous man that sent Marcel off the track.

For Christophe set the other boys on the straight and narrow when they thought of him. They wanted the tools to be like him, and in the scattered private schools around the town, here under a white teacher, there under a colored, they strove tensely, the lessons expensive, the classes select. They must be educated when they stepped off the boat, they had to be men.

And that Marcel would make the journey to Paris, that he would have his chance—all that was certain. A promise made by Monsieur Philippe at his birth was the guarantee. And sooner or later, at least once a year, that promise was reiterated. Cecile saw to that. She had no concern for her daughter Marie, she said, Marie would "do well." Lips pressed tight, she dismissed that subject abruptly. But in the warmest and best moments would broach the matter of her son. Marcel, lying awake on smothering summer nights when the mosquito netting, gleaming gold in the faint spluttering nightlight, became the only walls dividing them, would hear Monsieur Philippe murmur on the pillow, "I'll send the boy in style . . . " It was a vintage promise, a part of life. So why not work toward it?

But Marcel daydreamed in class, provoked the teacher with obscure questions, and the sight of his empty chair a dozen times in the last month filled everyone with a vague dread. He was too well liked for the others boys to enjoy it. And his best friend, Richard Lermontant, seemed rather miserable. But what made this fall from grace all the more confusing, especially to Richard, was that Marcel himself seemed not the least confused by it. He was hardly helpless in the face of youthful passion. He did not, for instance, court his sister's pretty friends and then, giggling, yank their hair. Nor did he pound his fist on tree trunks declaring, "I don't know what got into me!" And never once, in a welter of confusion, did he call on God to explain how he could make the races different colors, or demand an explanation for why the world was cruel.

Rather he seemed privy to some terrible secret that set him apart, and bound to calmly pursue his course.

Which this morning seemed hell-bent for disaster.

It was a warm summer day, and he had only caught his breath as he drew closer and closer to the volatile Juliet when she stopped at the fruit stands beneath the arcade. And putting his left hand up against the slender iron post in front of him, he pressed his lips against his hand and gazed at her with wide blue eyes. He did not realize it, but he seemed to want to hide behind the colonette, as if such a narrow thing could hide him, and he had covered all his face except his eyes.

There was pain in his eyes, but the kind that reveals itself in a flicker, the puckering of the eyelid underneath, a flinching at one's own thoughts. Looking at Juliet, he knew full well what he was expected to see, and understood full well what he, in fact, perceived. Not squalor and wickedness but some radiant and splendid spectacle of neglect that laid his heart waste. But this had been today a matter of glimpses. . . .

Running breathless to her gate from school, he'd pounded on it for the first time in his life, only to be told by a shouting neighbor that she'd gone to market. But he'd caught the first sight of her only a block away. And she was tall and he could trace her easily.

Now, when the flock of bonneted women broke between them, and she stepped out again into the cobblestone street, he saw her clearly for the first time.

He started, all of a piece, like a man jumping to the clang of a bell, and moved as if he might go up to her. Then he lapsed back, lips pressed again to the back of his hand, as she made her way under the clear sun to the iron fence of the square. He seemed lost to her in every detail and silently shuddered.

She was slow if not languid as she walked, her market basket riding gently on her arm, and as he had seen her a thousand times, fantastical, her frayed shawl a blaze of peacocks and silver against her red silk dress, flounces torn and dragging the stones, her fine brunette hair falling in hopeless tangles from the grip of a pearl comb. Diamonds sparkled on the fingers of her right hand with which she gathered her skirts at the curb, and as she turned toward the long row of sketches for sale on the pickets, Marcel could see her profile for an instant and the flash of the gold loop in her ear.

Suddenly, a great lumbering hack rattled by, obliterating her, and maddened, he darted across the street behind it, coming to a slapping halt so that she turned around.

Someone called his name. He didn't hear it, but then he did, and couldn't remember it. She was looking at him, and he had lapsed again into the utter passivity of a staring child.

Only a yard stood between them. It seemed in years he had never been so close to her, her amber face as smooth as a girl's, deepset black eyes fringed with lashes, the high smooth expanse of her forehead broken by a widow's peak from which her hair grew back in lustrous waves. She was mildly curious as she looked at him. Then, her thin rouged lips drew back into the curve of her cheek and the supple flesh around her eyes was etched with fine lines as she smiled.

A tiny heart pounded in Marcel's temple. Someone brushed his shoulder, yet he didn't move. Someone said his name.

But suddenly as if something had distracted her Juliet bowed her head, tilting it strangely to one side and groped with her fingers in her hair. She was searching for the comb as though it had begun to hurt her. And as she jerked it out and looked at it, all of her black hair fell down over her shoulders in a cascade.

A soft excited sound escaped Marcel's lips. Someone had a hold on his arm, but he merely flinched, stiffened, and let his eyes grow wide again, ignoring the young man at his side.

All he could feel was the pounding of his own heart and he had the distinct impression that the rush of horses and wheels in the street had become deafening. There was shouting somewhere, and from the riverfront before him came those echoing booms from the unloading ships. But he saw none of this. He was seeing only Juliet, though not right now. Rather it was another time, long long ago, before he was the villain he had become of late, the outcast. But it was a time so palpable that whenever it came back to him, it engulfed him and was memory no longer, but pure sensation. His tongue pressed against his teeth and he felt flushed and stunned. He might even be sick. And just for a moment he didn't know for certain where he was, which might lead to terror. But groping for a hold, he found the memory which was a spell.

Running home years ago, he'd stubbed his boot on a fallen lump of coal in the street and been thrown right into her arms. In fact he'd pushed her backwards as he gripped the taffeta of her soft waist and then seeing it was she, Juliet, let go in such panic he would have fallen if she hadn't clasped his shoulder. Looking up into her eyes like beads of jet, he saw the buttons all undone from her throat, and the mound of her naked breast pushed against the placket of shimmering cloth. There was a darkness there beneath the undercurve where he could see the soft meeting of chest and bosom. And an alien surge had made him shudder. He had felt her thumb against his cheek like sealskin, and then the open palm of her hand rubbing gently back and forth, back and forth against his tight curly hair. Her eyes seemed blind then. Her fine small waist was flesh beneath the cloth only, an astonishing nakedness. And the scent of spice and flowers lingered afterwards on his hands. He almost died.

He was almost dying now. And then and now, he watched baffled, weak, as she moved away from him like a tall ship, upstream.

"But this has nothing to do with it!" he whispered, the shame burning in his cheeks, unable to keep his lips from moving (he was a great one for talking right out loud to himself, and was forever relieved when others, coming upon him unawares assumed he had been singing). "It's Christophe," he went on. "I have to talk to her about Christophe!"

But the mere vision of her swaying skirts was stunning him again and he murmured in French out loud with a melodramatic air, "I *am* a criminal," and felt some mild relief at being the abject object of his own condemnation. Too many nights had he indulged himself thinking of that chance childhood collision—the naked breast, uncorseted waist, wild perfume—so that now he had to draw himself up like a gentleman who, having glimpsed an unclad lady at her bath, shuts the door and quickly walks away.

This was the Place d'Armes, someone was trying to break his arm.

He stared astonished at the breast buttons of Richard Lermontant, his best friend.

"No, go on, Richard," he said quickly, as if they'd been arguing all the while, "go on back to school," and craning his neck to see Juliet disappear in the throng at the market, tried to wrench himself free.

"You are telling *me* to go back to school?" demanded Richard, holding him fast. His voice was low and deep, all but a whisper on the word of emphasis. "Marcel, look at me!" It was always Richard's habit to lower his voice precisely at that point where others raise theirs, and it was invariably effective, perhaps because he was so tall. He towered over Marcel, though he was only sixteen. In fact, he towered over everyone in the street. "Monsieur De Latte's furious!" he confided drawing close. "You've got to come back with me now."

"No!" Marcel said shortly, and lurched forward freeing himself and stifling the urge to rub the upper part of his arm. Seldom in his life had he been touched except in anger, and he had a healthy distrust of being held, loathing it in fact, though it was impossible for him to loathe Richard. They were more than friends, and he simply couldn't bear to be angry with Richard or to have Richard angry with him. "Be a good friend to me," he turned pleading. "and go. I don't care what you tell Monsieur De Latte. Tell him anything." And he started off fast for the corner.

Richard overtook him quickly.

"But why are you doing this? What's the point of it?" he pleaded, his shoulders slightly bent so he could be near Marcel's ear. "You ran out in the middle of class, do you realize what you've done?"

"Yes, I realize it. I did it, I did it," Marcel said, blundering into the traffic of the riverfront street, so that he was at once forced back on the curb. "But let me go please." He could just make out the top of Juliet's head at the fish market. *"Give up on me, please!"*

Richard let him go, and clasping his hands behind his back he gained at once what seemed a characteristic composure so that nothing of the sixteen-year-old boy was left in him. In fact he had an ageless look most of the time so that strangers might think him twenty, perhaps older. He had never asked for his height, in fact, had prayed against it, but a manly spirit had some time ago invaded his long limbs; and as he stood very still with one foot forward and his shoulders only a little bent, his lean face with its prominent cheekbones and slanting black eyes made him appear at once majestic and exotic. He was darker than Marcel, all of an olive complexion, his hair wavy and black. But this suggested the Turk, the Spaniard perhaps, or even the Italian, and almost nothing of the French and the Senegalese from whom he was descended.

Gesturing with a languid hand, fingers sloping gracefully from the wrist, he whispered, "You have to come back, Marcel, you have to!" But Marcel was looking toward the market again where a great flock of birds rose suddenly from the tiled roof, looping and descending on the masts above the dock. His eyes narrowed. Juliet had emerged from the crowd feeding fish on her fingers to her cat.

Startled, Richard said, "You aren't following her!"

An involuntary look of distaste passed over his face, which he quickly banished, but not before Marcel had seen it. "But why?"

"What do you mean, why? You know why," Marcel said. "I have to ask her if it's true . . . I have to know now."

"This is all my fault," Richard murmured.

"Go back." Marcel started off again. And again Richard clutched his arm.

"She won't know, Marcel . . . and if she does what makes you think she'll tell you! She's not in her right mind!" he whispered, and glancing at her, dropped his eyes politely as if she were a cripple.

Her hair was in streams now like that of an immigrant, and she wandered through the crowd letting her feet find her path so that people all but stumbled over her as she crooned to the cat. Richard's thin, large-boned frame stiffened as he shifted his weight. The boy in him wanted to cry.

"You won't turn to stone, looking at her!" Marcel whispered. And astonished, Richard saw a vicious spark in Marcel's eyes, and heard a driving impatience in his voice.

"This is craziness," Richard muttered, and almost turned to go. Then he said, "If you don't come back with me now . . . you'll be sent home from school for good."

"For good?" Marcel reeled half off the curb. "Well then, good!" And he started across the street to her.

Richard was speechless. He stared beyond the row of crawling carts that worked against the crowds from the market, and as Marcel approached Christophe's mother, Richard went after him.

"Well, then give me back the clipping!" he said, his voice thick. "You know perfectly well it's Antoine's, I want it."

At once Marcel rummaged in his pockets and drew out a crumpled bit of newspaper with neatly trimmed edges. He tried desperately to smooth it in the palm of his hand. "I didn't mean to steal it," he said. "I was excited . . . I meant to put it back on your desk . . . "

Richard's face was dark with anger. He glanced from second to second at the figure of Juliet, and then at the ground.

"I would have brought it to you before supper," Marcel insisted. "You have to believe that."

"It's not even mine, it's Antoine's, and you stuffed it in your pocket and ran out."

"If you don't believe me," Marcel insisted, "you wound me in my heart."

"I know perfectly well where your heart is," Richard murmured, with a glance at the *mea culpa* fist Marcel touched to his breast. "And you're in for a lot more than pangs there, I'll tell you. You're going to be expelled!"

Marcel didn't even seem to understand.

"And suppose it's true," Richard went on, "suppose Christophe is coming back here . . . What kind of a recommendation is it—to be bounced out of Monsieur De Latte's school on your ear?"

Richard folded the clipping, but not without reading it quickly again. It seemed a flimsy piece of evidence to push Marcel to ruin. But, how splendid it had seemed that morning, when Antoine, Richard's cousin, cutting open the letter from Paris, had given it to Richard at the table. Christophe coming back at last. They had always dreamed of it, hoped for it, told themselves the day would come when he would learn of his mother's madness and if nothing else had done the trick, his love for her would bring him home. But there was so much more to it than that. One was left no room for fantasy, for speculation. It was spelled out plainly that Christophe Mercier planned no simple visit, but a real return. He was coming home to "found a school for the members of his race."

By the evening all the community of the *gens de couleur* would be aflame with it, this news which had sent Richard flying toward Monsieur De Latte's classroom to share it with Marcel. And now this turn had been taken, this bolting by Marcel through the open doorway with Monsieur De Latte shouting for order and cracking his stick on the lectern.

It seemed sour now, painful. A cloud hung over Richard that made the very streets dreary, like soot on the bricks.

But he looked up suddenly and was mortified. Juliet now a yard away was staring at them both. He felt his cheek flame. And Marcel was moving suddenly toward her! Richard turned, darting through the stagnant stream of mules and wagons until he was rushing fast along the Place d'Armes, headed back to school the way he'd come.

But it pounded in his head with every step: this is my fault, this is all my fault. I should have kept it till the right time. This is my fault.

1979

Zora Neale Hurston

Hoodoo

WINTER PASSED and caterpillars began to cross the road again. I had spend a year in gathering and culling over folktales. I loved it, but I had to bear in mind that there was a limit to the money to be spent on the project, and as yet, I had done nothing about hoodoo.

So I slept a night, and the next morning I headed my toenails toward Louisiana and New Orleans in particular.

New Orleans is now and has ever been the hoodoo capital of America. Great names in rites that vie with those of Hayti in deeds that keep alive the powers of Africa.

Hoodoo, or Voodoo, as pronounced by the whites, is burning with a flame in America, with all the intensity of a suppressed religion. It has its thousands of secret adherents. It adapts itself like Christianity to its locale, reclaiming some of its borrowed characteristics to itself, such as fire-worship as signified in the Christian church by the altar and the candles and the belief in the power of water to sanctify as in baptism.

Belief in magic is older than writing. So nobody knows how it started.

The way we tell it, hoodoo started way back there before everything. Six days of magic spells and mighty words and the world with its elements above and below was made. And now, God is leaning back taking a seventh day rest. When the eighth day comes around, He'll start to making new again.

Man wasn't made until around half-past five on the sixth day, so he can't know how anything was done. Kingdoms crushed and crumbled whilst man went gazing up into the sky and down into the hollows of the earth trying to catch God working with His hands so he could find out His secrets and learn how to accomplish and do. But no man yet has seen God's hand, nor yet His finger-nails. All they could know was that God made everything to pass and perish except stones. God made stones for memory. He builds a mountain Himself when He wants things not forgot. Then His voice is heard in rumbling judgment.

Moses was the first man who ever learned God's power-compelling words and it took him forty years to learn ten words. So he made ten plagues and ten commandments. But God gave him His rod for a present, and showed him the back part of His glory. Then too, Moses could walk out of the sight of man. But Moses never would have stood before the Burning Bush, if he had not married Jethro's daughter. Jethro was a great hoodoo man. Jethro could tell Moses could carry power as soon as he saw him. In fact he felt him coming. Therefore, he took Moses and crowned him and taught him. So Moses passed on beyond Jethro with his rod. He lifted it up and tore a nation out of Pharaoh's side, and Pharaoh couldn't help himself. Moses talked with the snake that lives in a hole right under God's foot-rest. Moses had fire in his head and a cloud in his mouth. The snake had told him God's making words. The words of doing and the words of obedience. Many a man thinks he is making something when he's only changing things around. But God let Moses make. And then Moses had so much power he made the eight winged angels split open a mountain to bury him in, and shut up the hole behind them.

And ever since the days of Moses, kings have been toting rods for a sign of power. But it's mostly sham-polish because no king has ever had the power of even one of Moses' ten words. Because Moses made a nation and a book, a thousand million leaves of ordinary men's writing couldn't tell what Moses said.

Then when the moon had dragged a thousand tides behind her, Solomon was a man. So Sheba, from her country where she was, felt him carrying power and therefore she came to talk with Solomon and hear him.

The Queen of Sheba was an Ethiopian just like Jethro, with power unequal to man. She didn't have to deny herself to give gold to Solomon. She had gold-making words. But she was thirsty, and the country where she lived was dry to her mouth. So she listened to her talking ring and went to see Solomon, and the fountain in his garden quenched her thirst.

So she made Solomon wise and gave him her talking ring. And Solomon built a room with a secret door and everyday he shut himself inside and listened to his ring. So he wrote down the ring-talk in books.

That's what the old ones said in ancient times and we talk it again.

I heard of Father Watson the "Frizzly Rooster" from afar, from people for whom he had "worked" and their friends, and from people who attended his meetings held twice a week in Myrtle Wreath Hall in New Orleans. His name is "Father" Watson, which in itself attests his Catholic leanings, though he is formally a Protestant.

On a given night I had a front seat in his hall. There were the usual camp-followers sitting upon the platform and bustling around performing chores. Two or three songs and a prayer were the preliminaries.

At last Father Watson appeared in a satin garment of royal purple, belted by a gold cord. He had the figure for wearing that sort of thing and he probably knew it. Between prayers and songs he talked, setting forth his powers. He could curse anybody he wished — and make the curse stick. He could remove curses, no matter who had laid them on whom. Hence his title The Frizzly Rooster. Many persons keep a frizzled chicken in the yard to locate and scratch up any hoodoo that may be buried for them. These chickens have, no doubt, earned this reputation by their ugly appearance — with all of their feathers set in backwards. He could "read" anybody at sight. He could "read" anyone who remained out of his sight if they but stuck two fingers inside the door. He could "read" anyone, no matter how far away, if he were given their height and color. He begged to be challenged.

He predicted the hour and the minute, nineteen years hence, when he should die — without even having been ill a moment in his whole life. God had told him.

He sold some small packets of love powders before whose powers all opposition must break down. He announced some new keys that were guaranteed to unlock every door and remove every obstacle in the way of success that the world knew. These keys had been sent to him by God through a small Jew boy. The old keys had been sent through a Jew man. They were powerful as long as they did not touch the floor—but if you ever dropped them, they lost their power. These new keys at five dollars each were not affected by being dropped, and were otherwise much more powerful.

I lingered after the meeting and made an appointment with him for the next day at his home.

Before my first interview with the Frizzly Rooster was fairly begun, I could understand his great following. He had the physique of Paul Robeson with the sex appeal and hypnotic what-ever-you-might-call-it of Rasputin. I could see that women would rise to flee from him but in mid-flight would whirl and end shivering at his feet. It was that way in fact.

His wife Mary knew how slight her hold was and continually planned to leave him.

"Only thing that's holding me here is this." She pointed to a large piece of brain-coral that was forever in a holy spot on the altar. "That's where his power is. If I could get me a piece, I could go start up a business all by myself. If I could only find a piece."

"It's very plentiful in South Florida," I told her. "But if that piece is so precious, and you're his wife, I'd take it and let *him* get another piece."

"Oh my God! Naw! That would be my end. He's too powerful. I'm leaving him," she whispered this stealthily. "You get me a piece of that—you know."

The Frizzly Rooster entered and Mary was a different person at once. But every time that she was alone with me it was "That on the altar, you know. When you back in Florida, get me a piece. I'm leaving this man to his women." Then a quick hush and forced laughter at her husband's approach.

So I became the pupil of Reverend Father Joe Watson, "The Frizzly Rooster," and his wife, Mary, who assisted him in all things. She was "round the altar"; that is while he talked with the clients, and usually decided on whatever "work" was to be done, she "set" the things on the altar and in the jars. There was one jar in the kitchen filled with honey and sugar. All the "sweet" works were set in this jar. That is, the names and the thing desired were written on paper and thrust into this jar to stay. Already four or five hundred slips of paper had accumulated in the jar. There was another jar called the "break up" jar. It held vinegar with some unsweetened coffee added. Papers were left in this one also.

When finally it was agreed that I should come to study with them, I was put to running errands such as "dusting" houses, throwing pecans, rolling apples, as the case might be; but I was not told why the thing was being done. After two weeks of this I was taken off this phase and initiated. This was the first step towards the door of the mysteries.

My initiation consisted of the Pea Vine Candle Drill. I was told to remain five days without sexual intercourse. I must remain indoors all day the day before the initiation and fast. I might wet my throat when necessary, but I was not to swallow water.

When I arrived at the house the next morning a little before nine, as per instruction, six other persons where there, so that there were nine of us—all in white except Father Watson who was in his purple robe. There was no talking. We went at once to the altar room. The altar was blazing. There were three candles around the vessel of holy water, three around the sacred sand pail, and one large cream candle burning in it. A picture of St. George and a large piece of brain coral were in the center. Father Watson dressed eight long blue candles and one black one, while the rest of us sat in the chairs around the wall. Then he lit the eight blue candles one by one from the altar and set them in the pattern of a moving serpent. Then I was called to the altar and both Father Watson and his wife laid hands on me. The black candle was placed in my hand; I was told to light it from all the other candles. I lit it at number one and pinched out the flame, and re-lit it at number two and so on till it had been lit by the eighth candle. Then I held the candle in my left hand, and by my right was conducted back to the altar by Father Watson. I was led through the maze of candles beginning at number eight. We circled numbers seven, five and three. When we reached the altar he lifted me upon the step. As I stood there, he called aloud, "Spirit! She's standing here without no home and no friends. She wants you to take her in." Then we began at number one and threaded back to number eight, circling three, five and seven. Then back to the altar again. Again he lifted me and placed me upon the step of the altar. Again the spirit was addressed as before. Then he lifted me down by placing his hands in my arm-pits. This time I did not walk at all. I was carried through the maze and I was to knock down each candle as I passed it with my foot. If I missed one, I was not to try again, but to knock it down on my way back to the altar. Arrived there the third time, I was lifted up and told to pinch out my black candle. "Now," Father told me, "you are made Boss of Candles. You have the power to light candles and put out candles, and to work with the spirits anywhere on earth."

Then all of the candles on the floor were collected and one of them handed to each of the persons present. Father took the black candle himself and we formed a ring. Everybody was given two matches each. The candles were held in our left hands, matches in the right; at a signal everybody stooped at the same moment, the matches scratched in perfect time and our candles lighted in concert. Then Father Watson walked rhythmically around the person at his right. Exchanged candles with her and went back to his place. Then that person did the same to the next so that the black candle went all around the circle and back to Father. I was then seated on a stool before the altar, sprinkled lightly with holy sand and water and confirmed as a Boss of Candles.

Then conversation broke out. We went into the next room and had a breakfast that was mostly fruit and smothered chicken. Afterwards the nine candles used in the ceremony were wrapped up and given to me to keep. They were to be used for lighting other candles only, not to be just burned in the ordinary sense.

In a few days I was allowed to hold consultations on my own. I felt insecure and said so to Father Watson.

"Of course you do now," he answered me, "but you have to learn and grow. I'm right here behind you. Talk to your people first, then come see me."

Within the hour a woman came to me. A man had shot and seriously wounded her husband and was in jail.

"But, honey," she all but wept, "they say ain't a thing going to be done with him. They say he got good white folks back of him and he's going to be let loose soon as the case is tried. I want him punished. Picking a fuss with my husband just to get chance to shoot him. We needs help. Somebody that can hit a straight lick with a crooked stick."

So I went in to the Frizzly Rooster to find out what I must do and he told me, "That a low fence." He meant a difficulty that was easily overcome.

"Go back and get five dollars from her and tell her to go home and rest easy. That man will be punished. When we get through with him, white folks or no white folks, he'll find a tough jury sitting on his case." The woman paid me and left in perfect confidence of Father Watson.

So he and I went into the workroom.

"Now," he said, "when you want a person punished who is already indicted, write his name on a slip of paper and put it in a sugar bowl or some other deep something like that. Now get your paper and pencil and write the name; alright now, you got it in the bowl. Now put in some red pepper, some black pepper—don't be skeered to put it in, it needs a lot. Put in one eightpenny nail, fifteen cents worth of ammonia and two door keys. You drop one key down in the bowl and you leave the other one against the side of the bowl. Now you got your bowl set. Go to your bowl every day at twelve o'clock and turn the key that is standing against the side of the bowl. That is to keep the man locked in jail. And every time you turn the key, add a little vinegar. Now I know this will do the job. All it needs is for you to do it in faith. I'm trusting this job to you entirely. Less see what you going to do. That can wait another minute. Come sit with me in the outside room and hear this woman out here that's waiting."

So we went outside and found a weakish woman in her early thirties that looked like somebody had dropped a sack of something soft on a chair.

The Frizzly Rooster put on his manner, looking like a brown, purple and gold throne-angel in a house.

"Good morning, sister er, er——"

"Murchison," she helped out.

"Tell us how you want to be helped, Sister Murchison."

She looked at me as if I was in the way and he read her eyes.

"She's alright, dear one. She's one of us. I brought her in with me to assist and help."

I thought still I was in her way but she told her business just the same.

"Too many women in my house. My husband's mother is there and she hates me and always puttin' my husband up to fight me. Look like I can't get her out of my house no ways I try. So I done come to you."

"We can fix that up in no time, dear one. Now go take a flat onion. If it was a man, I'd say a sharp pointed onion. Core the onion out, and write her name five times on paper and stuff it into the hole in the onion and close it back with the cut-out piece of onion. Now you watch when she leaves the house and then you roll the onion behind her before anybody else crosses the door-sill. And you make a wish at the same time for her to leave your house. She won't be there two weeks more." The woman paid and left.

That night we held a ceremony in the altar room on the case. We took a red candle and burnt it just enough to consume the tip. Then it was cut into three parts and the short lengths of candle were put into a glass of holy water. Then we took the glass and went at midnight to the door of the woman's house and the Frizzly Rooster held the glass in his hands and said, "In the name of the Father, in the name of the Son, in the name of the Holy Ghost." He shook the glass three times violently up and down, and the last time he threw the glass to the ground and broke it, and said, "Dismiss this woman from this place." We scarcely paused as this was said and done and we kept going and went home by another way because that was part of the ceremony.

Somebody came against a very popular preacher. "He's getting too rich and big. I want something done to keep him down. They tell me he's 'bout to get to be a bishop. I sho' would hate for that to happen. I got forty dollars in my pocket right now for the work."

So that night the altar blazed with the blue light. We wrote the preacher's name on a slip of paper with black ink. We took a small doll and ripped open its back and put in the paper with the name along with some bitter aloes and cayenne pepper and sewed the rip up again with the black thread. The hands of the doll were tied behind it and a black veil tied over the face and knotted behind it so that the man it represented would be blind and always do the things to keep himself from progressing. The doll was then placed in a kneeling position in a dark corner where it would not be disturbed. He would be frustrated as long as the doll was not disturbed.

When several of my jobs had turned out satisfactorily to Father Watson, he said to me, "You will do well, but you need the Black Cat Bone. Sometimes you have to be able to walk invisible. Some things must be done in deep secret, so you have to walk out of the sight of man."

First I had to get ready even to try this most terrible of experiences—getting the Black Cat Bone.

First we had to wait on the weather. When a big rain started, a new receptacle was set out in the yard. It could not be put out until the rain actually started for fear the sun might shine in it. The water must be brought inside before the weather faired off for the same reason. If lightning shone on it, it was ruined.

We finally got the water for the bath and I had to fast and "seek," shut in a room that had been purged by smoke. Twenty-four hours without food except a special wine that was fed to me every four hours. It did not make me drunk in the accepted sense of the word. I merely seemed to lose my body, my mind seemed very clear.

When dark came, we went out to catch a black cat. I must catch him with my own hands. Finding and catching black cats is hard work, unless one has been released for you to find. Then we repaired to a prepared place in the woods and a circle drawn and "protected" with nine horseshoes. Then the fire and the pot were made ready. A roomy iron pot with a lid. When the water boiled I was to toss in the terrified, trembling cat.

When he screamed, I was told to curse him. He screamed three times, the last time weak and resigned. The lid was clamped down, the fire kept vigorously alive. At midnight the lid was lifted. Here was the moment! The bones of the cat must be passed through my mouth until one tasted bitter.

Suddenly, the Rooster and Mary rushed in close to the pot and he cried, "Look out! This is liable to kill you. Hold your nerve!" They both looked fearfully around the circle. They communicated some unearthly terror to me. Maybe I went off in a trance. Great beast-like creatures thundered up to the circle from all sides. Indescribable noises, sights, feelings. Death was at hand! Seemed unavoidable! I don't know. Many times I have thought and felt, but I always have to say the same thing. I don't know. I don't know.

Before day I was home, with a small white bone for me to carry.

1935

Lafcadio Hearn

A Creole Mystery

THEY CAME together from Havana, mistress and servant. The mistress had a strange and serpentine sort of beauty; — the litheness of a snake in every movement; — the fascination of an ophidian; — and great eyes that flamed like black opals. One felt on meeting her that the embraces of lianas and of ivy were less potent to fetter than hers — and to fetter forever. Her voice was remarkably sweet, but had strangely deep tones in it; — and her laugh caused a feeling of unpleasant surprise. It was a mocking, weird, deep laugh, uttered without any change of features; there was no smile, no movement of the facial muscles; the lips simply opened and the laugh came pealing from her white throat, while the eyes, large, brilliant, and sinister with mockery, fixed themselves with motionless lids upon the face of the person present. But she seldom laughed.

None knew who she was. She was a mystery to the French people of the quarter. Her rooms were luxuriously furnished and hung in blue satin. At long intervals strangers called upon her — men of olivaceous complexion and hair tropically black with dead-blue lights in it. They spoke only in Spanish; and their interviews lasted far into the night. Sometimes they seemed to be gay. Gossipy people said they heard the popping of champagne corks; and a perfume of Havana tobacco floated out of the windows and hung about the shrubbery that enshrouded the veranda. Sometimes, however, there were sinister sounds as of men's voices raised in anger, and at intervals the deep laugh of the mysterious woman, long and loud and clear, and vibrant with mockery.

The servant was a mulattress, tall and solidly constructed as a caryatid of bronze. She was not less of a mystery than her mistress. She spoke French and Spanish with equal facility, but these only on rare occasions. Generally no mute in the seraglio of a Sultan could be more silent or more impassible. She never smiled. She never gossiped. She never seemed to hear or to see; yet she saw and heard all. Only a strange face could attract her attention—for a brief moment, during which she gazed upon it with an indescribable look that seemed potent enough to burn what it touched. It was a look that made its living object feel that his face was photographed in her brain and would be equally vivid there fifty years after. The foreigners who came were received by her in silence and without scrutiny. Their faces were doubtless familiar. None of them ever spoke to her. She seemed to be more than a Doppelgänger, and to appear in five or six different rooms at the same time. Nothing could transpire unperceived by her; though she seemed never to look at anything. Her feet were never heard. She moved like a phantom through the house, opening and closing doors noiselessly as a ghost. She always suddenly appeared when least expected. When looked for, she was never to be found. Her mistress never called her. When needed, she appeared to rise suddenly from the floor, like those Genii of Arabian fables summoned by a voiceless wish. She never played with the children; and these hushed their voices when she glided by them in silence. With a subtle intelligence seemingly peculiar to her, she answered questions before they were fully asked. She never seemed to sleep. Persons who visited the house were as certain to meet her at the entrance three hours before sunrise as at any other hours. She appeared to be surprised at nothing, and to anticipate everything. She was even a greater mystery, if possible, than her mistress.

At last the swarthy foreigners called more frequently and the interviews grew stormier. It was said that sometimes the conversations were held in Catalan; and that when Catalan was spoken there were angrier words and wickeder laughing. And one night the interviews were so terrible that all the old-fashioned French folks in the quarter put their heads out of the windows to listen. There were sounds as of broken glass and passionate blows given to the mahogany table. And the strange laughter suddenly ceased.

Next morning the postman calling to deliver a registered letter found the rooms empty. The spectral servant was gone. The sinister mistress was gone. The furniture was all there; and the only records of the night's mystery were two broken glasses and stains of wine on the rich carpet. The bed had been undisturbed. The clock still ticked on its marble pedestal. The wind moved the blue silk hangings. A drowsy perfume of woman lingered in the rooms like incense. The wardrobes retained their wealth of silks and laces. The piano remained open. A little Angora cat was playing with a spool of silk under the table. A broken fan lay on the luxuriously padded rockingchair; and a bouquet of camellias lay dying upon the mantelpiece.

The letter was never delivered. The rooms remained as they were, until mould and dust came to destroy the richness of their upholstery. The strangers never came back, nor did any ever hear what became of them The mystery remains unexplained. The letter remains in the dead-letter office. But I would like to open it and find out what is in it;—wouldn't you?

1880

John Kennedy Toole

A Confederacy of Dunces

A GREEN HUNTING cap squeezed the top of the fleshy balloon of a head. The green earflaps, full of large ears and uncut hair and the fine bristles that grew in the ears themselves, stuck out on either side like turn signals indicating two directions at once. Full, pursed lips protruded beneath the bushy black moustache and, at their corners, sank into little folds filled with disapproval and potato chip crumbs. In the shadow under the green visor of the cap Ignatius J. Reilly's supercilious blue and yellow eyes looked down upon the other people waiting under the clock at the D. H. Holmes department store, studying the crowd of people for signs of bad taste in dress. Several of the outfits, Ignatius noticed, were new enough and expensive enough to be properly considered offenses against taste and decency. Possession of anything new or expensive only reflected a person's lack of theology and geometry; it could even cast doubts upon one's soul.

Ignatius himself was dressed comfortably and sensibly. The hunting cap prevented head colds. The voluminous tweed trousers were durable and permitted unusually free locomotion. Their pleats and nooks contained pockets of warm, stale air that soothed Ignatius. The plaid flannel shirt made a jacket unnecessary while the muffler guarded exposed Reilly skin between earflap and collar. The outfit was acceptable by any theological and geometrical standards, however abstruse, and suggested a rich inner life.

Shifting from one hip to the other in his lumbering, elephantine fashion, Ignatius sent waves of flesh rippling beneath the tweed and flannel, waves that broke upon buttons and seams. Thus rearranged, he contemplated the long while that he had been waiting for his mother. Principally he considered the discomfort he was beginning to feel. It seemed as if his whole being was ready to burst from his swollen suede desert boots, and, as if to verify this, Ignatius turned his singular eyes toward his feet. The feet did indeed look swollen. He was prepared to offer the sight of those bulging boots to his mother as evidence of her thoughtlessness. Looking up, he saw the sun beginning to descend over the Mississippi at the foot of Canal Street. The Holmes clock said almost five. Already he was polishing a few carefully worded accusations designed to reduce his mother to repentance or, at least, confusion. He often had to keep her in her place.

She had driven him downtown in the old Plymouth, and while she was at the doctor's seeing about her arthritis, Ignatius had bought some sheet music at Werlein's for his trumpet and a new string for his lute. Then he had wandered into the Penny Arcade on Royal Street to see whether any new games had been installed. He had been disappointed to find the miniature mechanical baseball game gone. Perhaps it was only being repaired. The last time that he had played it the batter would not work and, after some argument, the management had returned his nickel, even though the Penny Arcade people had been base enough to suggest that Ignatius had himself broken the baseball machine by kicking it.

Concentrating upon the fate of the miniature baseball machine, Ignatius detached his being from the physical reality of Canal Street and the people around him and therefore did not notice the two eyes that were hungrily watching him from behind one of D. H. Holmes' pillars, two sad eyes shining with hope and desire.

Was it possible to repair the machine in New Orleans? Probably so. However, it might have to be sent to some place like Milwaukee or Chicago or some other city whose name Ignatius associated with efficient repair shops and permanently smoking factories. Ignatius hoped that the baseball game was being carefully handled in shipment, that none of its little players was being chipped or maimed by brutal railroad employees determined to ruin the railroad forever with damage claims from shippers, railroad employees who would subsequently go on strike and destroy the Illinois Central.

As Ignatius was considering the delight which the little baseball game afforded humanity, the two sad and covetous eyes moved toward him through the crowd like torpedoes zeroing in on a great woolly tanker. The policeman plucked at Ignatius' bag of sheet music.

"You got any identification, mister?" the policeman asked in a voice that hoped that Ignatius was officially unidentified.

"What?" Ignatius looked down upon the badge on the blue cap. "Who are you?"

"Let me see your driver's license."

"I don't drive. Will you kindly go away? I am waiting for my mother."

"What's this hanging our your bag?"

"What do you think it is, stupid? It's a string for my lute."

"What's that?" The policeman drew back a little. "Are you local?"

"Is it the part of the police department to harass me when this city is a flagrant vice capital of the civilized world?" Ignatius bellowed over the crowd in front of the store. "This city is famous for its gamblers, prostitutes, exhibitionists, anti-Christs, alcoholics, sodomites, drug addicts, fetishists, onanists, pornographers, frauds, jades, litterbugs, and lesbians, all of whom are only too well protected by graft. If you have a moment, I shall endeavor to discuss the crime problem with you, but don't make the mistake of bothering *me.*"

The policeman grabbed Ignatius by the arm and was struck on his cap with the sheet music. The dangling lute string whipped him on the ear.

"Hey," the policeman said.

"Take that!" Ignatius cried, noticing that a circle of interested shoppers was beginning to form.

Inside D. H. Holmes, Mrs. Reilly was in the bakery department pressing her maternal breast against a glass case of macaroons. With one of her fingers, chafed from many years of scrubbing her son's mammoth, yellowed drawers, she tapped on the glass case to attract the saleslady.

"Oh, Miss Inez," Mrs. Reilly called in that accent that occurs south of New Jersey only in New Orleans, that Hoboken near the Gulf of Mexico. "Over here, babe."

"Hey, how you making?" Miss Inez asked. "How you feeling, darling?"

"Not so hot," Mrs. Reilly answered truthfully.

"Ain't that a shame." Miss Inez leaned over the glass case and forgot about her cakes. "I don't feel so hot myself. It's my feet."

"Lord, I wisht I was that lucky. I got arthuritis in my elbow."

"Aw, no!" Miss Inez said with genuine sympathy. "My poor old poppa's got that. We make him go set himself in a hot tub fulla berling water."

"My boy's floating around in our tub all day long. I can't hardly get in my own bathroom no more."

"I thought he was married, precious."

"Ignatius? Eh, la la," Mrs. Reilly said sadly. "Sweetheart, you wanna gimme two dozen of them fancy mix?"

"But I thought you told me he was married," Miss Inez said while she was putting the cakes in a box.

"He ain't even got him a prospect. The little girl friend he had flew the coop."

"Well, he's got time."

"I guess so," Mrs. Reilly said disinterestedly. "Look, you wanna gimme half a dozen wine cakes, too? Ignatius gets nasty if we run outta cake."

"Your boy likes his cake, huh?"

"Oh, Lord, my elbow's killing me," Mrs. Reilly answered.

In the center of the crowd that had formed before the department store the hunting cap, the green radius of the circle of people, was bobbing about violently.

"I shall contact the mayor," Ignatius was shouting.

"Let the boy alone," a voice said from the crowd.

"Go get the strippers on Bourbon Street," an old man added. "He's a good boy. He's waiting for his momma."

"Thank you," Ignatius said haughtily. "I hope that all of you will bear witness to this outrage."

"You come with me," the policeman said to Ignatius with waning self-confidence. The crowd was turning into something of a mob, and there was no traffic patrolman in sight. "We're going to the precinct."

"A good boy can't even wait for his momma by D. H. Holmes." It was the old man again. "I'm telling you, the city was never like this. It's the communiss."

"Are you calling me a communiss?" the policeman asked the old man while he tried to avoid the lashing of the lute string. "I'll take you in, too. You better watch out who you calling a communiss."

"You can't aress me," the old man cried. "I'm a member of the Golden Age Club sponsored by the New Orleans Recreation Department."

"Let that old man alone, you dirty cop," a woman screamed. "He's prolly somebody's grampaw."

"I am," the old man said. "I got six grandchirren all studying with the sisters. Smart, too."

Over the heads of the people Ignatius saw his mother walking slowly out of the lobby of the department store carrying the bakery products as if they were boxes of cement.

"Mother!" he called. "Not a moment too soon. I've been seized."

Pushing through the people, Mrs. Reilly said, "Ignatius! What's going on here? What you done now? Hey, take your hands off my boy."

"I'm not touching him, lady," the policeman said. "Is this here your son?"

Mrs. Reilly snatched the whizzing lute string from Ignatius.

"Of course I'm her child," Ignatius said. "Can't you see her affection for me?"

"She loves her boy," the old man said.

"What you trying to do my poor child?" Mrs. Reilly asked the policeman. Ignatius patted his mother's hennaed hair with one of his huge paws. "You got plenty business picking on poor chirren with all the kind of people they got running in this town. Waiting for his momma and they try to arrest him."

"This is clearly a case for the Civil Liberties Union," Ignatius observed, squeezing his mother's drooping shoulder with the paw. "We must contact Myrna Minkoff, my lost love. She knows about those things."

"It's the communiss," the old man interrupted.

"How old is he?" the policeman asked Mrs. Reilly.

"I am thirty," Ignatius said condescendingly.

"You got a job?"

"Ignatius hasta help me at home," Mrs. Reilly said. Her initial courage was failing a little, and she began to twist the lute string with the cord on the cake boxes. "I got terrible arthuritis."

"I dust a bit," Ignatius told the policeman. "In addition, I am at the moment writing a lengthy indictment against our century. When my brain begins to reel from my literary labors, I make an occasional cheese dip."

"Ignatius makes delicious cheese dips," Mrs. Reilly said.

"That's very nice of him," the old man said. "Most boys are out running around all the time."

"Why don't you shut up?" the policeman said to the old man.

"Ignatius," Mrs. Reilly asked in a trembling voice, "what you done, boy?"

"Actually, Mother, I believe that it was he who started everything." Ignatius pointed to the old man with his bag of sheet music. "I was simply standing about, waiting for you, praying that the news from the doctor would be encouraging."

"Get that old man outta here," Mrs. Reilly said to the policeman. "He's making trouble. It's a shame they got people like him walking the streets."

"The police are all communiss," the old man said.

"Didn't I say for you to shut up?" the policeman said angrily.

"I fall on my knees every night to thank my God we got protection," Mrs. Reilly told the crowd. "We'd all be dead without the police. We'd all be laying in our beds with our throats cut open from ear to ear."

"That's the truth, girl," some woman answered from the crowd.

"Say a rosary for the police force." Mrs. Reilly was now addressing her remarks to the crowd. Ignatius caressed her shoulder wildly, whispering encouragement. "Would you say a rosary for a communiss?"

"No!" several voices answered fervently. Someone pushed the old man.

"It's true, lady," the old man cried. "He tried to arrest your boy. Just like in Russia. They're all communiss."

"Come on," the policeman said to the old man. He grabbed him roughly by the back of the coat.

"Oh, my god!" Ignatius said, watching the wan little policeman try to control the old man. "Now my nerves are totally frayed."

"Help!" the old man appealed to the crowd. "It's a takeover. It's a violation of the Constitution!"

"He's crazy, Ignatius," Mrs. Reilly said. "We better get outta here, baby." She turned to the crowd. "Run, folks. He might kill us all. Personally, I think maybe *he's* the communiss."

"You don't have to overdo it, Mother," Ignatius said as they pushed through the dispersing crowd and started walking rapidly down Canal Street. He looked back and saw the old man and the bantam policeman grappling beneath the department store clock. "Will you please slow down a bit? I think I'm having a heart murmur."

"Oh, shut up. How you think I feel? I shouldn't haveta be running like this at my age."

"The heart is important at any age, I'm afraid."

"They's nothing wrong with your heart."

"There will be if we don't go a little slower." The tweed trousers billowed around Ignatius' gargantuan rump as he rolled forward. "Do you have my lute string?"

Mrs. Reilly pulled him around the corner onto Bourbon Street, and they started walking down into the French Quarter.

"How come that policeman was after you, boy?"

"I shall never know. But he will probably be coming after us in a few moments, as soon as he has subdued that aged fascist."

"You think so?" Mrs. Reilly asked nervously.

"I would imagine so. He seemed determined to arrest me. He must have some sort of quota or something. I seriously doubt that he will permit me to elude him so easily."

"Wouldn't that be awful! You'd be all over the papers, Ignatius. The disgrace! You musta done something while you was waiting for me, Ignatius. I know you, boy."

"If anyone was ever minding his business, it was I," Ignatius breathed. "Please. We must stop. I think I'm going to have a hemorrhage."

"Okay." Mrs. Reilly looked at her son's reddening face and realized that he would very happily collapse at her feet just to prove his point. He had done it before. The last time that she had forced him to accompany her to mass on Sunday he had collapsed twice on the way to the church and had collapsed once again during the sermon about sloth, reeling out of the pew and creating an embarrassing disturbance. "Let's go in here and sit down."

She pushed him through the door of the Night of Joy bar with one of the cake boxes. In the darkness that smelled of bourbon and cigarette butts they climbed onto two stools. While Mrs. Reilly arranged her cake boxes on the bar, Ignatius spread his expansive nostrils and said, "My God, Mother, it smells awful. My stomach is beginning to churn."

"You wanna go back on the street? You want that policeman to take you in?"

Ignatius did not answer; he was sniffing loudly and making faces. A bartender, who had been observing the two, asked quizzically from the shadows, "Yes?"

"I shall have a coffee," Ignatius said grandly. "Chicory coffee with boiled milk."

"Only instant," the bartender said.

"I can't possibly drink that," Ignatius told his mother. "It's an abomination."

"Well, get a beer, Ignatius. It won't kill you."

"I may bloat."

"I'll take a Dixie 45," Mrs. Reilly said to the bartender.

"And the gentleman?" the bartender asked in a rich, assumed voice. "What is his pleasure?"

"Give him a Dixie, too."

"I may not drink it," Ignatius said as the bartender went off to open the beers.

"We can't sit in here for free, Ignatius."

"I don't see why not. We're the only customers. They should be glad to have us."

"They got strippers in here at night, huh?" Mrs. Reilly nudged her son.

"I would imagine so," Ignatius said coldly. He looked quite pained. "We might have stopped somewhere else. I suspect that the police will raid this place momentarily anyway." He snorted loudly and cleared his throat. "Thank God my mustache filters out some of the stench. My olfactories are already beginning to send out distress signals."

After what seemed a long time during which there was much tinkling of glass and closing of coolers somewhere in the shadows, the bartender appeared again and set the beers before them, pretending to knock Ignatius' beer into his lap. The Reillys were getting the Night of Joy's worst service, the treatment given unwanted customers.

"You don't by any chance have a cold Dr. Nut, do you?" Ignatius asked.

"No."

"My son loves Dr. Nut," Mrs. Reilly explained. "I gotta buy it by the case. Sometimes he sits himself down and drinks two, three Dr. Nuts at one time."

"I am sure that this man is not particularly interested," Ignatius said.

"Like to take that cap off?" the bartender asked.

"No, I wouldn't!" Ignatius thundered. "There's a chill in here."

"Suit yourself," the bartender said and drifted off into the shadows at the other end of the bar.

"Really!"

"Calm down," his mother said.

Ignatius raised the earflap on the side next to his mother.

"Well, I will lift this so that you won't have to strain your voice. What did the doctor tell you about your elbow or whatever it is?"

"It's gotta be massaged."

"I hope you don't want me to do that. You know how I feel about touching other people."

"He told me to stay out the cold as much as possible."

"If I could drive, I would be able to help you more, I imagine."

"Aw, that's okay, honey."

"Actually, even riding in a car affects me enough. Of course, the worst thing is riding on top in one of those Greyhound Scenicruisers. So high up. Do you remember the time that I went to Baton Rouge in one of those? I vomited several times. The driver had to stop the bus somewhere in the swamps to let me get off and walk around for a while. The other passengers were rather angry. They must have had stomachs of iron to ride in that awful machine. Leaving New Orleans also frightened me considerably. Outside of the city limits the heart of darkness, the true wasteland beings."

"I remember that, Ignatius," Mrs. Reilly said absently, drinking her beer in gulps. "You was really sick when you got back home."

"I felt better *then*. The worst moment was my arrival in Baton Rouge. I realized that I had a round-trip ticket and would have to return on the bus."

"You told me that, babe."

"The taxi back to New Orleans cost me forty dollars, but at least I wasn't violently ill during the taxi ride, although I felt myself beginning to gag several times. I made the driver go very slowly, which was unfortunate for him. The state police stopped him twice for being below the minimum highway speed limit. On the third time that they stopped him they took away his chauffeur's license. You see, they had been watching us on the radar all along."

Mrs. Reilly's attention wavered between her son and the beer. She had been listening to the story for three years.

"Of course," Ignatius continued, mistaking her mother's rapt look for interest, "that was the only time that I had ever been out of New Orleans in my life. I think that perhaps it was the lack of a center of orientation that might have upset me. Speeding along in that bus was like hurtling into the abyss. By the time we had left the swamps and reached those rolling hills near Baton Rouge, I was getting afraid that some rural rednecks might toss bombs at the bus. They love to attack vehicles, which are a symbol of progress, I guess."

"Well, I'm glad you didn't take the job," Mrs. Reilly said automatically, taking *guess* as her cue.

"I couldn't possibly take the job. When I saw the chairman of the Medieval Culture Department, my hands began breaking out in small white bumps. He was a totally soulless man. Then he made a comment about my not wearing a tie and made some smirky remark about the lumber jacket. I was appalled that so meaningless a person would dare such effrontery. That lumber jacket was one of the few creature comforts to which I've ever been really attached, and if I ever find the lunatic who stole it, I shall report him to the proper authorities."

Mrs. Reilly saw again the horrible, coffee-stained lumber jacket that she had always secretly wanted to give to the Volunteers of America along with several other pieces of Ignatius' favorite clothing.

"You see, I was so overwhelmed by the complete grossness of that spurious 'chairman' that I ran from his office in the middle of one of his cretinous ramblings and rushed to the nearest bathroom, which turned out to be the one for 'Faculty Men.' At any rate, I was seated in one of the booths, having rested the lumber jacket on top of the door of the booth. Suddenly I saw the jacket being whisked over the door. I heard footsteps. Then the door of the restroom closed. At the moment, I was unable to pursue the shameless thief, so I began to scream. Someone entered the bathroom and knocked at the door of the booth. It turned out to be a member of the campus security force, or so he said. Through the door I explained what had just happened. He promised to find the jacket and went away. Actually, as I have mentioned to you before, I have always suspected that he and the 'chairman' were the same person. Their voices sounded somewhat similar."

"You sure can't trust nobody nowadays, honey."

"As soon as I could, I fled from the bathroom, eager only to get away from that horrible place. Of course, I was almost frozen standing on that desolate campus trying to hail a taxi. I finally got one that agreed to take me to New Orleans for forty dollars, and the driver was selfless enough to lend me his jacket. By the time we arrived here, however, he was quite depressed about losing his license and had grown rather surly. He also appeared to be developing a bad cold, judging by the frequency of his sneezes. After all, we were on the highway for almost two hours."

"I think I could drink me another beer, Ignatius."

"Mother! In this forsaken place?"

"Just one, baby. Come on, I want another."

"We're probably catching something from these glasses. However, if you're quite determined about the thing, get me a brandy, will you?"

Mrs. Reilly signaled to the bartender, who came out of the shadows and asked, "Now what happened to you on that bus, bud? I didn't get the end of the story."

"Will you kindly tend the bar properly?" Ignatius asked furiously.

"It is your duty to silently serve when we call upon you. If we had wished to include you in our conversation, we would have indicated it by now. As a matter of fact, we are discussing rather urgent personal matters."

"The man's just trying to be nice, Ignatius. Shame on you."

"That in itself is a contradiction in terms. No one could possibly be nice in a den like this."

"We want two more beers."

"One beer and one brandy," Ignatius corrected.

"No more clean glasses," the bartender said.

"Ain't that a shame," Mrs. Reilly said. "Well, we can use the ones we got."

The bartender shrugged and went off into the shadows.

1960

John James Audubon

New Orleans Journal

Sunday January 7th 1821

AT NEW ORLEANS at Last—We arrived here about 8 o'clock this Morning; hundreds of Fish Crows hovering near the shipping and dashing down to the Watter Like Gulls for food—uttering a cry very much like the young of the *Common crow* when they first Leave the Nests—

Monday January 8th 1821

At Day breake, went to Market having received information that Much and great variety of game was brought to it—We found Many Malards, some teals, some American widgeons, Canada Geese, Snow Geese, Mergansers, Robins, Blue birds, Red wing Starlings, Tell-Tale Godwits—every thing selling extremely high: $1.25 for one pare of ducks, 1.50 for a Goose & Much surprised and diverted on finding a *Barred Owl* Cleaned and Exposed for Sale: Value 25 cts—I went to the review [celebrating the Battle of New Orleans], and will remember it and the 8th of January forever—My Pocket was rifled of my pocket Book.

I think the Knave who took it is now good deal disappointed and probably wishes I had it.

This evening one of our Men Called *Smith* fell over board drunk and Would have drowned if Providence had not interfered. A Woman heard the Noise and the Yawl of the S. Bt [steamboat] U. States saw him—

9th

My Spirits very Low—Weather Cloudy & Sultry—begun raining—Wrote to My Wife—Wished I had remained at Natchez—having found No Work to do remained on Board the Keel Boat opposite the French Market, the Dirtiest place in all the Cities of the United States.

12th

Early this Morning I Met an Italian, painter at the Theatre. I Shewed him the Drawing of the White Headed Eagle, he was much pleased, took me to his painting appartement at the Theatre, then to the Directors who very roughly offered me 100$ per Month to paint with Mons L'Italian.

I believe really now that my talents must be poor or else the country is.

Saturday 13th January 1821

I rose early tormented by many disagreable thoughts, nearly again without a cent, in a Busling City where no one cares a fig for a Man in my situation.

Sunday 14th January 1821

The Levee early was Crowded by people of all Sorts as well as Colors, the Market very aboundant, the Church Bell ringing (and) the Billiard Balls Knocking, the Guns heard all around. What a Display this is for a Steady Quaker of Philada or Cincinnati—the day was beautifull and the crowd Increased considerably—I saw however no handsome Woman and the Citron hue of allmost all is very disgusting to one who Likes the rosy Yankee or English Cheeks—

February 9th 1821

In walking this morning about a mile below this city I had the pleasure of remarking thousands of purple martins travelling eastwardly they flew high and circling feeding on incectes [insects] as they went they moved onwardly about ¼ miles an hour
Thermometer at 68, weather Drisly.
Hundreds of Coots where in the market this morning.

Monday 19th February 1821

Saw this Morning Three Immense flocks of *Bank Swallows* that past over Me with the Rapidity of a Storm, going Northeast—Their Cry was heard distinctly, and I knew them first by the Noise they made in the air coming from behind Me; the falling of their Dung resembled a heavy but thinly falling Snow; No appearance of any feeding While in our Sight—Which Lasted but a few Minutes—

Thursday New Orleans February 22d 1821

We at Last have left the Keel Boat and have moved on the hearth again—Our present situation is quite a Curious one to Me; the room we are in and for which We pay $10 per Month is situated in Barraks Street near the Corner of that & Royal Street—between Two Shops of Grocers and divided from them and our Yellow Landlady by Mere Board Partitions, receiving at once all the new Matter that Issues from the thundering Mouths of all these groups—the *Honest Woman* spoke much of honesty in Strangers and required one Month paid in Advance, this however I could not do, and satisfied her with one half—

Sunday March 11th 1821

Near our House a Mocking Bird regularly resorts to the South Angle of a Chimney top and salutes us with Sweetest Notes from the rising of the Moon until about Midnight, and every Morning from about 8 o'clock untill 11, when it flys to the Convent Garden to feed—I have remarked that Bird allways in the Same Spot and Same Position, and have been particularly pleased at hearing him (try to) Imitate the Watchman's Cry of *All's Well* that Issues from the fort about 3 Squares Distant, and so well has he sometimes performed that I Would have been mistaken if he not repeated too often in the Space of a 10 minutes.

March 15th Thursday 1821

I Make a Likeness to day for a Lady's Sadle [saddle] a thing I had not the Leass use for, but the Man I had Made a portrait for Wanted his Wife's Very Much and Could not Spare Money, and Not to disapoint him I sufered Myself to be Sadled—

March 16th Friday 1821

I took a Walk with my Gun this afternoon to see the Passage of Millions of *Golden Plovers* Coming from the North Est and going Nearly South—the distruction of these innocent fugitives from a Winter Storm above us was really astonishing—the Sportsmen are here more numerous and at the same time more expert at shooting on the Wing than any where in the U. States—On the first sight of these birds [the hunters] assembled in Parties of from 20 to 100 at Diferent places where they Knew by experience the birds [would] pass, and arranged themselves at equal distances, squatted on their hams—As a flock Came Near every man Called in a Masterly astonishing Manner, the Birds Imediately Lowered and Wheeled and coming about 40 to 50 yards run the Gantlet; every Gun goes off in Rotation, and so well aimed that I saw several times a flock of 100 or More Plovers destroyed [with] the exception of 5 or 6 [birds]—the Dogs after each Volcys, While the Shooters charged their Pieces, brought the Same to each Individual—this continued all day; when I Left One of those Lines of Sharp Shooters, then the Sun Setting, they appeared as Intent on Killing More as when I arrived at the spot at 4 o'clock—

A Man Near where I was seated had killed 63 dozens—from the firing before & behind us I would suppose that 400 Gunners where out. Supposing each Man to have Killed 30 Dozen that day 144,000 [plovers] must have been destroyed—On Enquiring if these Passages were frequent I was told that Six Years ago there was about such an Instance; imediately after 2 or 3 days of Very Warm Weather a blow from the Northeast brought them, Which Was Nearly the Same to day—some few [of the birds] Were fat but the Greatest Number Lean, and all that I opened showed no food—the femelles Eggs extremely small—

Saturday 17th March 1821

This Morning the Market Was plentifully suplied with Golden Plovers—I also saw a White Crane. Spent the day Walking about at the exception of an hour Drawing at a Likeness—

1821

Tennessee Williams

A Streetcar Named Desire

Scene One

T H E   E X T E R I O R   of a two-story corner building on a street in New Orleans which is named Elysian Fields and runs between the L & N tracks and the river. The section is poor but, unlike corresponding sections in other American cities, it has a raffish charm. The houses are mostly white frame, weathered grey, with rickety outside stairs and galleries and quaintly ornamented gables. This building contains two flats, upstairs and down. Faded white stairs ascend to the entrances of both.

It is first dark of an evening early in May. The sky that shows around the dim white building is a peculiarly tender blue, almost a turquoise, which invests the scene with a kind of lyricism and gracefully attenuates the atmosphere of decay. You can almost feel the warm breath of the brown river beyond the river warehouses with their faint redolences of bananas and coffee. A corresponding air is evoked by the music of Negro entertainers at a barroom around the corner. In this part of New Orleans you are practically always just around the corner, or a few doors down the street, from a tinny piano being played with the infatuated fluency of brown fingers. This "Blue Piano" expresses the spirit of the life which goes on here.

Two women, one white and one colored, are taking the air on the steps of the building. The white woman is Eunice, who occupies the upstairs flat; the colored woman a neighbor, for New Orleans is a cosmopolitan city where there is a relatively warm and easy intermingling of races in the old part of town.

Above the music of the "Blue Piano" the voices of people on the street can be heard overlapping.

BLANCHE:

Traveling wears me out.

STANLEY:

Well, take it easy.

[A cat screeches near the window. Blanche springs up.]

BLANCHE:

What's that?

STANLEY:

Cats . . . Hey, Stella!

STELLA [faintly, from the bathroom]:

Yes, Stanley.

STANLEY:

Haven't fallen in, have you? [He grins at Blanche. She tries unsuccessfully to smile back. There is a silence] I'm afraid I'll strike you as being the unrefined type. Stella's spoke of you a good deal. You were married once, weren't you?

[The music of the polka rises up, faint in the distance.]

BLANCHE:

Yes. When I was quite young.

STANLEY:

What happened?

BLANCHE:

The boy–the boy died. [She sinks back down] I'm afraid I'm–going to be sick!

[Her head falls on her arms.]

Scene Two

Blanche is bathing. Stella is completing her toilette. Blanche's dress, a flowered print, is laid out on Stella's bed.

Stanley enters the kitchen from outside, leaving the door open on the perpetual "blue piano" around the corner.

STANLEY:

What's all this monkey doings?

STELLA:

Oh, Stan! [She jumps up and kisses him which he accepts with lordly composure] I'm taking Blanche to Galatoire's for supper and then to a show, because it's your poker night.

STANLEY:

How about my supper, huh? I'm not going to no Galatoire's for supper!

STELLA:

I put you a cold plate on ice.

STANLEY:

Well, isn't that just dandy!

STELLA:

I'm going to try to keep Blanche out till the party breaks up because I don't know how she would take it. So we'll go to one of the little places in the Quarter afterwards and you'd better give me some money.

STANLEY:

Where is she?

STELLA:

She's soaking in a hot tub to quiet her nerves. She's terribly upset.

STANLEY:

Over what?

STELLA:

She's been through such an ordeal.

STANLEY:

Yeah?

STELLA:

Stan, we've – lost Belle Reve!

STANLEY:

The place in the country?

STELLA:

Yes.

STANLEY:

How?

STELLA [vaguely]:

Oh, it had to be – sacrificed or something. [There is a pause while Stanley considers. Stella is changing into her dress] When she comes in be sure to say something nice about her appearance. And, oh! Don't mention the baby. I haven't said anything yet. I'm waiting until she gets in a quieter condition.

STANLEY [ominously]:

So?

STELLA:

And try to understand her and be nice to her, Stan.

BLANCHE [singing in the bathroom]:

"From the land of the sky blue water,
They brought a captive maid!"

STELLA:

She wasn't expecting to find us in such a small place. You see I'd tried to gloss things over a little in my letters.

STANLEY:

So?

STELLA:

And admire her dress and tell her she's looking wonderful. That's important with Blanche. Her little weakness!

STANLEY:

Yeah. I get the idea. Now let's skip back a little to where you said the country place was disposed of.

STELLA:

Oh!—yes . . .

STANLEY:

How about that? Let's have a few more details on that subjeck.

STELLA:

It's best not to talk much about it until she's calmed down.

STANLEY:

So that's the deal, huh? Sister Blanche cannot be annoyed with business details right now!

STELLA:

You saw how she was last night.

STANLEY:

Uh-hum, I saw how she was. Now let's have a gander at the bill of sale.

STELLA:

I haven't seen any.

STANLEY:

She didn't show you no papers, no deed of sale or nothing like that, huh?

STELLA:

It seems like it wasn't sold.

STANLEY:

Well, what in hell was it then, give away? To charity?

STELLA:

Shhh! She'll hear you.

STANLEY:

I don't care if she hears me. Let's see the papers!

STELLA:

There weren't any papers, she didn't show any papers, I don't care about papers.

STANLEY:

Have you ever heard of the Napoleonic code?

STELLA:

No, Stanley, I haven't heard of the Napoleonic code and if I have, I don't see what it—

STANLEY:

Let me enlighten you on a point or two, baby.

STELLA:

Yes?

STANLEY:

In the state of Louisiana we have the Napoleonic code according to which what belongs to the wife belongs to the husband and vice versa. For instance if I had a piece of property, or you had a piece of property—

STELLA:

My head is swimming!

STANLEY:

All right. I'll wait till she gets through soaking in a hot tub and then I'll inquire if *she* is acquainted with the Napoleonic code. It looks to me like you have been swindled, baby, and when you're swindled under the Napoleonic code I'm swindled *too*. And I don't like to be *swindled*.

STELLA:

There's plenty of time to ask her questions later but if you do now she'll go to pieces again. I don't understand what happened to Belle Reve but you don't know how ridiculous you are being when you suggest that my sister or I or anyone of our family could have perpetrated a swindle on anyone else.

STANLEY:

Then where's the money if the place was sold?

STELLA:

Not sold—*lost, lost!*

[He stalks into bedroom, and she follows him.]

Stanley!

[He pulls open the wardrobe trunk standing in middle of room and jerks out an armful of dresses.]

STANLEY:

Open your eyes to this stuff! You think she got them out of a teacher's pay?

STELLA:

Hush!

STANLEY:

Look at these feathers and furs that she come here to preen herself in! What's this here? A solid-gold dress, I believe! And this one! What is these here? Fox-pieces! [He blows on them] Genuine fox fur-pieces, a half a mile long! Where are your fox-pieces, Stella? Bushy snow-white ones, no less! Where are your white fox-pieces?

STELLA:

Those are inexpensive summer furs that Blanche has had a long time.

STANLEY:

I got an acquaintance who deals in this sort of merchandise. I'll have him in here to appraise it. I'm willing to bet you there's thousands of dollars invested in this stuff here!

STELLA:

Don't be such an idiot, Stanley!

[He hurls the furs to the daybed. Then he jerks open small drawer in the trunk and pulls up a fist-full of costume jewelry.]

STANLEY:

And what have we here? The treasure chest of a pirate!

STELLA:

Oh, Stanley!

STANLEY:

Pearls! Ropes of them! What is this sister of yours, a deep-sea diver who brings up sunken treasures? Or is she the champion safe-cracker of all time! Bracelets of solid gold, too! Where are your pearls and gold bracelets?

STELLA:

Shhh! Be still, Stanley!

STANLEY:

And diamonds! A crown for an empress!

STELLA:

A rhinestone tiara she wore to a costume ball.

STANLEY:

What's rhinestone?

STELLA:

Next door to glass.

STANLEY:

Are you kidding? I have an acquaintance that works in a jewelry store. I'll have him in here to make an appraisal of this. Here's your plantation, or what was left of it, here!

STELLA:

You have no idea how stupid and horrid you're being! Now close that trunk before she comes out of the bathroom!

[He kicks the trunk partly closed and sits on the kitchen table.]

STANLEY:

The Kowalskis and the DuBois have different notions.

STELLA [angrily]:

Indeed they have, thank heavens!—*I'm* going outside.

[She snatches up her white hat and gloves and crosses to the outside door] You come out with me while Blanche is getting dressed.

STANLEY:

Since when do you give me orders?

STELLA:

Are you going to stay here and insult her?

STANLEY:

You're damn tootin' I'm going to stay here.

[Stella goes out to the porch. Blanche comes out of the bathroom in a red satin robe.]

BLANCHE [airily]:

Hello, Stanley! Here I am, all freshly bathed and scented, and feeling like a brand new human being!

[He lights a cigarette.]

STANLEY:

That's good.

BLANCHE [drawing the curtains at the windows]:

Excuse me while I slip on my pretty new dress!

STANLEY:

Go right ahead, Blanche.

[She closes the drapes between the rooms.]

BLANCHE:

I understand there's to be a little card party to which we ladies are cordially *not* invited!

STANLEY [ominously]:

Yeah?

[Blanche throws off her robe and slips into a flowered print dress.]

BLANCHE:

Where's Stella?

STANLEY:

Out on the porch.

BLANCHE:

I'm going to ask a favor of you in a moment.

STANLEY:

What could that be, I wonder?

BLANCHE:

Some buttons in back! You may enter!

[He crosses through drapes with a smoldering look.]

How do I look?

STANLEY:

You look all right.

BLANCHE:

Many thanks! Now the buttons!

STANLEY:

I can't do nothing with them.

BLANCHE:

You men with your big clumsy fingers. May I have a drag on your cig?

STANLEY:

Have one for yourself.

BLANCHE:

Why, thanks! . . . It looks like my trunk has exploded.

STANLEY:

Me an' Stella were helping you unpack.

BLANCHE:

Well, you certainly did a fast and thorough job of it!

STANLEY:

It looks like you raided some stylish shops in Paris.

BLANCHE:

Ha-ha! Yes—clothes are my passion!

STANLEY:

What does it cost for a string of fur-pieces like that?

BLANCHE:

Why, those were a tribute from an admirer of mine!

STANLEY:

He must have had a lot of—admiration!

BLANCHE:

Oh, in my youth I excited some admiration. But look at me now! [She smiles at him radiantly] Would you think it possible that I was once considered to be—attractive?

STANLEY:

Your looks are okay.

BLANCHE:

I was fishing for a compliment, Stanley.

STANLEY:

I don't go in for that stuff.

BLANCHE:

What—stuff?

STANLEY:

Compliments to women about their looks. I never met a woman that didn't know if she was good-looking or not without being told, and some of them give themselves credit for more than they've got. I once went out with a doll who said to me, "I am the glamorous type, I am the glamorous type!" I said, "So what?"

BLANCHE:

And what did she say then?

STANLEY:

She didn't say nothing. That shut her up like a clam.

BLANCHE:

Did it end the romance?

STANLEY:

It ended the conversation—that was all. Some men are took in by this Hollywood glamor stuff and some men are not.

BLANCHE:

I'm sure you belong in the second category.

STANLEY:

That's right.

BLANCHE:

I cannot imagine any witch of a woman casting a spell over you.

STANLEY:

That's—right.

BLANCHE:

You're simple, straightforward and honest, a little bit on the primitive side I should think. To interest you a woman would have to—[she pauses with an indefinite gesture.]

STANLEY [slowly]:

Lay . . . her cards on the table.

BLANCHE [smiling]:

Yes—yes—cards on the table. . . . Well, life is too full of evasions and ambiguities, I think. I like an artist who paints in strong, bold colors, primary colors. I don't like pinks and creams and I never cared for wishy-washy people. That was why, when you walked in here last night, I said to myself—"My sister has married a man!"—Of course that was all that I could tell about you.

STANLEY [booming]:

Now let's cut the re-bop!

BLANCHE [pressing hands to her ears]:

Ouuuuu!

STELLA [calling from the steps]:

Stanley! You come out here and let Blanche finish dressing!

BLANCHE:

I'm through dressing, honey.

STELLA:

Well, you come out, then.

STANLEY:

Your sister and I are having a little talk.

BLANCHE [lightly]:

Honey, do me a favor. Run to the drug-store and get me a lemon-coke with plenty of chipped ice in it!—Will you do that for me, Sweetie?

STELLA [uncertainly]:

Yes. [She goes around the corner of the building.]

BLANCHE:

The poor little thing was out there listening to us, and I have an idea she doesn't understand you as well as I do. . . . All right; now, Mr. Kowalski, let us proceed without any more double-talk. I'm ready to answer all questions. I've nothing to hide. What is it?

STANLEY:

There is such a thing in this State of Louisiana as the Napoleonic code, according to which whatever belongs to my wife is also mine—and vice versa.

BLANCHE:

My, but you have an impressive judicial air!

[She sprays herself with her atomizer; then playfully sprays him with it. He seizes the atomizer and slams it down on the dresser. She throws back her head and laughs.]

STANLEY:

If I didn't know that you was my wife's sister I'd get ideas about you!

BLANCHE:

Such as what!

STANLEY:

Don't play so dumb. You know what!—Where's the papers?

BLANCHE:

Papers?

STANLEY:

Papers! That stuff people write on!

BLANCHE:

Oh, papers, papers! Ha-ha! The first anniversary gift, all kinds of papers!

STANLEY:

I'm talking of legal papers. Connected with the plantation.

BLANCHE:

There *were* some papers.

STANLEY:

You mean they're no longer existing?

BLANCHE:

They probably are, somewhere.

STANLEY:

But not in the trunk.

BLANCHE:

Everything that I own is in that trunk.

STANLEY:

They why don't we have a look for them? [He crosses to the trunk, shoves it roughly open and begins to open compartments.]

BLANCHE:

What in the name of heaven are you thinking of! What's in the back of that little boy's mind of yours? That I am absconding with something, attempting some kind of treachery on my sister?—Let me do that! It will be faster and simpler . . . [She crosses to the trunk and takes out a box] I keep my papers mostly in this tin box. [She opens it.]

STANLEY:

What's them underneath? [He indicates another sheaf of paper.]

BLANCHE:

These are love-letters, yellowing with antiquity, all from one boy. [He snatches them up. She speaks fiercely] Give those back to me!

STANLEY:

I'll have a look at them first!

BLANCHE:

The touch of your hands insults them!

STANLEY:

Don't pull that stuff!

[He rips off the ribbon and starts to examine them. Blanche snatches them from him, and they cascade to the floor.]

BLANCHE:

Now that you've touched them I'll burn them!

STANLEY [staring, baffled]:
What in hell are they?

BLANCHE [on the floor gathering them up]:
Poems a dead boy wrote. I hurt him the way that you would like to hurt me, but you can't! I'm not young and vulnerable any more. But my young husband was and I—never mind about that! Just give them back to me!

STANLEY:

What do you mean by saying you'll have to burn them?

BLANCHE:

I'm sorry, I must have lost my head for a moment. Everyone has something he won't let others touch because of their—intimate nature . . .

[She now seems faint with exhaustion and she sits down with the strong box and puts on a pair of glasses and goes methodically through a large stack of papers.]

Ambler & Ambler. Hmmmmm. . . . Crabtree. . . . More Ambler & Ambler.

STANLEY:

What is Ambler & Ambler?

BLANCHE:

A firm that made loans on the place.

STANLEY:

Then it *was* lost on a mortgage?

BLANCHE [touching her forehead]:
That must've been what happened.

STANLEY:

I don't want no ifs, ands or buts! What's all the rest of them papers?

[She hands him the entire box. He carries it to the table and starts to examine the papers.]

BLANCHE [picking up a large envelope containing more papers]:
There are thousands of papers, stretching back over hundreds of years, affecting Belle Reve as, piece by piece, our improvident grandfathers and father and uncles and brothers exchanged the land for their epic fornications—to put it plainly! [She removes her glasses with an exhausted laugh] The four-letter word deprived us of our plantation, till finally all that was left—and Stella can verify that!—was the house itself and about twenty acres of ground, including a graveyard, to which now all but Stella and I have retreated. [She pours the contents

of the envelope on the table] Here all of them are, all papers! I hereby endow you with them! Take them, peruse them—commit them to memory, even! I think it's wonderfully fitting that Belle Reve should finally be this bunch of old papers in your big, capable hands! . . . I wonder if Stella's come back with my lemon-coke . . .

[She leans back and closes her eyes.]

STANLEY:

I have a lawyer acquaintance who will study these out.

BLANCHE:

Present them to him with a box of aspirin tablets.

STANLEY [becoming somewhat sheepish]:

You see, under the Napoleonic code—a man has to take an interest in his wife's affairs—especially now that she's going to have a baby.

[Blanche opens her eyes. The "blue piano" sounds louder.]

BLANCHE:

Stella? Stella going to have a baby? [dreamily] I didn't know she was going to have a baby!

[She gets up and crosses to the outside door. Stella appears around the corner with a carton from the drugstore.]

[Stanley goes into the bedroom with the envelope and the box.]

[The inner rooms fade to darkness and the outside wall of the house is visible. Blanche meets Stella at the foot of the steps to the sidewalk.]

BLANCHE:

Stella, Stella for Star! How lovely to have a baby! [She embraces her sister. Stella returns the embrace with a convulsive sob. Blanche speaks softly] Everything is all right; we thrashed it out. I feel a bit shaky, but I think I handled it nicely. I laughed and treated it all as a joke, called him a little boy and laughed—and flirted! Yes—I was flirting with your husband, Stella!

[Steve and Pablo appear carrying a case of beer.]

The guests are gathering for the poker party.

[The two men pass between them, and with a short, curious stare at Blanche, they enter the house.]

STELLA:

I'm sorry he did that to you.

BLANCHE:

He's just not the sort that goes for jasmine perfume! But maybe he's what we need to mix with our blood now that we've lost Belle Reve and have to go on without Belle Reve to protect us . . . How pretty the sky is! I ought to go there on a rocket that never comes down.

[A tamale Vendor calls out as he rounds the corner.]

VENDOR:

Red hot! Red hots!

[Blanche utters a sharp, frightened cry and shrinks away; then she laughs breathlessly again.]

BLANCHE:

Which way do we—go now—Stella?

VENDOR:

Re-e-d ho-o-ot!

BLANCHE:

The Blind are—leading the blind!

[They disappear around the corner, Blanche's desperate laughter ringing out once more.]

[Then there is a bellowing laugh from the interior of the flat.]

[Then the "blue piano" and the hot trumpet sound louder.]

1947

Truman Capote

Dazzle

S HE FASCINATED me.

She fascinated everyone, but most people were ashamed of their fascination, especially the proud ladies who presided over some of the grander households of New Orleans' Garden District, the neighborhood where the big plantation owners lived, the shipowners and oil operators, the richest professional men. The only persons not secretive about their fascination with Mrs. Ferguson were the servants of these Garden District families. And, of course, some of the children, who were too young or guileless to conceal their interest.

I was one of those children, an eight-year-old boy temporarily living with Garden District relatives. However, as it happened, I did keep my fascination to myself, for I felt a certain guilt: I had a secret, something that was bothering me, something that was really worrying me very much, something I was afraid to tell anybody, anybody—I couldn't imagine what their reaction would be, it was such an odd thing that was worrying me, that had been worrying me for almost two years. I had never heard of anyone with a problem like the one that was troubling me. On the one hand it seemed maybe silly; on the other . . .

I wanted to tell my secret to Mrs. Ferguson. Not want to, but felt I had to. Because Mrs. Ferguson was said to have magical powers. It was said, and believed by many serious-minded people, that she could tame errant husbands, force proposals from reluctant suitors, restore lost hair, recoup squandered fortunes. In short, she was a witch who could make wishes come true. I had a wish.

Mrs. Ferguson did not seem clever enough to be capable of magic. Not even card tricks. She was a plain woman who might have been forty but was perhaps thirty; it was hard to tell, for her round Irish face, with its round full-moon eyes, had few lines and little expression. She was a laundress, probably the only white laundress in New Orleans, and an artist at her trade: the great ladies of the town sent for her when their finest laces and linens and silks required attention. They sent for her for other reasons as well: to obtain desires—a new lover, a certain marriage for a daughter, the death of a husband's mistress, a codicil to a mother's will, an invitation to be Queen of Comus, grandest of the Mardi Gras galas. It was not merely as a laundress that Mrs. Ferguson was courted. The source of her success, and principal income, was her alleged abilities to sift the sands of daydreams until she produced the solid stuff, golden realities.

Now, about this wish of my own, the worry that was with me from first thing in the morning until last thing at night: it wasn't anything I could just straight out ask her. It required the right time, a carefully prepared moment. She seldom came to our house, but when she did I stayed close by, pretending to watch the delicate movements of her thick ugly fingers as they handled lace-trimmed napkins, but really attempting to catch her eye. We never talked; I was too nervous and she was too stupid. Yes, stupid. It was just something I sensed; powerful witch or not, Mrs. Ferguson was a stupid woman. But now and again our eyes did lock, and dumb as she was, the intensity, the *fascination* she saw in my gaze told her that I desired to be a client. She probably thought I wanted a bike, or a new air rifle; anyway, she wasn't about to concern herself with a kid like me. What could I give her? So she would turn her tiny lips down and roll her full-moon eyes elsewhere.

About this time, early December in 1932, my paternal grand-mother arrived for a brief visit. New Orleans has cold winters; the chilly humid winds from the river drift deep into your bones. So my grand-mother, who was living in Florida, where she taught school, had wisely brought with her a fur coat, one she had borrowed from a friend. It was made of black Persian lamb, the belonging of a rich woman, which my grandmother was not. Widowed young, and left with three sons to raise, she had not had an easy life, but she never complained. She was an admirable woman; she had a lively mind, and a sound, sane one as well. Due to family circumstances, we rarely met, but she wrote often and sent me small gifts. She loved me and I wanted to love her, but until she died, and she lived beyond ninety, I kept my distance, behaved indifferently. She felt it, but she never knew what caused my apparent coldness, nor did anyone else, for the reason was part of an intricate guilt, faceted as the dazzling yellow stone dangling from a slender gold-chain necklace that she often wore. Pearls would have suited her better, but she attached great value to this somewhat theatrical gewgaw, which I understood her own grandfather had won in a card game in Colorado.

Of course the necklace wasn't valuable; as my grandmother always scrupulously explained to anyone who inquired, the stone, which was the size of a cat's paw, was not a "gem" stone, not a canary diamond, nor even a topaz, but a chunk of rock-crystal deftly faceted and tinted dark yellow. Mrs. Ferguson, however, was unaware of the trinket's true worth, and when one afternoon, during the course of my grandmother's stay, the plump youngish witch arrived to stiffen some linen, she seemed spellbound by the brilliant bit of glass swinging from the thin chain around my grandmother's neck. Her ignorant moon eyes glowed, and that's a fact: they truly glowed. I now had no difficulty attracting her attention; she studied me with an interest absent heretofore.

As she departed, I followed her into the garden, where there was a century-old wisteria arbor, a mysterious place even in winter when the foliage had shriveled, stripping this leaf-tunnel of its concealing shadows. She walked under it and beckoned to me.

Softly, she said: "You got something on your mind?"

"Yes."

"Something you want done? A favor?"

I nodded; she nodded, but her eyes shifted nervously: she didn't want to be seen talking to me.

She said: "My boy will come. He will tell you."

"When?"

But she said hush, and hurried out of the garden. I watched her waddle off into the dusk. It dried my mouth to think of having all my hopes pinned on this stupid woman. I couldn't eat supper that night; I didn't sleep until dawn. Aside from the thing that was worrying me, now I had a whole lot of new worries. If Mrs. Ferguson did what I wanted her to do, then what about my clothes, what about my name, where would I go, who would I be? Holy smoke, it was enough to drive you crazy! Or was I already crazy? That was part of the problem:

I must be crazy to want Mrs. Ferguson to do this thing I wanted her to do. That was one reason why I couldn't tell anybody: they would think I was crazy. Or something worse. I didn't know what that something worse could be, but instinctively I felt that people saying I was crazy, my family and their friends and the other kids, might be the least of it.

Because of fear and superstition combined with greed, the servants of the Garden District, some of the snobbiest mammies and haughtiest housemen who ever tread a parquet floor, spoke of Mrs. Ferguson with respect. They also spoke of her in quiet tones, and not only because of her peculiar gifts, but because of her equally peculiar private life, various details of which I had gradually collected by eaves-dropping on the tattletale of these elegant blacks and mulattoes and Creoles, who considered themselves the real royalty of New Orleans, and certainly superior to any of their employers. As for Mrs. Ferguson —she was not a madame, merely a mamselle: an unmarried woman with a raft of children, at least six, who came from East Texas, one of those redneck hamlets across the border from Shreveport. At the age of fifteen she had been tied to a hitching post in front of the town post office and publicly flogged with a horsewhip by her own father. The reason for this terrible punishment was a child she had borne, a boy with green eyes but unmistakably the product of a black father. With the baby, who was called Skeeter and was now fourteen and said to be a devil himself, she came to New Orleans and found work as a house-keeper for an Irish Catholic priest, whom she seduced, had a second baby by, abandoned for another man, and went on from there, living with a succession of handsome lovers, men she could only have succeeded in acquiring through potions poured into their wine, for after all, without her particular powers, who was she? White trash from East Texas who carried on with black men, the mother of six bastards, a laundress, a servant herself. And yet they respected her; even Mme. Jouet, the head mammy of the Vacarro family, who owned the United Fruit Company, always addressed her civilly.

Two days after my conversation with Mrs. Ferguson, a Sunday, I accompanied my grandmother to church, and as we were walking home, a matter of a few blocks, I noticed that someone was following us: a well-built boy with tobacco-colored skin and green eyes. I knew at once that it was the infamous Skeeter, the boy whose birth had caused his mother to be flogged, and I knew that he was bringing me a message. I felt nauseated, but also elated, almost tipsy, enough so to make me laugh.

Merrily, my grandmother asked: "Ah, you know a joke?"

I thought: No, but I know a secret. However, I only said: "It was just something the minister said."

"Really? I'm glad you found some humor. It struck me as a very dry sermon. But the choir was good."

I refrained from making the following comment: "Well, if they're just going to talk about sinners and hell, when they don't know what hell is, they ought to ask me to preach the sermon. I could tell them a thing or two."

"Are you happy here?" my grandmother asked, as if it were a question she had been considering ever since her arrival. "I know it's been difficult. The divorce. Living here, living there. I want to help; I don't know how."

"I'm fine. Everything's hunky-dory."

But I wished she'd shut up. She did, with a frown. So at least I'd got one wish. One down and one to go.

When we reached home my grandmother, saying she felt the start of a migraine and might try to ward it off with a pill and a nap, kissed me and went inside the house. I raced through the garden toward the old wisteria arbor and hid myself inside it, like a bandit in a bandit's cave waiting for a confederate.

Soon Mrs. Ferguson's son arrived. He was tall for his age, just shy of six feet, and muscular as a dockworker. He resembled his mother in no respect. It wasn't only his dark coloring; his features were nicely defined, the bone structure quite precise—his father must have been a handsome man. And unlike Mrs. Ferguson, his emerald eyes were not dumb comic-strip dots, but narrow and mean, weapons, bullets threatingly aimed and primed to explode. I wasn't surprised when, not many years later, I heard he'd committed a double murder in Houston and died in the electric chair at Texas State Prison.

He was natty, dressed like the adult sharp-guy hoodlums who lounged around the waterfront hangouts: Panama hat, two-toned shoes, a tight stained white linen suit that some much slighter man must have given him. An impressive cigar jutted from his handker-chief pocket: a Havana Castle Morro, the connoisseur's cigar Garden District gentlemen served along with their after-dinner absinthe and framboise. Skeeter Ferguson lit his cigar with movie-gangster show-manship, constructed an impeccable smoke ring, blew it straight into my face, and said: "I've come to get you."

"*Now?*"

"Just as soon as you bring me the old lady's necklace."

It was useless to stall, but I tried: "What necklace?"

"Save your breath. Go get it and then we'll head somewhere. Or else we won't. And you'll never have another chance."

"But she's wearing it!"

Another smoke ring, professionally manufactured, effortlessly projected. "How you get it ain't none of my beeswax. I'll just be right here. Waiting."

"But it may take a long time. And suppose I can't do it?"

"You will. I'll wait till you do."

The house sounded empty when I entered through the kitchen door, and except for my grandmother, it was; everyone else had driven off to visit a newly married cousin who lived across the river. After calling my grandmother's name, and hearing silence, I tiptoed upstairs and listened at her bedroom door. She must be asleep. Accepting the risk, I inched the door open.

The curtains were drawn and the room dark except for the hot shine of coal burning inside a porcelain stove. My grandmother was lying in bed with covers drawn up to her chin; she must have taken the headache pill, for her breathing was deep and even. Still, I drew back the quilt covering her with the meticulous stealth of a robber tumbling the dials of a bank safe. Her throat was naked; she was wearing only an undergarment, a pink slip. I found the necklace on a bureau; it was lying in front of a photograph of her three sons, one of them my father. I hadn't seen him for so long that I'd forgotten what he looked like—and after today, I'd probably never see him again. Or if I did, he wouldn't know who I was. But I had no time to think about that. Skeeter Ferguson was waiting for me, standing inside the wisteria arbor tapping his foot and sucking on his millionaire's cigar. Nevertheless, I hesitated.

I had never stolen anything before; well, some Hershey bars from the candy counter at the movies, and a few books I'd not returned to the public library. But this was so important. My grandmother would forgive me if she knew why I had to steal the necklace. No, she wouldn't forgive me; nobody would forgive me if they knew *exactly* why. But I had no choice. It was like Skeeter said: if I didn't do it now, his mother would never give me another chance. And the thing that was worrying me would go on and on, maybe forever and forever. So I took it. I stuffed it in my pocket and fled the room without even closing the door. When I rejoined Skeeter, I didn't show him the necklace, I just told him I had it, and his green eyes grew greener, turned nastier, as he issued one of his big shot smoke rings and said: "Sure you do. You're just a born rascal. Like me."

First we walked, then we took a trolley car down Canal Street, usually so crowded and cheerful but spooky now with the stores closed and a Sabbath stillness hovering over it like a funeral cloud. At Canal and Royal we changed trolleys and rode all the way across the French Quarter, a familiar neighborhood where many of the longer-established families lived, some with purer lineage than any names the Garden District could offer. Eventually we started walking again; we walked miles. The stiff churchgoing shoes I was still wearing hurt, and now I didn't know where we were, but wherever it was I didn't like it. It was no use questioning Skeeter Ferguson, for if you did, he smiled and whistled, or spit and smiled and whistled. I wonder if he whistled on his way to the electric chair.

I really had no idea where we were; it was a section of the city I'd not seen before. And yet there was nothing unusual about it, except that there were fewer white faces around than one was accustomed to, and the farther we walked the scarcer they became: an occasional white resident surrounded by blacks and Creoles. Otherwise it was an ordinary collection of humble wooden structures, rooming houses with peeling paint, modest family homes, mostly poorly kept but with some exceptions. Mrs. Ferguson's house, when at last we reach it, was one of the exceptions.

It was an old house but a *real* house, with seven or eight rooms; it didn't look as though the first strong breeze from the Gulf would blow it away. It was painted an ugly brown, but at least the paint was not sun-blistered and flaking. And it stood inside a well-tended yard that contained a big shade tree—a chinaberry tree with old rubber tires, several of them, suspended on ropes from its branches: swings for children. And there were other playthings scattered around the yard: a tricycle, buckets, and little shovels for making mud pies—evidence of Mrs. Ferguson's fatherless brood. A mongrel puppy held captive by a chain attached to a stake began bouncing about and yapping the second he glimpsed Skeeter.

Skeeter said: "Here we are. Just open the door and walk in."

"Alone?"

"She's expectin' you. Do what I tell you. Walk right in. And if you catch her in the middle of a hump, keep your eyes open; that's how I got to be a champion humper."

The last remark, meaningless to me, ended with a chuckle, but I followed his instructions, and as I started toward the front door, glanced back at him. It didn't seem possible, but he was already gone, and I never saw him again—or if I did, I don't remember it.

The door opened directly into Mrs. Ferguson's parlor. At least it was furnished as a parlor (a couch, easy chairs, two wicker rocking chairs, maplewood side tables), though the floor was covered with a brown kitchen linoleum that perhaps was meant to match the color of the house. When I came into the room Mrs. Ferguson was tilting to and fro in one of the rocking chairs, while a good-looking young man, a Creole not many years older than Skeeter, rocked away in the other. A bottle of rum rested on a table between them, and they were both drinking from glasses filled with the stuff. The young man, who was not introduced to me, was wearing only an undershirt and somewhat unbuttoned bell-bottom sailor's trousers. Without a word he stopped rocking, stood up, and swaggered down a hall, taking the rum bottle with him. Mrs. Ferguson listened until she heard a door close.

Then all she said was: "Where is it?"

I was sweating. My heart was acting funny. I felt as though I had run a hundred miles and lived a thousand years in just the last few hours.

Mrs. Ferguson stilled her chair, and repeated herself: "Where is it?"

"Here. In my pocket."

She held out a thick red hand, palm up, and I dropped the necklace into it. Rum had already done something to alter the usual dullness of her eyes; the dazzling yellow stone did more. She turned it this way and that, staring at it; I tried not to, I tried to think of other things, and found myself wondering if she had scars on her back, lash marks.

"Am I expected to guess?" she asked, never removing her gaze from the bijou dangling from its fragile gold chain. "Well? Am I supposed to tell you why you are here? What it is you want?"

She didn't know, she couldn't, and suddenly I didn't want her to. I said: "I like to tap-dance."

For an instant her attention was diverted from the sparkling new toy.

"I want to be a tap dancer. I want to run away. I want to go to Hollywood and be in the movies." There was some truth in this; running away to Hollywood was high on my list of escape-fantasies. But that wasn't what I'd decided not to tell her, after all.

"Well," she drawled. "You sure are pretty enough to be in picture shows. Prettier than any boy ought to be."

So she *did* know. I heard myself shouting: "Yes! Yes! That's it!"

"That's what? And stop hollering. I'm not deaf."

"I don't want to be a boy. I want to be a girl."

It began as a peculiar noise, a strangled gurgling far back in her throat that bubbled into laughter. Her tiny lips stretched and widened; drunken laughter spilled out of her mouth like vomit, and it seemed to be spurting all over me—laughter that sounded like vomit smells.

"Please, please. Mrs. Ferguson, you don't understand. I'm very worried. I'm worried all the time. There's something wrong. Please. You've got to understand."

She went on rocking with laughter and her rocking chair rocked with her.

Then I said: "You *are* stupid. Dumb and stupid." And I tried to grab the necklace away from her.

The laughter stopped as though she had been struck by lightning: a storm overtook her face, total fury. Yet when she spoke her voice was soft and hissing and serpentine: "You don't know what you want boy. I'll show you what you want. Look at me, boy. Look here. I'll show you what you want."

"Please. I don't want anything."

"Open your eyes, boy."

Somewhere in the house a baby was crying.

"Look at me, boy. Look here."

What she wanted me to look at was the yellow stone. She was holding it above her head, and slightly swinging it. It seemed to have gathered up all the light in the room, accumulated a devastating brilliance that plunged everything else into blackness. Swing, spin, dazzle, dazzle.

"I hear a baby crying."

"That's you you hear."

"Stupid woman. Stupid. Stupid."

"Look here, boy."

Spindazzlespinspindazzledazzledazzle.

It was still daylight, and it was still Sunday, and here I was back in the Garden District, standing in front of my house. I don't know how I got there. Someone must have brought me, but I don't know who; my last memory was the noise of Mrs. Ferguson's laughter returning.

Of course, a huge commotion was made over the missing necklace. The police were not called, but the whole household was upside down for days; not an inch was left unsearched. My grandmother was very upset. But even if the necklace had been of high value, a jewel that could have been sold and assured her of comfort the rest of her life, I still would not have accused Mrs. Ferguson. For if I did, she might reveal what I'd told her, the thing I never told anyone again, not ever. Finally it was decided that a thief had stolen into the house and taken the necklace while my grandmother slept. Well, that was the truth. Everyone was relieved when my grandmother concluded her visit and returned to Florida. It was hoped that the whole sad affair of the missing jewel would soon be forgotten.

But it was not forgotten. Forty-four years evaporated, and it was not forgotten. I became a middle-aged man, riddled with quirks and quaint notions. My grandmother died, still sane and sound of mind despite her great age.

A cousin called to inform me of her death, and to ask when I would be arriving for the funeral; I said I'd let her know. I was ill with grief, inconsolable; and it was absurd, out of all proportion. My grandmother was not someone I had loved. Yet how I grieved! But I did not travel to the funeral, nor even send flowers. I stayed home and drank a quart of vodka. I was very drunk, but I can remember answering the telephone and hearing my father identify himself. His old man's voice trembled with more than the weight of years; he vented the pent-up wrath of a lifetime, and when I remained silent, he said: "You sonofabitch. She died with your picture in her hand." I said "I'm sorry," and hung up. What was there to say? How could I explain that all through the years any mention of my grandmother, any letter from her or thought of her, evoked Mrs. Ferguson? Her laughter, her fury, the swinging, spinning yellow stone: spindazzledazzle.

1975

William Thackeray

A Mississippi Bubble

N EW ORLEANS, in spring-time—just when the orchards were flushing over with peach-blossoms, and the sweet herbs came to flavor the juleps—seemed to me the city of the world where you can eat and drink the most and suffer the least. At Bordeaux itself, claret is not better to drink than at New Orleans. It was all good—believe an expert Robert—from the half-dollar Médoc of the public hotel table, to the private gentleman's choicest wine. Claret is, somehow, good in that gifted place at dinner, at supper, and at breakfast in the morning. It is good: it is super-abundant—and there is nothing to pay. Find me speaking ill of such a country! When I do, *pone me pigris campis:* smother me in a desert, or let the Mississippi or Garonne drown me! At that comfortable tavern on Pontchartrain we had a *bouillabaisse* than which a better was never eaten at Marseilles: and not the least headache in the morning, I give you my word; on the contrary, you only wake with a sweet refreshing thirst for claret and water. They say there is fever there in the autumn: but not in the spring-time, when the peach-blossoms blush over the orchards, and the sweet herbs come to flavor the juleps.

I was bound from New Orleans to Saint Louis; and our walk was constantly on the Levee, whence we could see a hundred of those huge white Mississippi steamers at their moorings in the river: "Look," said my friend Lochlomond to me, as we stood one day on the quay—"look at that post! Look at that coffee-house behind it! Sir, last year a streamer blew up in the river yonder, just where you see those men pulling off in the boat. By that post where you are standing a mule was cut in two by a fragment of the burst machinery, and a bit of the chimney stove in the first-floor window of that coffee-house killed a Negro, who was cleaning knives in the top room!" I looked at the post, at the coffee-house window, at the steamer in which I was going to embark, at my friend, with a pleasing interest not divested of melancholy.

These incidents give a queer zest to the voyage down the life stream in America. When our huge, tall, white, pasteboard castle of a steamer began to work up stream, every limb in her creaked, and groaned, and quivered, so that you might fancy she would burst right off. Would she hold together, or would she split into ten million of shivers. O my home and children! Would your humble servant's body be cut in two across yonder chain on the Levee, or be precipitated into yonder first-floor, so as to damage the chest of a black man cleaning boots at the window? It has happened; and if to a mule, why not to a more docile animal? On our journey up the Mississippi, I give you my honour we were on fire three times, and burned our cook-room down. The deck at night was a great firework—the chimney spouted myriads of stars, which fell blackening on our garments, sparkling on to the deck, or gleaming into the mighty stream through which we labored—the mighty yellow stream with all its snags.

How I kept up my courage through these dangers shall now be narrated. The excellent landlord of the Saint Charles Hotel, when I was going away, begged me to accept two bottles of the very finest Cognac, with his compliments; and I found them in my state-room with my luggage. My friend Lochlomond came to see me off, and as he squeezed my hand at parting, "Roundabout," says he, "the wine mayn't be very good on board, so I have brought a dozen-case of the Médoc which you liked:" and we grasped together the hands of friendship and farewell. Whose boat is this pulling up to the ship? It is our friend Glenlivat, who gave us the dinner on Lake Pontchartrain. "Roundabout," says he, "we have tried to do what we could for you, my boy; and it has been done *de bon coeur*" (I detect a kind tremulousness in the good fellow's voice as he speaks). "I say—hem!—the a—the wine isn't too good on board, so I've brought you a dozen of Médoc for your voyage, you know. And God bless you; and when I come to London in May I shall come and see you. Hallo! Here's Johnson come to see you off, too!"

Well, as I am a miserable sinner, when Johnson grasped my

hand, he said, "Mr. Roundabout, you can't be sure of the wine on board these steamers, so I thought I would bring you a little case of that light claret which you liked at my house." *Et de trois!* No wonder I could face the Mississippi with so much courage supplied to me! Where are you, honest friends, who gave me of your kindness and your cheer? May I be considerably boiled, blown up, and snagged, if I speak hard words of you. May claret turn sour ere I do!

1856

M. Dumont

Indian Troubles and Hangmen

NEW ORLEANS, during these early years, was not tranquil. One day a woman, whose head was turned by the brandy she had been taking, came running into the city from the Bayou St. John with streaming hair, crying that the Indians had made a descent on the Bayou and massacred all the settlers there, and were actually pursuing her. This woman was joined by some others, about as wise, and the noise increasing, the alarm soon spread to all quarters. The muster was beat, all ran to arms, and assembled in the great square. Here they were formed into companies, and powder and ball delivered to each. The ladies meanwhile fled to the churches, or to the vessels moored before the town. The terror was general; all thought they were lost, without anybody's knowing on which side the enemy were. The commandant-general sent out a large scouting party to bring him correct information. This body at first advanced with great caution for fear of being surprised, but after a lapse of two hours, it was found that it was all nothing, that this great trouble had no better foundation than two or three shots fired by some hunters in the woods.

Soon after this false alarm there was one much better founded, and which might have resulted seriously. For some time a secret plot had been brewing among the Negro slaves. Excited underhand by the Indians, or perhaps wishing to imitate them and recover their liberty, they had formed the design of making away with their masters and butchering the garrison. The plan was bold, and they alone never could have succeeded, but who knows whether the Indians would not have lent a hand? Be that as it may, they had already concerted the manner of executing their guilty project, and the plot was ready to be put in action, when a Negro woman, belonging to a surgeon named Brosset, told her master, and discovered all about it. He prudently questioned her, learned the names of the chiefs in the conspiracy, and the manner in which they were to act. Their plan was for each first to kill his master at night as he was going to bed: then being masters of all the keys, they would soon have guns, powder and lead, which would enable them to get rid of the troops on guard without difficulty. After committing to writing all he could get from the woman, the surgeon communicated it to the commandant-general, who, on this information, immediately arrested the leaders in the conspiracy, with some Negro women also denounced. They were put in dungeons, and separately examined; and, on the avowal which they made on their dark design, were all condemned, some to be broken on the wheel, others to be hung as examples for the rest.

Yet after this execution the commandant-general saw that it was not enough to have extinguished this first fire by the death of the most guilty, unless the probable consequences were also prevented; and as he could not discover whether the Negroes had been excited by the Indians or not, he resolved to embroil them with each other to prevent all danger on that side. With this view he ordered most of the Negroes before him, told them that they were all traitors, and that he was going to hang them all, as he had learned that they were in league with the Indians to exterminate the French. On this they protested innocence, cried for mercy, and offered, if permitted, to march themselves against the Indians and destroy them. The general having thus gained his end, armed them with hatchets, bayonets and knives, and let them attack a little tribe called the Chouachas, ordering them to kill only the men and to spare the women and children. His orders were fulfilled, the Negroes attacked the village, killed seven or eight men whom they found there, the rest being at the chase. This single expedition rendered the Indians mortal enemies of the Negroes.

It would be wrong to suppose the Negroes I have so often mentioned to be natives of Louisiana. They are blacks, from the coast of Guinea, sent into the province by the company, and distributed to the colonists at a thousand livres apiece, payable in three years in colonial produce.* When a slave vessel arrived it was visited by surgeons, who

*In 1712 there were but twenty Negroes in the colony. The first large importation was made under the auspices of the Western Company in June, 1719; and during the existence of the company and for several years afterwards, their agents continued to supply the demand at the

separated the healthy from the sick, and put the latter under treatment. The former were then divided in this way: Such settlers as were named to have Negroes went to the commissary-ordinator, and drew from a bag a ticket, whose number denoted the Negro man or woman who fell to them, each Negro having a number around his neck. As for the sick, they were sold at auction, and as there were always settlers who could not get healthy ones, the biddings ran so high that the sick brought as much as the others.

These Negroes are fed in their masters' houses, with rice, maize, or other food of the country. Some of these slaves can really rejoice at having fallen into good hands; but there are many, too, who suffer. They are sent to work at daybreak, either in the fields, or at something else; in the course of the morning they have half an hour for breakfast, and at half-past eleven they go to the house to get their dinner, and then work again from two till sunset, when they come home again, and then, sometimes, must break rice or Indian corn to make bread. Those who have many Negro slaves, and are consequently looked upon as lords in the country, do not take the trouble to lead them to work themselves; for this purpose they hire a Frenchman, who manages and watches them. Sometimes a trusted Negro holds this place and he then carries a whip as a mark of distinction. The Negro women go to work like the men; and when nursing children, carry them on their backs, and follow the rest.

Most of the slaves clear grounds and cultivate them on their own account, raising cotton, tobacco &c., which they sell. Some give their Negroes Saturday and Sunday to themselves, and during that time the master does not give them any food; they then work for other Frenchmen who have no slaves, and who pay them. Those who live in or near the capital generally turn their two hours at noon to account by making faggots to sell in the city; others sell ashes, or fruits that are in season. Some of these Negroes have behaved so well as to gain their freedom, and have begun plantations in imitation of the French.

As the race of hangmen has not yet emigrated, and a well-ordered government must have them, they had to choose one of the

---

rate of three to five hundred annually. The average price for a Negro man was about one hundred and fifty dollars; and for a woman, about one hundred and twenty dollars.

company's Negroes to fill that post in the early part of the establishment of the colony. His name was Johnny; when he was called and they had explained their wish, he tried to get clear of it, although they promised him his liberty. But when he saw that they would force him to it, he exclaimed: "Well! that is right, wait a moment," and running to his cabin, took an axe, and laying his arm on a block, cut off his hand, and returning to the meeting showed his maimed limb, and his consequent inability to exercise the office with which they would have honored him. It is easy to imagine the effect produced by this action: the first thought was to save his life; he was put in the hands of surgeons, cured, and made commander of the company's Negroes. As for the office, another less delicate was found, who accepted it as the price of his freedom, so that the hangman in the colony is a Negro.

1730

Ishmael Reed

Mumbo Jumbo

A   T R U E   S P O R T ,   the mayor of New Orleans, spiffy in his patent-leather brown and white shoes, his plaid suit, the Rudolph Valentino parted-down-the-middle hair style, sits in his office. Sprawled upon his knees is Zuzu, local doo-wack-a-doo and voo-do-dee-odo fizgig. A slatternly floozy, her green, sequined dress quivers.

Work has kept Your Honor late.

The Mayor passes the flask of bootlegged gin to Zuzu. She takes a sip and continues to spread sprawl and behave skittishly. Loose. She is inhaling from a Chesterfield cigarette in a shameless brazen fashion.

The telephone rings.

The Mayor removes his hand and picks up the receiver; he recognizes at once the voice of his poker pardner on the phone.

Harry, you'd better get down here quick. What was once dormant is now a Creeping Thing.

The Mayor stands up and Zuzu lands on the floor. Her posture reveals a small flask stuck in her garter as well as some healthily endowed gams.

What's wrong, Harry?

I gots to git down to the infirmary, Zuzu, something awful is happening, the Thing has stirred in its moorings. The Thing that my Grandfather and his generation of Harrys had thought was nothing but a false alarm.

The Mayor, dragging the woman by the fox skins hanging from her neck, leaves city hall and jumps into his Stutz Bearcat parked at the curb. They drive until they reach St. Louis Cathedral where 19th-century HooDoo Queen Marie Laveau was a frequent worshiper; its location was about 10 blocks from Place Congo. They walk up the steps and the door's Judas Eye swings open.

Joe Sent Me.

What's going on, hon? Is this a speakeasy? Zuzu inquires in her cutesy-poo drawl.

The door opens to a main room of the church which has been converted into an infirmary. About 22 people lie on carts. Doctors are rushing back and forth; they wear surgeon's masks and white coats. Doors open and shut.

1 man approaches the Mayor who is walking from bed to bed examining the sleeping occupants, including the priest of the parish.

What's the situation report, doc? the Mayor asks.

We have 22 of them. The only thing that seems to anesthetize them is sleep.

When did it start?

This morning. We got reports from down here that people were doing "stupid sensual things," were in a state of "uncontrollable frenzy," were wriggling like fish, doing something called the "Eagle Rock" and the "Sassy Bump"; were cutting a mean "Mooche," and "lusting after relevance." We decoded this coon mumbo jumbo. We knew that something was Jes Grewing just like the 1890s flair-up. We thought that the local infestation area was Place Congo so we put our antipathetic substances to work on it, to try to drive it out; but it started to play hide and seek with us, a case occurring in 1 neighborhood and picking up in another. It began to leapfrog all about us.

But can't you put it under 1 of them microscopes? Lock it in? Can't you protective-reaction the dad-blamed thing? Look I got an election coming up—

To blazes with your election, man! Don't you understand, if this Jes Grew becomes pandemic it will mean the end of Civilization As We Know It?

That serious?

Yes. You see, it's not 1 of those germs that break bleed suck gnaw or devour. It's nothing we can bring into focus or categorize; once we call it 1 thing it forms into something else.

No man. This is a *psychic epidemic,* not a lesser germ like typhoid yellow fever or syphilis. We can handle those. This belongs under some ancient Demonic Theory of Disease.

Well, what about the priest?

We tried him but it seized him too. He was shouting and carrying on like any old coon wench with a bass drum.

What about the patients, did you ask any of them about how they knew it?

Yes, 1, Harry. When we thought it was physical we examined his output, and drinking water to determine if we could find some normal germ. We asked him questions, like what he had seen.

What *did* he see?

He said he saw Nkulu Kulu of the Zulu, a locomotive with a red green and black python entwined in its face, Johnny Canoeing up the tracks.

Well Clem, how about his feelings? How did he feel?

He said he felt like the gut heart and lungs of Africa's interior. He said he felt like the Kongo: "Land of the Panther." He said he felt like "deserting his master," as the Kongo is "prone to do." He said he felt he could dance on a dime.

Well, his hearing, Clem. His hearing.

He said he was hearing shank bones, jew's harps, bagpipes, flutes, conch horns, drums, banjos, kazoos.

Go on go on and then what did he say?

He started to speak in tongues. There are no isolated cases in this thing. It knows no class no race no consciousness. It is self-propagating and you can never tell when it will hit.

Well doc, did you get other opinions?

Who do you think some of those other cases are? 6 of them are some of the most distinguished bacteriologists epidemiologists and chemists from the University.

There is a commotion outside. The Mayor rushes out to see Zuzu rejoicing. Slapping the attendants who are attempting to placate her. The people on carts suddenly leap up and do their individual numbers. The Mayor feels that uncomfortable sensation at the nape and soon he is doing something resembling the symptoms of Jes Grew, and the Doctor who rushes to his aid starts slipping dipping gliding on out of doors and into the streets. Shades of windows fly up. Lights flick on in buildings. And before you know it the whole quarter is in convulsions from Jes Grew's entrance into the Govi of New Orleans; the charming city, the amalgam of Spanish French and African culture, is out-of-its head. By morning there are 10,000 cases of Jes Grew.

§

The foolish Wallflower Order hadn't learned a damned thing. They thought that by fumigating the Place Congo in the 1890s when people were doing the Bamboula the Cacta the Babouille the Counjaille the Juba the Congo and the VooDoo that this would put an end to it. That it was merely a fad. But they did not understand that the Jes Grew epidemic was unlike physical plagues. Actually Jes Grew was an anti-plague. Some plagues caused the body to waste away; Jes Grew enlivened the host. Other plagues were accompanied by bad air (malaria). Jes Grew victims said that the air was as clear as they had ever seen it and that there was the aroma of roses and perfumes which had never before enticed their nostrils. Some plagues arise from decomposing animals, but Jes Grew is electric as life and is characterized by ebullience and ecstasy. Terrible plagues were due to the wrath of God; but Jes Grew is the delight of the gods.

So Jes Grew is seeking its words. Its text. For what good is a liturgy without a text? In the 1890s the text was not available and Jes Grew was out there all alone. Perhaps the 1920s will also be a false alarm and Jes Grew will evaporate as quickly as it appeared again broken-hearted and double-crossed (+ +).

> Once the band starts, everybody starts swaying from one side of the street to the other, especially those who drop in and follow the ones who have been to the funeral. These people are known as "the second line" and they may be anyone passing along the street who wants to hear the music. *The spirit hits them and they follow.*
>
> (My italics)
>
> Louis Armstrong

Mumbo Jumbo

[Mandingo *mā-mā-gyo-mbō*, "magician who makes the troubled spirits of ancestors go away": *mā-mā*, grandmother + *gyo*, trouble +*mbo*, to leave.]

The American Heritage Dictionary of the English Language

1972

William Faulkner

Absalom, Absalom!

"THEY WENT to New Orleans. They rode through the bright cold of that Christmas day, to the River and took the steamboat, it still Henry doing the leading, the bringing, as he always did until the very last, when for the first time during their entire relationship Bon led and Henry followed. He didn't have to go. He had voluntarily made himself a pauper but he could have gone to his grandfather since although he was probably better mounted than any other at the University, not excepting Bon himself, he probably had very little money beyond what he could raise hurriedly on his horse and what valuables he happened to have on his body when he and Bon rode away. No, he didn't have to go, and he doing the leading this time too, and Bon riding beside him trying to find out from him what had happened. Bon knew of course what Sutpen had discovered in New Orleans, but he would need to know just what, just how much, Sutpen had told Henry, and Henry not telling him, doubtless with the new mare which he probably knew he would have to surrender, sacrifice too, along with all the rest of his life, inheritance, going fast now and his back rigid and irrevocably turned upon the house, his birthplace and all the familiar scenes of his childhood and youth which he had repudiated for the sake of that friend with whom, despite the sacrifice which he had just made out of love and loyalty, he still could not be perfectly frank. Because he knew that what Sutpen had told him was true. He must have known that at the very instant when he gave his father the lie. So he dared not ask Bon to deny it; he dared not, you see. He could face poverty, disinheritance, but he could not have borne that lie from Bon. Yet he went to New Orleans. He went straight there, to the only place, the very place, where he could not help but prove conclusively the very statement which, coming from his father, he had called a lie. He went there for that purpose; he went there to prove it. And Bon, riding beside him, trying to find out what Sutpen had told him,—Bon who for a year and a half now had been watching Henry ape his clothing and speech, who for a year and a half now had seen himself as the object of that complete and abnegant devotion which only a youth, never a woman, gives to another youth or a man; who for exactly a year now had seen the sister succumb to that same spell which the brother had already succumbed to, and this with no volition on the seducer's part, without so much as the lifting of a finger, as though it actually were the brother who had put the spell on the sister, seduced her to his own vicarious image which walked and breathed with Bon's body. Yet here is the letter, sent four years afterward, written on a sheet of paper salvaged from a gutted house in Carolina, with stove polish found in some captured Yankee stores; four years after she had had any message from him save the messages from Henry that he (Bon) was still alive. So whether Henry now knew about the other woman or not, he would now have to know. Bon realised that. I can imagine them as they rode, Henry still in the fierce repercussive flush of vindicated loyalty, and Bon, the wiser, the shrewder even if only from wider experience and a few more years of age, learning from Henry without Henry's being aware of it, what Sutpen had told him. Because Henry would have to know now. And I dont believe it was just to preserve Henry as an ally, for the crisis of some future need. It was because Bon not only loved Judith after his fashion but he loved Henry too and I believe in a deeper sense than merely after his fashion. Perhaps in his fatalism he loved Henry the better of the two, seeing perhaps in the sister merely the shadow, the woman vessel with which to consummate the love whose actual object was the youth:—this cerebral Don Juan who, reversing the order, had learned to love what he had injured; perhaps it was even more than Judith or Henry either: perhaps the life, the existence, which they represented. Because who knows what picture of peace he might have seen in that monotonous provincial backwater; what alleviation and escape for a parched traveller who had travelled too far at too young an age, in this granite-bound and simple country spring.

"And I can imagine how Bon told Henry, broke it to him. I can imagine Henry in New Orleans, who had not yet even been to

Memphis, whose entire worldly experience consisted of sojourns at other houses, plantations, almost interchangeable with his own, where he followed the same routine which he did at home—the same hunting and cockfighting, the same amateur racing of horses on crude homemade tracks, horses sound enough in blood and lineage yet not bred to race and perhaps not even thirty minutes out of the shafts of a trap or perhaps even a carriage; the same square dancing with identical and also interchangeable provincial virgins, to music exactly like that at home, the same champagne, the best doubtless yet crudely dispensed out of the burlesqued pantomime elegance of negro butlers who (and likewise the drinkers who gulped it down like neat whiskey between flowering and unsubtle toasts) would have treated lemonade the same way. I can imagine him, with his puritan heritage—that heritage peculiarly Anglo-Saxon—of fierce proud mysticism and the ability to be ashamed of ignorance and inexperience, in that city foreign and paradoxical, with its atmosphere at once fatal and languorous, at once feminine and steelhard—this grim humorless yokel out of a granite heritage where even the houses, let alone clothing and conduct, are built in the image of a jealous and sadistic Jehovah, put suddenly down in a place whose denizens had created their All-Powerful and His supporting hierarchy-chorus of beautiful saints and handsome angels in the image of their houses and personal ornaments and voluptuous lives. Yes, I can imagine how Bon led up to it, to the shock: the skill, the calculation, preparing Henry's puritan mind as he would have prepared a cramped and rocky field and planted it and raised the crop which he wanted. It would be the fact of the ceremony, regardless of what kind, that Henry would balk at: Bon knew this. It would not be the mistress or even the child, not even the negro mistress and even less the child because of that fact, since Henry and Judith had grown up with a negro half sister of their own; not the mistress to Henry, certainly not the nigger mistress to a youth with Henry's background, a young man grown up and living in a milieu where the other sex is separated into three sharp divisions, separated (two of them) by a chasm which could be crossed but one time and in but one direction—ladies, women, females—the virgins whom gentlemen someday married, the courtesans to whom they went while on sabbaticals to the cities, the slave girls and women upon whom that first caste rested and to whom in certain cases it doubtless owed the very fact of its virginity;—not this to Henry, young, strong-blooded, victim of the hard celibacy of riding and hunting to heat and make importunate the blood of a young man, to which he and his kind were forced to pass time away, with girls of his own class interdict and inaccessible and women of the second class just as inaccessible because of money and distance, and hence only the slave girls, the housemaids neated and cleaned by white mistresses or perhaps girls with sweating bodies out of the fields themselves and the young man rides up and beckons the watching overseer and says Send me Juno or Missylena or Chlory and then rides on into the trees and dismounts and waits. No: it would be the ceremony, a ceremony entered into, to be sure, with a negro, yet still a ceremony; this is what Bon doubtless thought. So I imagine him the way he did it: the way in which he took the innocent and negative plate of Henry's provincial soul and intellect and exposed it by slow degrees to this esoteric milieu, building gradually toward the picture which he desired it to retain, accept. I can see him corrupting Henry gradually into the purlieus of elegance, with no foreword, no warning, the postulation to come after the fact, exposing Henry slowly to the surface aspect—the architecture a little curious, a little femininely flamboyant and therefore to Henry opulent, sensuous, sinful; the inference of great and easy wealth measured by steamboat loads in place of a tedious inching of sweating human figures across cotton fields; the flash and glitter of a myriad carriage wheels, in which women, enthroned and immobile and passing rapidly across the vision, appeared like painted portraits beside men in linen a little finer and diamonds a little brighter and in broadcloth a little trimmer and with hats raked a little more above faces a little more darkly swaggering than any Henry had ever seen before: and the mentor, the man for whose sake he had repudiated not only blood and kin but food and shelter and clothing too, whose clothing and walk and speech he had tried to ape, along with his attitude toward women and his ideas of honor and pride too, watching him with that cold and catlike inscrutable calculation, watching the picture resolve and become fixed and then telling Henry, 'But that's not it. That's just the base, the foundation. It can belong to anyone':

and Henry, 'You mean, this is not it? That it is above this, higher than this, more select than this?': and Bon, 'Yes. This is only the foundation. This belongs to anybody.': a dialogue without words, speech, which would fix and then remove without obliterating one line the picture, this background, leaving the background, the plate prepared and innocent again: the plate docile, with that puritan's humility toward anything which is a matter of sense rather than logic, fact, the man, the struggling and suffocating heart behind it saying *I will believe! I will! I will! Whether it is true or not, I will believe!* waiting for the next picture which the mentor, the corruptor, intended for it: that next picture, following the fixation and acceptance of which the mentor would say again, perhaps with words now, still watching the sober and thoughtful face but still secure in his knowledge and trust in that puritan heritage which must show disapproval instead of surprise or even despair and nothing at all rather than have the disapprobation construed as surprise or despair: 'But even this is not it': and Henry, 'You mean, it is still higher than this, still above this?' Because he (Bon) would be talking now, lazily, almost cryptically, stroking onto the plate himself now the picture which he wanted there; I can imagine how he did it—the calculation, the surgeon's alertness and cold detachment, the exposures brief, so brief as to be cryptic, almost staccato, the plate unaware of what the complete picture would show, scarce-seen yet ineradicable:—a trap, a riding horse standing before a closed and curiously monastic doorway in a neighborhood a little decadent, even a little sinister, and Bon mentioning the owner's name casually—this, corruption subtly anew by putting into Henry's mind the notion of one man of the world speaking to another, that Henry knew that Bon believed that Henry would know even from a dis-jointed word what Bon was talking about, and Henry the puritan who must show nothing at all rather than surprise or incomprehension;—a façade shuttered and blank, drowsing in steamy morning sunlight, invested by the bland and cryptic voice with something of secret and curious and unimaginable delights. Without his knowing what he saw it was as though to Henry the blank and scaling barrier in dissolving produced and revealed not comprehension to the mind, the intellect which weighs and discards, but striking instead straight and true to some primary blind and mindless foundation of all young male living dream and hope—a row of faces like a bazaar of flowers, the supreme apotheosis of chattelry, of human flesh bred of the two races for that sale—a corridor of doomed and tragic flower faces walled between the grim duenna row of old women and the elegant shapes of young men trim predatory and (at the moment) goatlike: this seen by Henry quickly, exposed quickly and then removed, the mentor's voice still bland, pleasant, cryptic, postulating still the fact of one man of the world talking to another about something they both understand, depending upon, counting upon still, the puritan's provincial horror of revealing surprise or ignorance, who knew Henry so much better than Henry knew him, and Henry not showing either, suppressing still that first cry of terror and grief, *I will believe! I will! I will!* Yes, that brief, before Henry had had time to know what he had seen, but now slowing: now would come the instant for which Bon had builded:—a wall, unscalable, a gate ponderously locked, the sober and thoughtful country youth just waiting, looking, not yet asking why? or what? the gate of solid beams in place of the lacelike iron grilling and they passing on, Bon knocking at a small adjacent doorway from which a swarthy man resembling a creature out of an old woodcut of the French Revolution erupts, concerned, even a little aghast, looking first at the daylight and then at Henry and speaking to Bon in French which Henry does not understand and Bon's teeth glinting for an instant before he answers in French: 'With Him? An American? He is a guest; I would have to let him choose weapons and I decline to fight with axes. No, no; not that. Just the key.' Just the key; and now, the solid gates closed behind them instead of before, no sight or evidence above the high thick walls of the low city and scarce any sound of it, the labyrinthine mass of oleander and jasmine, lantana and mimosa walling yet again the strip of bare earth combed and curried with powdered shell, raked and immaculate and only the most recent of the brown stains showing now, and the voice—the mentor, the guide standing aside now to watch the grave provincial face—casually and pleasantly anecdotal: 'The customary way is to stand back to back, the pistol in your right hand and the corner of the other cloak in your left. Then at the signal you begin to walk and when you feel the cloak tauten you turn and fire. Though there are some now and then, when the blood is especially hot or when it is still peasant blood, who prefer knives and one cloak. They face one another inside the same cloak, you see, each holding the other's wrist with the left hand. But that was never my way';–casual, chatty, you see, waiting for the countryman's slow question, who knew already now before he asked it: 'What would you–they be fighting for?'"

1936

Ellen Gilchrist

Rich

TOM AND Letty Wilson were rich in everything. They were rich in friends because Tom was a vice-president of the Whitney Bank of New Orleans and liked doing business with his friends, and because Letty was vice-president of the Junior League of New Orleans and had her picture in *Town and Country* every year at the Symphony Ball.

The Wilsons were rich in knowing exactly who they were because every year from Epiphany to Fat Tuesday they flew the beautiful green and gold and purple flag outside their house that meant that Letty had been queen of the Mardi Gras the year she was a debutante. Not that Letty was foolish enough to take the flag seriously.

Sometimes she was even embarrassed to call the yardman and ask him to come over and bring his high ladder.

"Preacher, can you come around on Tuesday and put up my flag?" she would ask.

"You know I can," the giant black man would answer. "I been saving time to put up your flag. I won't forget what a beautiful queen you made that year."

"Oh, hush, Preacher. I was a skinny little scared girl. It's a wonder I didn't fall off the balcony I was so scared. I'll see you on Monday." And Letty would think to herself what a big phony Preacher was and wonder when he was going to try to borrow some more money from them.

Tom Wilson considered himself a natural as a banker because he loved to gamble and wheel and deal. From the time he was a boy in a small Baptist town in Tennessee he had loved to play cards and match nickels and lay bets.

In high school he read *The Nashville Banner* avidly and kept an eye out for useful situations such as the lingering and suspenseful illnesses of Pope Pius.

"Let's get up a pool on the day the Pope will die," he would say to the football team, "I'll hold the bank." And because the Pope took a very long time to die with many close calls there were times when Tom was the richest left tackle in Franklin, Tennessee.

Tom had a favorite saying about money. He had read it in the *Reader's Digest* and attributed it to Andrew Carnegie. "Money," Tom would say, "is what you keep score with. Andrew Carnegie."

Another way Tom made money in high school was performing as an amateur magician at local birthday parties and civic events. He could pull a silver dollar or a Lucky Strike cigarette from an astonished six-year-old's ear or from his own left palm extract a seemingly endless stream of multicolored silk chiffon or cause an ordinary piece of clothesline to behave like an Indian cobra.

He got interested in magic during a convalescence from German measles in the sixth grade. He sent off for books of magic tricks and practiced for hours before his bedroom mirror, his quick clever smile flashing and his long fingers curling and uncurling from the sleeves of a black dinner jacket his mother had bought at a church bazaar and remade to fit him.

Tom's personality was too flamboyant for the conservative Whitney Bank, but he was cheerful and cooperative and when he made a mistake he had the ability to turn it into an anecdote.

"Hey, Fred," he would call to one of his bosses. "Come have lunch on me and I'll tell you a good one."

They would walk down St. Charles Avenue to where it crosses Canal and turns into Royal Street as it enters the French Quarter. They would walk into the crowded, humid excitement of the quarter, admiring the girls and watching the Yankee tourists sweat in their absurd spun-glass leisure suits, and turn into the side door of Antoine's or breeze past the maitre d' at Galatoire's or Brennan's.

When a red-faced waiter in funereal black had seated them at a choice table, Tom would loosen his Brooks Brothers' tie, turn his handsome brown eyes on his guest, and begin.

"That bunch of promoters from Dallas talked me into backing an idea to videotape all the historic sights in the quarter and rent the tapes to hotels to show on closed-circuit television. Goddamit, Fred, I could just see those fucking tourists sitting around their hotel rooms on rainy days ordering from room service and taking in the Cabildo and the Presbytere on T.V." Tom laughed delightedly and waved his glass of vermouth at an elegantly dressed couple walking by the table.

"Well, they're barely breaking even on that one, and now they want to buy up a lot of soft porn movies and sell them to motels in Jefferson Parish. What do you think? Can we stay with them for a few more months?"

Then the waiter would bring them cold oysters on the half shell and steaming pompano *en papillote* and a wine steward would serve them a fine Meursault or a Piesporter, and Tom would listen to whatever advice he was given as though it were the most intelligent thing he had ever heard in his life.

Of course he would be thinking, "You stupid, impotent son of a bitch. You scrawny little frog bastard, I'll buy and sell you before it's over. I've got more brains in my balls than the whole snotty bunch of you."

"Tom, you always throw me off my diet," his friend would say, "dammed if you don't."

"I told Letty the other day," Tom replied, "that she could just go right ahead and spend her life worrying about being buried in her wedding dress, but I didn't hustle my way to New Orleans all the way from north Tennessee to eat salads and melba toast. Pass me the French bread."

Letty fell in love with Tom the first time she laid eyes on him. He came to Tulane on a football scholarship and charmed his way into a fraternity of wealthy New Orleans boys famed for its drunkenness and its wild practical jokes. It was the same old story. Even the second, third, and fourth generation blue bloods of New Orleans need an infusion of new genes now and then.

The afternoon after Tom was initiated he arrived at the fraternity house with two Negro painters and sat in the low-hanging branches of a live oak tree overlooking Henry Clay Avenue directing them in painting an official-looking yellow-and-white-striped pattern on the street in front of the property. "D-R-U-N-K," he yelled to his painters, holding on to the enormous limb with one hand and pushing his black hair out of his eyes with the other. "Paint it to say D-R-U-N-K Z-O-N-E."

Letty stood near the tree with a group of friends watching him. He was wearing a blue shirt with the sleeves rolled up above his elbows, and a freshman beanie several sizes too small was perched on his head like a tipsy sparrow.

"I'm wearing this goddamn beanie forever," Tom yelled. "I'm wearing this beanie until someone brings me a beer," and Letty took the one she was holding and walked over to the tree and handed it to him.

One day a few weeks later, he commandeered a Bunny Bread truck while it was parked outside the fraternity house making a delivery. He picked up two friends and drove the truck madly around the Irish Channel, throwing fresh loaves of white and whole-wheat and rye bread to the astonished housewives.

"Steal from the rich, give to the poor," Tom yelled, and his companions gave up trying to reason with him and helped him yell.

"Free bread, free cake," they yelled, handing out powdered doughnuts and sweet rolls to a gang of kids playing baseball on a weed-covered vacant lot.

They stopped off at Darby's, an Irish bar where Tom made bets on races and football games, and took on some beer and left off some cinnamon rolls.

"Tom, you better go turn that truck in before they catch you," Darby advised, and Tom's friends agreed, so they drove the truck to the second-precinct police headquarters and turned themselves in. Tom used up half a year's allowance paying the damages, but it made his reputation.

In Tom's last year at Tulane a freshman drowned during a hazing accident at the Southern Yacht Club, and the event frightened Tom. He had never liked the boy and had suspected him of being involved with the queers and nigger lovers who hung around the philosophy department and the school newspaper. The boy had gone to prep school in the East and brought weird-looking girls to rush parties. Tom had resisted the temptation to blackball him as he was well connected in uptown society.

After the accident, Tom spent less time at the fraternity house and more time with Letty, whose plain sweet looks and expensive clothes excited him.

"I can't go in the house without thinking about it," he said to Letty. "All we were doing was making them swim from pier to pier carrying martinis. I did it fifteen times the year I pledged."

"He should have told someone he couldn't swim very well," Letty answered. "It was an accident. Everyone knows it was an accident. It wasn't your fault." And Letty cuddled up close to him on the couch, breathing as softly as a cat.

Tom had long serious talks with Letty's mild, alcoholic father, who held a seat on the New York Stock Exchange, and in the spring of the year Tom and Letty were married in the Cathedral of Saint Paul with twelve bridesmaids, four flower girls, and seven hundred guests. It was pronounced a marriage made in heaven, and Letty's mother ordered masses said in Rome for their happiness.

They flew to New York on the way to Bermuda and spent their wedding night at the Sherry Netherland Hotel on Fifth Avenue. At least half a dozen of Letty's friends had lost their virginity at the same address, but the trip didn't seem prosaic to Letty.

She stayed in the bathroom a long time gazing at her plain face in the oval mirror and tugging at the white lace nightgown from the Lylian Shop, arranging it now to cover, now to reveal her small breasts. She crossed herself in the mirror, suddenly giggled, then walked out into the blue and gold bedroom as though she had been going to bed with men every night of her life. She had been up until three the night before reading a book on sexual intercourse. She offered her small unpainted mouth to Tom. Her pale hair smelled of Shalimar and carnations and candles. Now she was safe. Now life would begin.

"Oh, I love you. I love, I love, I love you," she whispered over and over. Tom's hands touching her seemed a strange and exciting passage that would carry her simple dreamy existence to a reality she had never encountered. She had never dreamed anyone so interesting would marry her.

Letty's enthusiasm and her frail body excited him, and he made love to her several times before he asked her to remove her gown.

The next day they breakfasted late and walked for a while along the avenue. In the afternoon Tom explained to his wife what her clitoris was and showed her some of the interesting things it was capable of generating, and before the day was out Letty became the first girl in her crowd to break the laws of God and the Napoleonic Code by indulging in oral intercourse.

Fourteen years went by and the Wilsons' luck held. Fourteen years is a long time to stay lucky even for rich people who don't cause trouble for anyone.

Of course, even among the rich there are endless challenges, unyielding limits, rivalry, envy, quirks of fortune. Letty's father grew increasingly incompetent and sold his seat on the exchange, and Letty's irresponsible brothers went to work throwing away the money in Las Vegas and L.A. and Zurich and Johannesburg and Paris and anywhere they could think of to fly to with their interminable strings of mistresses.

Tom envied them their careless, thoughtless lives and he was annoyed that they controlled their own money while Letty's was tied up in some mysterious trust, but he kept his thoughts to himself as he did his obsessive irritation over his growing obesity.

"Looks like you're putting on a little weight there," a friend would observe.

"Good, good," Tom would say, "makes me look like a man. I got a wife to look at if I want to see someone who's skinny."

He stayed busy gambling and hunting and fishing and being the life of the party at the endless round of dinners and cocktail parties and benefits and Mardi Gras functions that consume the lives of the Roman Catholic hierarchy that dominates the life of the city that care forgot.

Letty was preoccupied with the details of their domestic life and her work in the community. She took her committees seriously and actually believed that the work she did made a difference in the lives of other people.

The Wilsons grew rich in houses. They lived in a large Victorian house in the Garden District, and across Lake Ponchartrain they had another Victorian house to stay in on the weekends, with a private beach surrounded by old moss-hung oak trees. Tom bought a duck camp in

Plaquemines Parish and kept an apartment in the French quarter in case one of his business friends fell in love with his secretary and needed someplace to be alone with her. Tom almost never used the apartment himself. He was rich in being satisfied to sleep with his own wife.

The Wilsons were rich in common sense. When five years of a good Catholic marriage went by and Letty inexplicably never became pregnant, they threw away their thermometers and ovulation charts and litmus paper and went down to the Catholic adoption agency and adopted a baby girl with curly black hair and hazel eyes. Everyone declared she looked exactly like Tom. The Wilsons named the little girl Helen and, as the months went by, everyone swore she even walked and talked like Tom.

About the same time Helen came to be the Wilsons' little girl, Tom grew interested in raising Labrador retrievers. He had large wire runs with concrete floors built in the side yard for the dogs to stay in when he wasn't training them on the levee or at the park lagoon. He used all the latest methods of training Labs, including an electric cattle prod given to him by Chalin Perez himself and live ducks supplied by a friend on the Audubon Park Zoo Association Committee.

"Watch this, Helen," he would call to the little girl in the stroller, "watch this." And he would throw a duck into the lagoon with its secondary feathers neatly clipped on the left side and its feet tied loosely together, and one of the Labs would swim out into the water and carry it safely back and lay it at his feet.

As so often happens when childless couples are rich in common sense, before long Letty gave birth to a little boy, and then to twin boys, and finally to another little Wilson girl. The Wilsons became so rich in children the neighbors all lost count.

"Tom," Letty said, curling up close to him in the big walnut bed, "Tom, I want to talk to you about something important." The new baby girl was three months old. "Tom I want to talk to Father Delahoussaye and ask him if we can use some birth control. I think we have all the children we need for now."

Tom put his arms around her and squeezed her until he wrinkled her new green linen B. H. Wragge, and she screamed for mercy.

"Stop it," she said, "be serious. Do you think it's all right to do that?"

Then Tom agreed with her that they had had all the luck with children they needed for the present, and Letty made up her mind to call the cathedral and make an appointment. All her friends were getting dispensations so they would have time to do their work at the Symphony League and the Thrift Shop and the New Orleans Museum Association and the PTAs of the private schools.

All the Wilson children were in good heath except Helen. The pediatricians and psychiatrists weren't certain what was wrong with Helen. Helen couldn't concentrate on anything. She didn't like to share and she went through stages of biting other children at the Academy of the Sacred Heart of Jesus.

The doctors decided it was a combination of prenatal brain damage and dyslexia, a complicated learning disability that is a fashionable problem with children in New Orleans.

Letty felt like she spent half her life sitting in offices talking to people about Helen. The office she sat in most often belonged to Dr. Zander. She sat there twisting her rings and avoiding looking at the box of Kleenex on Dr. Zander's desk. It made her feel like she was sleeping in a dirty bed even to think of plucking a Kleenex from Dr. Zander's container and crying in a place where strangers cried. She imagined his chair was filled all day with women weeping over terrible and sordid things like their husbands running off with their secretaries or their children not getting into the right clubs and colleges.

"I don't know what we're going to do with her next," Letty said. "If we let them hold her back a grade it's just going to make her more self-conscious than ever."

"I wish we knew about her genetic background. You people have pull with the sisters. Can't you find out?"

"Tom doesn't want to find out. He says we'll just be opening a can of worms. He gets embarrassed even talking about Helen's problem."

"Well," said Dr. Zander, crossing his short legs and settling his steel-rimmed glasses on his nose like a tiny bicycle stuck on a hill, "let's start her on Dexedrine."

So Letty and Dr. Zander and Dr. Mullins and Dr. Pickett and Dr. Smith decided to try an experiment. They decided to give Helen five milligrams of Dexedrine every day for twenty days each month, taking her off the drug for ten days in between.

"Children with dyslexia react to drugs strangely," Dr. Zander said. "If you give them tranquilizers it peps them up, but if you give them Ritalin or Dexedrine it calms them down and makes them able to think straight."

"You may have to keep her home and have her tutored on the days she is off the drug," he continued, "but the rest of the time she should be easier to live with." And he reached over and patted Letty on the leg and for a moment she thought it might all turn out all right after all.

Helen stood by herself on the playground of the beautiful old pink-brick convent with its drooping wrought-iron balconies covered with ficus. She was watching the girl she liked talking with some other girls who were playing jacks. All the little girls wore blue-and-red-plaid skirts and navy blazers or sweaters. They looked like a disorderly marching band. Helen was waiting for the girl, whose name was Lisa, to decide if she wanted to go home with her after school and spend the afternoon. Lisa's mother was divorced and worked downtown in a department store, so Lisa rode the streetcar back and forth from school and could go anywhere she liked until 5:30 in the afternoon. Sometimes she went home with Helen so she wouldn't have to ride the streetcar. Then Helen would be so excited the hours until school let out would seem to last forever.

Sometimes Lisa liked her and wanted to go home with her and other times she didn't but she was always nice to Helen and let her stand next to her in lines.

Helen watched Lisa walking toward her. Lisa's skirt was two inches shorter than those of any of the other girls, and she wore high white socks that made her look like a skater. She wore a silver identification bracelet and Revlon nail polish.

"I'll go home with you if you get your mother to take us to get an Icee," Lisa said. "I was going last night but my mother's boyfriend didn't show up until after the place closed so I was going to walk to Manny's after school. Is that O.K.?"

"I think she will," Helen said, her eyes shining. "I'll go call her up and see."

"Naw, let's just go swing. We can ask her when she comes." Then Helen walked with her friend over to the swings and tried to be patient waiting for her turn.

The Dexedrine helped Helen concentrate and it helped her get along better with other people, but it seemed to have an unusual side effect. Helen was chubby and Dr. Zander had led the Wilsons to believe the drug would help her lose weight, but instead she grew even fatter. The Wilsons were afraid to force her to stop eating for fear they would make her nervous, so they tried to reason with her.

"Why can't I have any ice cream?" she would say. "Daddy is fat and he eats all the ice cream he wants." She was leaning up against Letty, stroking her arm and petting the baby with her other hand. They were in an upstairs sitting room with the afternoon sun streaming in through the French windows. Everything in the room was decorated with different shades of blue, and the curtains were white and old-fashioned blue-and-white-checked ruffles.

"You can have ice cream this evening after dinner," Letty said, "I just want you to wait a few hours before you have it. Won't you do that for me?"

"Can I hold the baby for a while?" Helen asked, and Letty allowed her to sit in the rocker and hold the baby and rock it furiously back and forth crooning to it.

"Is Jennifer beautiful, Mother?" Helen asked.

"She's O.K., but she doesn't have curly black hair like you. She just has plain brown hair. Don't you see, Helen, that's why we want you stop eating between meals, because you're so pretty and we don't want you to get too fat. Why don't you go outside and play with Tim and try not to think about ice cream so much?"

"I don't care," Helen said, "I'm only nine years old and I'm hungry. I want you to tell the maids to give me some ice cream now," and she handed the baby to her mother and ran out of the room.

The Wilsons were rich in maids, and that was a good thing

because there were all those children to be taken care of and cooked for and cleaned up after. The maids didn't mind taking care of the Wilson children all day. The Wilsons' house was much more comfortable than the ones they lived in, and no one cared whether they worked very hard or not as long as they showed up on time so Letty could get to her meetings. The maids left their own children with relatives or at home watching television, and when they went home at night they liked them much better than if they had spent the whole day with them.

The Wilson house had a wide white porch across the front and down both sides. It was shaded by enormous oak trees and furnished with swings and wicker rockers. In the afternoons the maids would sit on the porch and other maids from around the neighborhood would come up pushing prams and strollers and the children would all play together on the porch and in the yard. Sometimes the maids fixed lemonade and the children would sell it to passersby from a little stand.

The maids hated Helen. They didn't care whether she had dyslexia or not. All they knew was that she was a lot of trouble to take care of. One minute she would be as sweet as pie and cuddle up to them and say she loved them and the next minute she wouldn't do anything they told her.

"You're a nigger, nigger, nigger, and my mother said I could cross St. Charles Avenue if I wanted to," Helen would say, and the maids would hold their lips together and look into each other's eyes.

One afternoon the Wilson children and their maids were sitting on the porch after school with some of the neighbors' children and maids. The baby was on the porch in a bassinet on wheels and a new maid was looking out for her. Helen was in the biggest swing and was swinging as high as she could go so that none of the other children could get in the swing with her.

"Helen," the new maid said, "it's Tim's turn in the swing. You been swinging for fifteen minutes while Tim's been waiting. You be a good girl now and let Tim have a turn. You too big to act like that."

"You're just a high yeller nigger," Helen called, "and you can't make me do anything." And she swung up higher and higher.

This maid had never had Helen call her names before and she had a quick temper and didn't put up with children calling her a nigger. She walked over to the swing and grabbed the chain and stopped it from moving.

"You say you're sorry for that, little fat honky white girl," she said, and made as if to grab Helen by the arms, but Helen got away and started running, calling over her shoulder, "nigger, can't make me do anything."

She was running and looking over her shoulder and she hit the bassinet and it went rolling down the brick stairs so fast none of the maids or children could stop it. It rolled down the stairs and threw the baby onto the sidewalk and the blood from the baby's head began to move all over the concrete like a little ruby lake.

The Wilsons' house was on Philip Street, a street so rich it even had its own drugstore. Not some tacky chain drugstore with everything on special all the time, but a cute drugstore made out of a frame bungalow with gingerbread trim. Everything inside cost twice as much as it did in a regular drugstore, and the grown people could order any kind of drugs they needed and a green Mazda pickup would bring them right over. The children had to get their drugs from a fourteen-year-old pusher in Audubon Park named Leroi, but they could get all the ice cream and candy and chewing gum they wanted from the drugstore and charge it to their parents.

No white adults were at home in the houses where the maids worked so they sent the children running to the drugstore to bring the druggist to help with the baby. They called the hospital and ordered an ambulance and they called several doctors and they called Tom's bank. All the children who were old enough ran to the drugstore except Helen. Helen sat on the porch steps staring down at the baby with the maids hovering over it like swans, and she was crying and screaming and beating her hands against her head. She was in one of the periods when she couldn't have Dexedrine. She screamed and screamed, but none of the maids had time to help her. They were too busy with the baby.

"Shut up, Helen," one of the maids called. "Shut up that goddamn screaming. This baby is about to die."

A police car and the local patrol service drove up. An ambulance arrived and the yard filled with people. The druggist and one of the maids rode off in the ambulance with the baby. The crowd in the yard swarmed and milled and swam before Helen's eyes like a parade.

Finally they stopped looking like people and just looked like spots of color on the yard. Helen ran up the stairs and climbed under her cherry four-poster bed and pulled her pillows and her eiderdown comforter under it with her. There were cereal boxes and an empty ice cream carton and half a tin of English cookies under the headboard. Helen was soaked with sweat and her little Lily playsuit was tight under the arms and cut into her flesh. Helen rolled up in the comforter and began to dream the dream of the heavy clouds. She dreamed she was praying, but the beads of the rosary slipped through her fingers so quickly she couldn't catch them and it was cold in the church and beautiful and fragrant, then dark, then light, and Helen was rolling in the heavy clouds that rolled her like biscuit dough. Just as she was about to suffocate they rolled her face up to the blue air above the clouds. Then Helen was a pink kite floating above the houses at evening. In the yards children were playing and fathers were driving up and baseball games were beginning and the sky turned gray and closed upon the city like a lid.

And now the baby is alone with Helen in her room and the door is locked and Helen ties the baby to the table so it won't fall off.

"Hold still, Baby, this will just be a little shot. This won't hurt much. This won't take a minute." And the baby is still and Helen begins to work on it.

Letty knelt down beside the bed. "Helen, please come out from under there. No one is mad at you. Please come out and help me, Helen. I need you to help me."

Helen held on tighter to the slats of the bed and squeezed her eyes shut and refused to look at Letty.

Letty climbed under the bed to touch the child. Letty was crying and her heart had an anchor in it that kept digging in and sinking deeper and deeper.

Dr. Zander came into the bedroom and knelt beside the bed and began to talk to Helen. Finally he gave up being reasonable and wiggled his small gray-suited body under the bed and Helen was lost in the area of arms that tried to hold her.

Tom was sitting in the bank president's office trying not to let Mr. Saunders know how much he despised him or how much it hurt and mattered to him to be listening to a lecture. Tom thought he was too old to have to listen to lectures. He was tired and he wanted a drink and he wanted to punch the bastard in the face.

"I know, I know," he answered, "I can take care of it. Just give me a month or two. You're right. I'll take care of it."

And he smoothed the pants of his cord suit and waited for the rest of the lecture.

A man came into the room without knocking. Tom's secretary was behind him.

"Tom, I think your baby has had an accident. I don't know any details. Look, I've called for a car. Let me go with you."

Tom ran up the steps of his house and into the hallway full of neighbors and relatives. A girl in a tennis dress touched him on the arm, someone handed him a drink. He ran up the winding stairs to Helen's room. He stood in the doorway. He could see Letty's shoes sticking out from under the bed. He could hear Dr. Zander talking. He couldn't go near them.

"Letty," he called, "Letty, come here, my god, come out from there."

No one came to the funeral but the family. Letty wore a plain dress she would wear any day and the children all wore their school clothes.

The funeral was terrible for the Wilsons, but afterward they went home and all the people from the Garden District and from all over town started coming over to cheer them up. It looked like the biggest cocktail party ever held in New Orleans. It took four rented butlers just to serve the drinks. Everyone wanted to get in on the Wilsons' tragedy.

In the months that followed the funeral Tom began to have sinus headaches for the first time in years. He was drinking a lot and smoking again. He was allergic to whiskey, and when he woke up in the morning his nose and head were so full of phlegm he had to vomit before he could think straight.

He began to have trouble with his vision.

One November day the high yellow windows of the Shell Oil Building all turned their eyes upon him as he stopped at the corner of Poydras and Carondelet to wait for a streetlight, and he had to pull the car over to a curb and talk to himself for several minutes before he could drive on.

He got back all the keys to his apartment so he could go there and be alone and think. One afternoon he left work at two o'clock and drove around Jefferson Parish all afternoon drinking Scotch and eating potato chips.

Not as many people at the bank wanted to go out to lunch with him anymore. They were sick and tired of pretending his expensive mistakes were jokes.

One night Tom was gambling at the Pickwick Club with a poker group and a man jokingly accused him of cheating. Tom jumped up from the table, grabbed the man and began hitting him with his fists. He hit the man in the mouth and knocked out his new gold inlays.

"You dirty little goddamn bond peddler, you son of a bitch! I'll kill you for that," Tom yelled, and it took four waiters to hold him while the terrified man made his escape. The next morning Tom resigned from the club.

He started riding the streetcar downtown to work so he wouldn't have to worry about driving his car home if he got drunk. He was worrying about money and he was worrying about his gambling debts, but most of the time he was thinking about Helen. She looked so much like him that he believed people would think she was his illegitimate child. The more he tried to talk himself into believing the baby's death was an accident, the more obstinate his mind became.

The Wilson children were forbidden to take the Labs out of the kennels without permission. One afternoon Tom came home earlier than usual and found Helen sitting in the open door of one of the kennels playing with a half-grown litter of puppies. She was holding one of the puppies and the others were climbing all around her and spilling out onto the grass. She held the puppy by its forelegs, making it dance in the air, then letting it drop. Then she would gather it in her arms and hold it tight and sing to it.

Tom walked over to the kennel and grabbed her by an arm and began to paddle her as hard as he could.

"Goddamn you, what are you trying to do? You know you aren't supposed to touch those dogs. What in the hell do you think you're doing?"

Helen was too terrified to scream. The Wilsons never spanked their children for anything.

"I didn't do anything to it. I was playing with it," she sobbed.

Letty and the twins came running out of the house and when Tom saw Letty he stopped hitting Helen and walked in through the kitchen door and up the stairs to the bedroom. Letty gave the children to the cook and followed him.

Tom stood by the bedroom window trying to think of something to say to Letty. He kept his back turned to her and he was making a nickel disappear with his left hand. He thought of himself at Tommie Keenen's birthday party wearing his black coat and hat and doing his famous rope trick. Mr. Keenen had given him fifteen dollars. He remembered sticking the money in his billfold.

"My god, Letty, I'm sorry. I don't know what the shit's going on. I thought she was hurting the dog. I know I shouldn't have hit her and there's something I need to tell you about the bank. Kennington is getting sacked. I may be part of the housecleaning."

"Why didn't you tell me before? Can't Daddy do anything?"

"I don't want him to do anything. Even if it happens it doesn't have anything to do with me. It's just bank politics. We'll say I quit. I want to get out of there anyway. That fucking place is driving me crazy."

Tom put the nickel in his pocket and closed the bedroom door. He could hear the maid down the hall comforting Helen. He didn't give a fuck if she cried all night. He walked over to Letty and put his arms around her. He smelled like he'd been drinking for a week. He reached under her dress and pulled down her pantyhose and her underpants and began kissing her face and hair while she stood awkwardly with the pants and hose around her feet like a halter. She was trying to cooperate.

She forgot that Tom smelled like sweat and whiskey. She was thinking about the night they were married. Every time they made love Letty pretended it was as that night. She had spent thousands of nights in a bridal suite at the Sherry Netherland Hotel in New York City.

Letty lay on the walnut bed leaning into a pile of satin pillows and twisting a gold bracelet around her wrist. She could hear the children playing outside. She had a headache and her stomach was queasy, but she was afraid to take a Valium or an aspirin. She was waiting for the doctor to call her back and tell her if she was pregnant. She already knew what he was going to say.

Tom came into the room and sat by her on the bed.

"What's wrong?"

"Nothing's wrong. Please don't do that. I'm tired."

"Something's wrong."

"Nothing's wrong. Tom, please leave me alone."

Tom walked out through the French windows and onto a little balcony that overlooked the play yard and the dog runs. Sunshine flooded Philip Street, covering the houses and trees and dogs and children with a million volts a minute. It flowed down to hide in the roots of trees, glistening on the cars, baking the street, and lighting Helen's rumpled hair where she stooped over the puppy. She was singing a little song. She had made up the song she was singing.

"The baby's dead. The baby's dead. The baby's gone to heaven."

"Jesus God," Tom muttered. All up and down Philip Street fathers were returning home from work. A jeep filled with teenagers came tearing past and threw a beer can against the curb.

Six or seven pieces of Tom's mind sailed out across the street and stationed themselves along the power line that zigzagged back and forth along Philip Street between the live oak trees.

The pieces of his mind sat upon the power line like a row of black starlings. They looked him over.

Helen took the dog out of the buggy and dragged it over to the kennel.

"Jesus Christ," Tom said, and the pieces of his mind flew back to him as swiftly as they had flown away and entered his eyes and ears and nostrils and arranged themselves in their proper places like parts of a phrenological head.

Tom looked at his watch. It said 6:15. He stepped back into the bedroom and closed the French windows. A vase of huge roses from the garden hid Letty's reflection in the mirror.

"I'm going to the camp for the night. I need to get away. Besides, the season's almost over."

"All right," Letty answered. "Who are you going with?"

"I think I'll take Helen with me. I haven't paid any attention to her for weeks."

"That's good," Letty said, "I really think I'm getting a cold. I'll have a tray up for supper and try to get some sleep."

Tom moved around the room, opening drawers and closets and throwing some gear into a canvas duffel bag. He changed into his hunting clothes.

He removed the guns he needed from a shelf in the upstairs den and cleaned them neatly and thoroughly and zipped them into their carriers.

"Helen," he called from the downstairs porch. "Bring the dog in the house and come get on some play clothes. I'm going to take you to the duck camp with me. You can take the dog."

"Can we stop and get beignets?" Helen called back, coming running at the invitation.

"Sure we can, honey. Whatever you like. Go get packed. We'll leave as soon as dinner is over."

It was past 9:00 at night. They crossed the Mississippi River from the New Orleans side on the last ferry going to Algier's Point. There was an offshore breeze and a light rain fell on the old brown river. The Mississippi River smelled like the inside of a nigger cabin, powerful and fecund. The smell came in Tom's mouth until he felt he could chew it.

He leaned over the railing and vomited. He felt better and walked back to the red Chevrolet pickup he had given himself for a birthday present. He thought it was chic for a banker to own a pickup.

Helen was playing with the dog, pushing him off the seat and laughing when he climbed back on her lap. She had a paper bag of doughnuts from the French Market and was eating them and licking the powdered sugar from her fingers and knocking the dog off the seat.

She wasn't the least bit sleepy.

"I'm glad Tim didn't get to go. Tim was bad at school, that's why he had to stay home, isn't it? The sisters called Momma. I don't like Tim. I'm glad I got to go by myself." She stuck her fat arms out the window and rubbed Tom's canvas hunting jacket. "This coat feels hard. It's all dirty. Can we go up in the cabin and talk to the pilot?"

"Sit still, Helen."

"Put the dog in the back, he's bothering me." She bounced up and down on the seat. "We're going to the duck camp. We're going to the duck camp."

The ferry docked. Tom drove the pickup onto the blacktop road past the city dump and on into Plaquemines Parish.

They drove into the brackish marshes that fringe the Gulf of Mexico where it extends in ragged fingers along the coast below and to the east of New Orleans. As they drove closer to the sea the hardwoods turned to palmetto and water oak and willow.

The marshes were silent. Tom could smell the glasswort and black mangrove, the oyster and shrimp boats.

He wondered if it were true that children and dogs could penetrate a man's concealment, could know him utterly.

Helen leaned against his coat and prattled on.

In the Wilson house on Philip Street Tim and the twins were cuddled up by Letty, hearing one last story before they went to bed.

A blue wicker tray held the remains of the children's hot chocolate. The china cups were a confirmation present sent to Letty from Limoges, France.

Now she was finishing reading a wonderful story by Ludwig Bemelmans about a little convent girl in Paris named Madeline who reforms the son of the Spanish ambassador, putting an end to his terrible habit of beheading chickens on a miniature guillotine.

Letty was feeling better. She had decided God was just trying to make up to her for Jennifer.

§

The camp was a three-room wooden shack built on pilings out over Bayou Lafouche, which runs through the middle of the parish.

The inside of the camp was casually furnished with old leather office furniture, hand-me-down tables and lamps, and a walnut poker table from Neiman-Marcus. Photographs of hunts and parties were tacked around the walls. Over the poker table were pictures of racehorses and their owners and an assortment of ribbons won in races.

Tom laid the guns down on the bar and opened a cabinet over the sink in the part of the room that served as a kitchen. The nigger hadn't come to clean up after the last party and the sink was piled with half-washed dishes. He found a clean glass and a bottle of Tanqueray gin and sat down behind the bar.

Helen was across the room on the floor finishing the beignets and trying to coax the dog to come closer. He was considering it. No one had remembered to feed him.

Tom pulled a new deck of cards out of a drawer, broke the seal, and began to shuffle them.

Helen came and stood by the bar. "Show me a trick, Daddy. Make the queen disappear. Show me how to do it."

"Do you promise not to tell anyone the secret? A magician never tells his secrets."

"I won't tell, Daddy, please show me, show me now."

Tom spread out the cards. He began to explain the trick.

"All right, you go here and here, then here. Then pick up these in just the right order, but look at the people while you do it, not at the cards."

"I'm going to do it for Lisa."

"She's going to beg you to tell the secret. What will you do then?"

"I'll tell her a magician never tells his secrets."

Tom drank the gin and poured some more.

"Now let me do it to you, Daddy."

"Not yet, Helen. Go sit over there with the dog and practice it where I can't see what you're doing. I'll pretend I'm Lisa and don't know what's going on."

Tom picked up the Kliengunther 7 mm. Magnum rifle and shot the dog first, splattering its brains all over the door and walls. Without pausing, without giving her time to raise her eyes from the red and gray and black rainbow of the dog, he shot the little girl.

The bullet entered her head from the back. Her thick body rolled across the hardwood floor and lodged against a hat rack from Jody Mellon's old office in the Hibernia Bank Building. One of her arms landed on a pile of old *Penthouse* magazines and her disordered brain flung its roses north and east and south and west and rejoined the order from which it casually arose.

Tom put down the rifle, took a drink of the thick gin, and, carrying the pistol, walked out onto the pier through the kitchen door. Without removing his glasses or his hunting cap he stuck the .38 Smith and Wesson revolver against his palate and splattered his own head all over the new pier and the canvas covering of the Boston Whaler. His body struck the boat going down and landed in eight feet of water beside a broken crab trap left over from the summer.

A pair of deputies from the Plaquemines Parish sheriff's office found the bodies.

Everyone believed it was some terrible inexplicable mistake or accident.

No one believed that much bad luck could happen to a nice lady like Letty Dufrechou Wilson, who never hurt a flea or gave anyone a minute's trouble in her life.

No one believed that much bad luck could get together between the fifteenth week after Pentecost and the third week in Advent.

No one believed a man would kill his own little illegitimate dyslexic daughter just because she was crazy.

And no one, not even the district attorney of New Orleans, wanted to believe a man would shoot a $3,000 Labrador retriever sired by Super Chief out of Prestidigitation.

1981

Mark Twain

Southern Sports

IN THE North one hears the war mentioned, in social conversation, once a month; sometimes as often as once a week; but as a distinct subject for talk, it has long ago been relieved of duty. There are sufficient reasons for this. Given a dinner company of six gentlemen to-day, it can easily happen that four of them – and possibly five – were not in the field at all. So the chances are four to two, or five to one, that the war will at no time during the evening become the topic of conversation; and the chances are still greater that if it become the topic it will remain so but a little while. If you add six ladies to the company, you have added six people who saw so little of the dread realities of the war that they ran out of talk concerning them years ago, and now would soon weary of the war topic if you brought it up.

The case is very different in the South. There, every man you meet was in the war; and every lady you meet saw the war. The war is the great chief topic of conversation. The interest in it is vivid and constant; the interest in other topics is fleeting. Mention of the war will wake up a dull company and set their tongues going, when nearly any other topic would fail. In the South, the war is what A.D. is elsewhere: they date from it. All day long you hear things 'placed' as having happened since the waw; or du'in' the waw; or befo' the waw; or right aftah the waw; or 'bout two yeahs or five yeahs or ten yeahs befo' the waw or aftah the waw. It shows how intimately every individual was visited, in his own person, by that tremendous episode. It gives the inexperienced stranger a better idea of what a vast and comprehensive calamity invasion is than he can ever get by reading books at the fireside.

At a club one evening, a gentleman turned to me and said, in an aside –

'You notice, of course, that we are nearly always talking about the war. It isn't because we haven't anything else to talk about, but because nothing else has so strong an interest for us. And there is another reason: In the war, each of us, in his own person, seems to have sampled all the different varieties of human experience; as a consequence, you can't mention an outside matter of any sort but it will certainly remind some listener of something that happened during the war—and out he comes with it. Of course that brings the talk back to the war. You may try all you want to, to keep other subjects before the house, and we may all join in and help, but there can be but one result: the most random topic would load every man up with war reminiscences, and *shut* him up, too; and talk would be likely to stop presently, because you can't talk pale inconsequentialities when you've got a crimson fact or fancy in your head that you are burning to fetch out.'

The poet was sitting some little distance away; and presently he began to speak—about the moon.

The gentleman who had been talking to me remarked in an 'aside': 'There, the moon is far enough from the seat of war, but you will see that it will suggest something to somebody about the war; in ten minutes from now the moon, as a topic, will be shelved.'

The poet was saying he had noticed something which was a surprise to him; had had the impression that down here, toward the equator, the moonlight was much stronger and brighter than up North; had had the impression that when he visited New Orleans, many years ago, the moon—

Interruption from the other end of the room—

'Let me explain that. Reminds me of an anecdote. Everything is changed since the war, for better or for worse; but you'll find people down here born grumblers, who see no change except the change for the worse. There was an old negro woman of this sort. A young New-Yorker said in her presence, "What a wonderful moon you have down here!" She sighed and said, "Ah, bless yo' heart, honey, you ought to seen dat moon befo' de waw!"'

The new topic was dead already. But the poet resurrected it, and gave it a new start.

A brief dispute followed, as to whether the difference between Northern and Southern moonlight really existed or was only imagined. Moonlight talk drifted easily into talk about artificial methods of dispelling darkness. Then somebody remembered that when Farragut advanced upon Port Hudson on a dark night—and did not wish to assist the aim of the Confederate gunners—he carried no battle-lanterns, but painted the decks of his ships white, and thus created a dim but valuable light, which enabled his own men to grope their way around with considerable facility. At this point the war got the floor again—the ten minutes not quite up yet.

I was not sorry, for war talk by men who have been in a war is always interesting; whereas moon talk by a poet who has not been in the moon is likely to be dull.

We went to a cockpit in New Orleans on a Saturday afternoon. I had never seen a cock-fight before. There were men and boys there of all ages and all colours, and of many languages and nationalities. But I noticed one quite conspicuous and surprising absence: the traditional brutal faces. There were no brutal faces. With no cock-fighting going on, you could have played the gathering on a stranger for a prayer-meeting; and after it began, for a revival—provided you blindfolded your stranger—for the shouting was something prodigious.

A negro and a white man were in the ring; everybody else outside. The cocks were brought in in sacks; and when time was called, they were taken out by the two bottle-holders, stroked, caressed, poked toward each other, and finally liberated. The big black cock plunged instantly at the little grey one and struck him on the head with his spur. The grey responded with spirit. Then the Babel of many-tongued shoutings broke out, and ceased not thenceforth. When the cocks had been fighting some little time, I was expecting them momently to drop dead, for both were blind, red with blood, and so exhausted that they frequently fell down. Yet they would not give up, neither would they die. The negro and the white man would pick them up every few seconds, wipe them off, blow cold water on them in a fine spray, and take their heads in their mouths and hold them there a moment—to warm back the perishing life perhaps; I do not know. Then, being set down again, the dying creatures would totter gropingly about, with dragging wings, find each other, strike a guesswork blow or two, and fall exhausted once more.

I did not see the end of the battle. I forced myself to endure it as long as I could, but it was too pitiful a sight; so I made frank confession to that effect, and we retired. We heard afterward that the black cock died in the ring, and fighting to the last.

Evidently there is abundant fascination about this 'sport' for such as have had a degree of familiarity with it. I never saw people enjoy anything more than this gathering enjoyed this fight. The case was the same with old grey-heads and with boys of ten. They lost themselves in frenzies of delight. The 'cocking-main' is an inhuman sort of entertainment, there is no question about that; still, it seems a much more respectable and far less cruel sport than fox-hunting— for the cocks like it; they experience, as well as confer enjoyment; which is not the fox's case.

We assisted—in the French sense—at a mule race, one day. I believe I enjoyed this contest more than any other mule there. I enjoyed it more than I remember having enjoyed any other animal race I ever saw. The grand stand was well filled with the beauty and the chivalry of New Orleans. That phrase is not original with me. It is the Southern reporter's. He has used it for two generations. He uses it twenty times a day, or twenty thousand times a day; or a million times a day—according to the exigencies. He is obliged to use it a million times a day, if he have occasion to speak of respectable men and women that often; for he has no other phrase for such service except that single one. He never tires of it; it always has a fine sound to him. There is a kind of swell mediæval bulliness and tinsel about it that pleases his gaudy barbaric soul. If he had been in Palestine in the early times, we should have had no references to 'much people' out of him. No, he would have said 'the beauty and the chivalry of Galilee' assembled to hear the Sermon on the Mount. It is likely that the men and women of the South are sick enough of that phrase by this time, and would like a change, but there is no immediate prospect of their getting it.

The New Orleans editor has a strong, compact, direct, un-flowery style; wastes no words, and does not gush. Not so with his average correspondent. In the Appendix I have quoted a good letter, penned by a trained hand; but the average correspondent hurls a style which differs from that. For instance—

The 'Times-Democrat' sent a relief-steamer up one of the bayous, last April. This steamer landed at a village, up there somewhere, and the Captain invited some of the ladies of the village to make a short trip with him. They accepted and came aboard, and the steamboat shoved out up the creek. That was all there was 'to it.' And that is all that the editor of the 'Times-Democrat' would have got out of it. There was nothing in the thing but statistics, and he would have got nothing else out of it. He would probably have even tabulated them, partly to secure perfect clearness of statement, and partly to save space. But his special correspondent knows other methods of handling statistics. He just throws off all restraint and wallows in them—

> 'On Saturday, early in the morning, the beauty of the place graced our cabin, and proud of her fair freight the gallant little boat glided up the bayou.'

Twenty-two words to say the ladies came aboard and the boat shoved out up the creek, is a clean waste of ten good words, and is also destructive of compactness of statement.

The trouble with the Southern reporter is—Women. They unsettle him; they throw him off his balance. He is plain, and sensible, and satisfactory, until a woman heaves in sight. Then he goes all to pieces; his mind totters, he becomes flowery and idiotic. From reading the above extract, you would image that this student of Sir Walter Scott is an apprentice, and knows next to nothing about handling a pen. On the contrary, he furnishes plenty of proofs, in his long letter, that he knows well enough how to handle it when the women are not around to give him the artificial-flower complaint. For instance—

> 'At 4 o'clock ominous clouds began to gather in the southeast, and presently from the Gulf there came a blow which increased in severity every moment. It was not safe to leave the landing then, and there was a delay. The oaks shook off long tresses of their mossy beards to the tugging of the wind, and the bayou in its ambition put on miniature waves in mocking of much larger bodies of water. A lull permitted a start, and homewards we steamed, an inky sky overhead

and a heavy wind blowing. As darkness crept on, there were few on board who did not wish themselves nearer home.'

There is nothing the matter with that. It is good description, compactly put. Yet there was great temptation, there, to drop into lurid writing.

But let us return to the mule. Since I left him, I have rummaged around and found a full report of the race. In it I find confirmation of the theory which I broached just now—namely, that the trouble with the Southern reporter is Women: Women, supplemented by Walter Scott and his knights and beauty and chivalry, and so on. This is an excellent report, as long as the women stay out of it. But when they intrude, we have this frantic result—

'It will be probably a long time before the ladies' stand presents such a sea of foam-like loveliness as it did yesterday. The New Orleans women are always charming, but never so much so as at this time of the year, when in their dainty spring costumes they bring with them a breath of balmy freshness and an odour of sanctity unspeakable. The stand was so crowded with them that, walking at their feet and seeing no possibility of approach, many a man appreciated as he never did before the Peri's feeling at the Gates of Paradise, and wondered what was the priceless boon that would admit him to their sacred presence. Sparkling on their white-robed breasts or shoulders were the colours of their favourite knights, and were it not for the fact that the doughty heroes appeared on unromantic mules, it would have been easy to imagine one of King Arthur's gala-days.'

There were thirteen mules in the first heat; all sorts of mules, they were; all sorts of complexions, gaits, dispositions, aspects. Some were handsome creatures, some were not; some were sleek, some hadn't had their fur brushed lately; some were innocently gay and frisky; some were full of malice and all unrighteousness; guessing from looks, some of them thought the matter on hand was war, some thought it was a lark, the rest took it for a religious occasion. And each mule acted according to his convictions. The result was an absence of harmony well compensated by a conspicuous presence of variety—variety of a picturesque and entertaining sort.

All the riders were young gentlemen in fashionable society. If the reader has been wondering why it is that the ladies of New Orleans attend so humble an orgy as a mule-race, the thing is explained now. It is a fashion-freak; all connected with it are people of fashion.

It is great fun, and cordially liked. The mule-race is one of the marked occasions of the year. It has brought some pretty fast mules to the front. One of these had to be ruled out, because he was so fast that he turned the thing into a one-mule contest, and robbed it of one of its best features—variety. But every now and then somebody disguises him with a new name and a new complexion, and rings him in again.

The riders dress in full jockey costumes of bright-coloured silks, satins, and velvets.

The thirteen mules got away in a body, after a couple of false starts, and scampered off with prodigious spirit. As each mule and each rider had a distinct opinion of his own as to how the race ought to be run, and which side of the track was best in certain circumstances, and how often the track ought to be crossed, and when a collision ought to be accomplished, and when it ought to be avoided, these twenty-six conflicting opinions created a most fantastic and picturesque confusion, and the resulting spectacle was killingly comical.

Mile heat; time 2:22. Eight of the thirteen mules distanced. I had a bet on a mule which would have won if the procession had been reversed. The second heat was good fun; and so was the 'consolation race for beaten mules,' which followed later; but the first heat was the best in that respect.

I think that much the most enjoyable of all races is a steamboat race; but, next to that, I prefer the gay and joyous mule-rush. Two red-hot steamboats raging along, neck-and-neck, straining every nerve—that is to say, every rivet in the boilers—quaking and shaking and groaning from stem to stern, spouting white steam from the pipes, pouring black smoke from the chimneys, raining down sparks, parting the river into long breaks of hissing foam—this is sport that makes a body's very liver curl with enjoyment. A horse-race is pretty tame and colourless in comparison. Still, a horse-race might be well enough, in its way, perhaps, if it were not for the tiresome false starts. But then, nobody is ever killed. At least, nobody was ever killed when I was at a horse-race. They have been crippled, it is true; but this is little to the purpose.

1884

Carl Sandburg

A Scar for Abraham Lincoln

I N T H E year 1825, ox teams and pack horses came through Gentryville carrying people on their way to a place on the Wabash River they called New Harmony. A rich English business man named Robert Owen had paid $132,000.00 for land and $50,000.00 for livestock, tools, and merchandise, and had made a speech before the Congress at Washington telling how he and his companions were going to try to find a new way for people to live their lives together, without fighting, cheating, or exploiting each other, where work would be honorable yet there would be time for play and learning; they would share and share alike, each for all and all for each. In January, 1826, Owen himself with a party of 30 people came down the Ohio River in what was called the "boatload of knowledge."

More ox wagons and pack horses coming past the Gentryville crossroads; about a thousand people were joined in Owen's scheme at New Harmony on the Wabash. The scheme lighted up Abe Lincoln's heart. But Tom Lincoln had other plans for his son Abe.

Across the next three years the boy grew longer of leg and arm, tougher of bone and sinew, with harder knuckles and joints. James Gentry, with the largest farms in the Pigeon Creek clearings, and a landing on the Ohio River, was looking the big boy over. He believed Abe could take his pork, flour, meal, bacon, potatoes, and produce to trade down the Mississippi River, for cotton, tobacco, and sugar. Young Abe was set to work on a flatboat; he cut the oaks for a double bottom of stout planks, and a deck shelter, two pairs of long oars at bow and stern, a check-post, and a setting pole for steering.

As the snow and ice began to melt, a little before the first frogs started shrilling, in that year of 1828, they loaded the boat and pushed off.

In charge of the boat Mr. Gentry had placed his son Allen, and in charge of Allen he had placed Abe Lincoln, to hold his own against any half horse, half alligator bush-whackers who might try to take the boat or loot it, and leave the bones of those they took it from, at Cave-in-Rock on the Illinois shore, or other spots where the skeletons of flatboatmen had been found years after the looters sold the cargo down the river. The honesty of Abe, of course, had been the first point Mr. Gentry considered; and the next point had been whether he could handle the boat in the snags and sandbars. The two young men pushed off on their trip of a thousand miles to New Orleans, on a wide, winding waterway, where the flatboats were tied up at night to the river-bank, and floated and poled by day amid changing currents, strings of other flatboats, and in the paths of the proud white steamboats.

Whitecaps rose and broke with their foam feathers, a mile, two miles, beyond the limit of eyesight, as fresh winds blew along the Ohio River. Cave-in-Rock was passed on the Illinois shore, with its sign, "Wilson's Liquor Vault and House of Entertainment," with a doorway 25 feet high, 80 feet wide, and back of that entrance a cavern 200 feet deep, a 14-foot chimney leading to an upper room, where one time later were found 60 human skeletons, most of them rivermen lured and trapped by the Wilson gang that camped at Hurricane Island near by.

Timber-covered river bluffs stood up overlooking the river like plowmen resting big shoulders between the plow-handles; twisted dumps and runs of clay banks were like squatters who had lost hope and found rheumatism and malaria; lone pine trees had silhouetted their dry arms of branches on reefs where they dissolved and reappeared in river-mist lights as if they struggled to tell some secret of water and sky before going under.

The nineteen-year-old husky from Indiana found the Mississippi River tricky with sandbars, shoals, and islands scattered along with the look of arithmetic numbers. Sudden rains, shifting winds, meant new handling of oars. A rising roar and rumble of noise might be rough water ahead or some whimsical current tearing through fallen tree-branches at the river side. A black form seems to be floating upriver through a gray drizzle; the coming out of the sun shows it is an island point, standing still; the light and air play tricks with it.

The bends of the river ahead must be watched with ready oars and sweeps or the flatboat naturally heads in to shore. Strong winds crook the course of the boat, sometimes blowing it ashore; one of the crew must hustle off in a rowboat, tie a hawser to a tree or stump, while another man on the big boat has a rope at the checkpost; and they slow her down. Warning signals must be given at night, by waving lantern or firewood, to other craft.

So the flatboat, "the broadhorn," went down the Father of Waters, four to six miles an hour, the crew frying their own pork and cornmeal cakes, washing their own shirts, sewing on their own buttons.

Below Baton Rouge, among the sugar plantations known as the "Sugar Coast," they tied up at the plantation of Madame Duquesne one evening, put their boat in order, spoke their good nights to any sweet stars in the sky, and dropped off to sleep. They woke to find seven Negroes on board trying to steal the cargo and kill the crew; the long-armed Indiana husky swung a crab-tree club, knocked them galley-west, chased them into the woods, and came back to the boat and laid a bandanna on a gash over the right eye that left a scar for life as it healed. Then they cut loose the boat and moved down the river.

At New Orleans they traded, sold the rest of their cargo of potatoes, bacon, hams, flour, apples, jeans, in exchange for cotton, tobacco, and sugar, and sold the flatboat for what it would bring as lumber. And they lingered and loitered a few days, seeing New Orleans, before taking steamer north.

On the streets and by-streets of that town, which had floated the flags of French, British, and American dominion, young Abraham Lincoln felt the pulses of a living humanity with far heartbeats in wide, alien circles over the earth: English sailors who sang "Ranzo" and "Boney," "Hangin' Johnny" and "O Fare-you-well, My Bonny Young Girls"; Dutchmen and French in jabber and exclamative; Swedes, Norwegians, and Russians with blond and reddish mustaches and whiskers; Spaniards and Italians with knives and red silk handkerchiefs; New York, Philadelphia, Boston, Rome, Amsterdam, become human facts; it was London those men came from, ejaculating, "'Ow can ye blime me?"

Women in summer weather wearing slippers and boots; creoles with dusks of eyes; quadroons and octoroons with elusive soft voices;

streets lined with saloons where men drank with men or chose from the women sipping their French wine or Jamaica rum at tables, sending quiet signals with their eyes or openly slanging the sailors, teamsters, roustabouts, rivermen, timber cruisers, crap-shooters, poker sharps, squatters, horse thieves, poor whites; bets were laid on steamboat races; talk ran fast about the construction, then going on, of the New Orleans & Pontchartrain Railroad, to be one of the first steam railroads in America and the world; slaves passed handcuffed into gangs headed for cotton fields of one, two, six thousand acres in size; and everywhere was talk about niggers, good and bad niggers, how to rawhide the bad ones with mule whips or bring 'em to N' Orleans and sell 'em; and how you could trust your own children with a good nigger.

As young Abe Lincoln and Allen Gentry made their way back home to the clearings of Pigeon Creek, Indiana, the tall boy had his thoughts. He had crossed half the United States, it seemed, and was back home after three months' vacation with eight dollars a month pay in his pocket and a scar over the right eye.

1926

Kate Chopin

Cavanelle

I WAS ALWAYS sure of hearing something pleasant from Cavanelle across the counter. If he was not mistaking me for the freshest and prettiest girl in New Orleans, he was reserving for me some bit of silk, or lace, or ribbon of a nuance marvelously suited to my complexion, my eyes or my hair! What an innocent, delightful humbug Cavanelle was! How well I knew it and how little I cared! For when he had sold me the confection or bit of dry-goods in question, he always began to talk to me of his sister Mathilde, and then I knew that Cavanelle was an angel.

I had known him long enough to know why he worked so faithfully, so energetically and without rest—it was because Mathilde had a voice. It was because of her voice that his coats were worn till they were out of fashion and almost out at elbows. But for a sister whose voice needed only a little training to rival that of the nightingale, one might do such things without incurring reproach.

"You will believe, madame, that I did not know you las' night at the opera? I remark' to Mathilde, 'tiens! Mademoiselle Montreville,' an' I only rec'nize my mistake when I finally adjust my opera glass . . . . . . I guarantee you will be satisfied, madame. In a year from now you will come an' thank me for having secu' you that bargain in a poult-de-soie. . . . . Yes, yes; as you say, Tolville was in voice. But," with a shrug of the narrow shoulders and a smile of commiseration that wrinkled the lean olive cheeks beneath the thin beard, "but to hear that cavatina render' as I have heard it render' by Mathilde, is another affair! A quality, madame, that moves, that penetrates. Perhaps not yet enough volume, but that will accomplish itself with time, when she will become more robus' in health. It is my intention to sen' her for the summer to Gran' Isle; that good air an' surf bathing will work miracles. An artiste, voyez vous, it is not to be treated like a human being of every day; it needs des petits soins; perfec' res' of body an' mind; good red wine an' plenty. . . . . oh yes, madame, the stage; that is our intention; but never with my consent in light opera. Patience is what I counsel to Mathilde. A little more stren'th; a little dev'lopment of the chest to give that soupçon of compass which is lacking, an' gran' opera is what I aspire for my sister."

I was curious to know Mathilde and to hear her sing; and thought it a great pity that a voice so marvelous as she doubtless possessed should not gain the notice that might prove the step toward the attainment of her ambition. It was such curiosity and a half-formed design or desire to interest myself in her career that prompted me to inform Cavanelle that I should greatly like to meet his sister; and I asked permission to call upon her the following Sunday afternoon.

Cavanelle was charmed. He otherwise would not have been Cavanelle. Over and over I was given the most minute directions for finding the house. The green car—or was it the yellow or blue one? I can no longer remember. But it was near Goodchildren street, and would I kindly walk this way and turn that way? At the corner was an ice dealer's. In the middle of the block, their house—one story; painted yellow; a knocker; a banana tree nodding over the side fence. But indeed, I need not look for the banana tree, the knocker, the number or anything, for if I but turn the corner in the neighborhood of five o'clock I would find him planted at the door awaiting me.

And there he was! Cavanelle himself; but seeming to me not himself; apart from the entourage with which I was accustomed to associate him. Every line of his mobile face, every gesture emphasized the welcome which his kind eyes expressed as he ushered me into the small parlor that opened upon the street.

"Oh, not that chair, madame! I entreat you. This one, by all means. Thousan' times more comfortable."

"Mathilde! Strange; my sister was here but an instant ago. Mathilde! Où es tu donc?" Stupid Cavanelle! He did not know when I had already guessed it—that Mathilde had retired to the adjoining room at my approach, and would appear after a sufficient delay to give an appropriate air of ceremony to our meeting.

And what a frail little piece of mortality she was when she did appear! At beholding her I could easily fancy that when she stepped outside of the yellow house, the zephyrs would lift her from her feet and, given a proper adjustment of the balloon sleeves, gently waft her in the direction of Goodchildren street, or wherever else she might want to go.

Hers was no physique for grande opera—certainly no stage presence; apparently so slender a hold upon life that the least tension might snap it. The voice which could hope to overcome these glaring disadvantages would have to be phenomenal.

Mathilde spoke English imperfectly, and with embarrassment, and was glad to lapse into French. Her speech was languid, unaffectedly so; and her manner was one of indolent repose; in this respect offering a striking contrast to that of her brother. Cavanelle seemed unable to rest. Hardly was I seated to his satisfaction than he darted from the room and soon returned followed by a limping old black woman bringing in a sirop d'orgeat and layer cake on a tray.

Mathilde's face showed feeble annoyance at her brother's want of savoir vivre in thus introducing the refreshments at so early a stage of my visit.

The servant was one of those cheap black women who abound in the French quarter, who speak Creole patois in preference to English, and who would rather work in a petit ménage in Goodchildren street for five dollars a month than for fifteen in the fourth district. Her presence, in some unaccountable manner, seemed to reveal to me much of the inner working of this household. I pictured her early morning visit to the French market, where picayunes were doled out sparingly, and lagniappes gathered in with avidity.

I could see the neatly appointed dinner table; Cavanelle extolling his soup and bouillie in extravagant terms; Mathilde toying with her papabotte or chicken-wing, and pouring herself a demi-verre from her very own half-bottle of St. Julien; Pouponne, as they called her, mumbling and grumbling through habit, and serving them as faithfully as a dog through instinct. I wondered if they knew that Pouponne "played the lottery" with every spare "quarter" gathered from a judicious management of lagniappe. Perhaps they would not have cared, or have minded, either, that she as often consulted the Voudoo priestess around the corner as her father confessor.

My thoughts had followed Pouponne's limping figure from the

room and it was with an effort I returned to Cavanelle twirling the piano stool this way and that way. Mathilde was languidly turning over scores, and the two warmly discussing the merits of a selection which she had evidently decided upon.

The girl seated herself at the piano. Her hands were thin and anæmic, and she touched the keys without firmness or delicacy. When she had played a few introductory bars, she began to sing. Heaven only knows what she sang; it made no difference then, nor can it make any now.

The day was a warm one, but that did not prevent a creepy chilliness seizing hold of me. The feeling was generated by disappointment, anger, dismay and various other disagreeable sensations which I cannot find names for. Had I been intentionally deceived and misled? Was this some impertinent pleasantry on the part of Cavanelle? Or rather had not the girl's voice undergone some hideous transformation since her brother had listened to it? I dreaded to look at him, fearing to see horror and astonishment depicted on his face. When I did look, his expression was earnestly attentive and beamed approval of the strains to which he meaasured time by a slow, satisfied motion of the hand.

The voice was thin to attenuation, I fear it was not even true. Perhaps my disappointment exaggerated its simple deficiencies into monstrous defects. But it was an unsympathetic voice that never could have been a blessing to possess or to listen to.

I cannot recall what I said at parting—doubtless conventional things which were not true. Cavanelle politely escorted me to the car, and there I left him with a hand-clasp which from my side was tender with sympathy and pity.

"Poor Cavanelle! poor Cavanelle!" The words kept beating time in my brain to the jingle of the car bells and the regular ring of the mule's hoofs upon the cobble stones. One moment I resolved to have a talk with him in which I would endeavor to open his eyes to the folly of thus casting his hopes and the substance of his labor to the winds. The next instant I had decided that chance would possibly attend to Cavanelle's affair less clumsily than I could. "But all the same," I wondered, "is Cavanelle a fool? is he a lunatic? is he under a hypnotic spell?" And then—strange that I did not think of it before—I realized that Cavanelle loved Mathilde intensely, and we all know that love is blind, but a god just the same.

Two years passed before I saw Cavanelle again. I had been absent that length of time from the city. In the meanwhile Mathilde had died. She and her little voice—the apotheosis of insignificance—were no more. It was perhaps a year after my visit to her that I read an account of her death in a New Orleans paper. Then came a momentary pang of commiseration for my good Cavanelle. Chance had surely acted here the part of a skillful though merciless surgeon; no temporizing, no half measures. A deep, sharp thrust of the scalpel; a moment of agonizing pain; then rest, rest; convalescence; health; happiness! Yes, Mathilde had been dead a year and I was prepared for great changes in Cavanelle.

He had lived like a hampered child who does not recognize the restrictions hedging it about, and lives a life of pathetic contentment in the midst of them. But now all that was altered. He was, doubtless, regaling himself with the half-bottles of St. Julien, which were never before for him; with, perhaps, an occasional petit souper at Moreau's, and there was no telling what little pleasures beside.

Cavanelle would certainly have bought himself a suit of clothes or two of modern fit and finish. I would find him with a brightened eye, a fuller cheek, as became a man of his years; perchance, even a waxed moustache! So did my imagination run rampant with me.

And after all, the hand which I clasped across the counter was that of the self-same Cavanelle I had left. It was no fuller, no firmer. There were even some additional lines visible through the thin, brown beard.

"Ah, my poor Cavanelle! you have suffered a grievous loss since we parted." I saw in his face that he remembered the circumstances of our last meeting, so there was no use in avoiding the subject. I had rightly conjectured that the wound had been a cruel one, but in a year such wounds heal with a healthy soul.

He could have talked for hours of Mathilde's unhappy taking-off, and if the subject had possessed for me the same touching fascination which it held for him, doubtless, we would have done so, but—

"And how is it now, mon ami? Are you living in the same place? running your little ménage as before, my poor Cavanelle?"

"Oh, yes, madame, except that my Aunt Félicie is making her home with me now. You have heard me speak of my aunt—No? You never have heard me speak of my Aunt Félicie Cavanelle of Terrebonne! That, madame, is a noble woman who has suffer' the mos' cruel affliction, an' deprivation, since the war.—No, madame, not in good health, unfortunately, by any means. It is why I esteem that a blessed privilege to give her declining years those little comforts, ces petits soins, that is a woman's right to expec' from men."

I knew what "des petits soins" meant with Cavanelle; doctors' visits, musical little jaunts across the lake, friandises of every description showered upon "Aunt Félicie," and he himself relegated to the soup and bouillie which typified his prosaic existence.

I was unreasonably exasperated with the man for awhile, and would not even permit myself to notice the beauty in texture and design of the mousseline de laine which he had spread across the counter in tempting folds. I was forced to restrain a brutal desire to say something stinging and cruel to him for his fatuity.

However, before I had regained the street, the conviction that Cavanelle was a hopeless fool seemed to reconcile me to the situation and also afforded me some diversion.

But even this estimate of my poor Cavanelle was destined not to last. By the time I had seated myself in the Prytania street car and passed up my nickel, I was convinced that Cavanelle was an angel.

1970

John Dos Passos

Funiculi Funicula

CHARLEY STAYED all summer in Louisville working at the Wiggins Repair Shops. He roomed with an Italian named Grassi who'd come over to escape military service. Grassi read the papers every day and was very much afraid the U. S. would go into the war. Then he said he'd have to hop across the border to Mexico. He was an anarchist and a quiet sort of guy who spent the evenings singing low to himself and playing the accordion on the lodginghouse steps. He told Charley about the big Fiat factories at Torino where he'd worked, and taught him to eat spaghetti and drink red wine and to play *Funiculi funicula* on the accordion. His big ambition was to be an airplane pilot. Charley picked up with a Jewish girl who worked as sorter in a tobacco warehouse. Her name was Sarah Cohen but she made him call her Belle. He liked her well enough but he was careful to make her understand that he wasn't the marrying kind. She said she was a radical and believed in free love, but that didn't suit him much either. He took her to shows and took her out walking in Cherokee Park and bought her an amethyst brooch when she said amethyst was her birthstone.

When he thought about himself he felt pretty worried. Here he was doing the same work day after day, with no chance of making better money or getting any schooling or seeing the country. When winter came on he got restless. He'd rescued an old Ford roadster that they were going to tow out to the junkheap and had patched it up with discarded spare parts.

He talked Grassi into going down to New Orleans with him. They had a little money saved up and they'd run down there and get a job and be there for the Mardi Gras. The first day that he'd felt very good since he left St. Paul was the sleety January day they pulled out of Louisville with the engine hitting on all four cylinders and a pile of thirdhand spare tires in the back, headed south.

They got down through Nashville and Birmingham and Mobile, but the roads were terrible and they had to remake the car as they went along and they almost froze to death in a blizzard near Guntersville and had to lay over for a couple of days, so that by the time they'd gotten down to Bay St. Louis and were bowling along the shore road under a blue sky and feeling the warm sun and seeing palms and banana-trees and Grassi was telling about Vesuvio and Bella Napoli and his girl in Torino that he'd never see again on account of the bastardly capitalista war, their money had run out. They got into New Orleans with a dollar five between them and not more than a teacupful of gasoline in the tank, but by a lucky break Charley managed to sell the car as it stood for twenty-five dollars to a colored undertaker.

They got a room in a house near the levee for three dollars a week. The landlady was a yellowfaced woman from Panama and there was a parrot on the balcony outside their room and the sun was warm on their shoulders walking along the street. Grassi was very happy. "This is lika the Italia," he kept saying. They walked around and tried to find out about jobs but they couldn't seem to find out about anything except that Mardi Gras was next week. They walked along Canal Street that was crowded with colored people, Chinamen, pretty girls in brightcolored dresses, racetrack hangerson, tall elderly men in palmbeach suits. They stopped to have a beer in a bar open to the street with tables along the outside where all kinds of men sat smoking cigars and drinking. When they came out Grassi bought an afternoon paper. He turned pale and showed the headline, WAR WITH GERMANY IMMINENT. "If America go to war with Germany cops will arrest all Italian man to send back to Italy for fight, see? My friend tell who work in consule's office; tell me, see? I will not go fight in capitalista war." Charley tried to kid him along, but a worried set look came over Grassi's face and as soon as it was dark he left Charley saying he was going back to the flop and going to bed.

Charley walked round the streets alone. There was a warm molasses smell from the sugar refineries, whiffs of gardens and garlic and pepper and oil cookery. There seemed to be women everywhere, in bars, standing round streetcorners, looking out invitingly behind shutters ajar in all the doors and windows; but he had twenty dollars on him and was afraid one of them might lift it off him, so he just walked around until he was tired and then went back to the room, where he found Grassi already asleep with the covers over his head.

It was late when he woke up. The parrot was squawking on the gallery outside the window, hot sunlight filled the room. Grassi was not there.

Charley had dressed and was combing his hair when Grassi came in looking very much excited. He had taken a berth as donkey-engineman on a freighter bound for South America. "When I get Buenos Aires goodby and no more war," he said. "If Argentina go to war, goodby again." He kissed Charley on the mouth, and insisted on giving him his accordion and there were tears in his eyes when he went off to join the boat that was leaving at noon.

Charley walked all over town inquiring at garages and machineshops if there was any chance of a job. The streets were broad and dusty, bordered by low shuttered frame houses, and distances were huge. He got tired and dusty and sweaty. People he talked to were darned agreeable but nobody seemed to know where he could get a job. He decided he ought to stay through the Mardi Gras anyway and then he would go up North again. Men he talked to told him to go to Florida or Birmingham, Alabama, or up to Memphis or Little Rock, but everybody agreed that unless he wanted to ship as a seaman there wasn't a job to be had in the city. The days dragged along warm and slow and sunny and smelling of molasses from the refineries. He spent a great deal of time reading in the public library or sprawled on the levee watching the niggers unload the ships. He had too much time to think and he worried about what he was going to do with himself. Nights he couldn't sleep well because he hadn't done anything all day to tire him.

One night he heard guitarmusic coming out of a joint called "The Original Tripoli," on Chartres Street. He went in and sat down at a table and ordered drinks. The waiter was a Chink. Couples were dancing in a kind of wrestling hug in the dark end of the room. Charley decided that if he could get a girl for less than five seeds he'd take one on. Before long he found himself setting up a girl who said her name was Liz to drinks and a feed. She said she hadn't had anything to eat all day. He asked her about Mardi Gras and she said it was a bum time because the cops closed everything up tight. "They rounded up all the waterfront hustlers last night, sent every last one of them up the river." "What they do with 'em?" "Take 'em up to Memphis and turn 'em loose . . . ain't a jail in the state would hold all the floosies in this town." They laughed and had another drink and then they danced. Charley held her tight. She was a skinny girl with little pointed breasts and big hips. "Jez, baby, you've got some action," he said after they'd been dancing a little while. "Ain't it ma business to give the boys a good time?" He liked the way she looked at him. "Say, baby, how much do you get?" "Five bucks." "Jez, I ain't no millionaire . . . and didn't I set you up to some eats?" "Awright, sugar-popper; make it three."

They had another drink. Charley noticed that she took some kind of lemonade each time. "Don't you ever drink anything, Liz?" "You can't drink in this game, dearie; first thing you know I'd be givin' it away."

There was a big drunken guy in a dirty undershirt looked like a ships' stoker reeling round the room. He got hold of Liz's hand and made her dance with him. His big arms tattooed blue and red folded right round her. Charley could see he was mauling and pulling at her dress as he danced with her. "Quit that, you son of a bitch," she was yelling. That made Charley sore and he went up and pulled the big guy away from her. The big guy turned and swung on him. Charley ducked and hopped into the center of the floor with his dukes up. The big guy was blind drunk, as he let fly another haymaker Charley put his foot out and the big guy tripped and fell on his face upsetting a table and a little dark man with a black mustache with it. In a second the dark man was on his feet and had whipped out a machete. The Chinks ran round mewing like a lot of damn gulls. The proprietor, a fat Spaniard in an apron, had come out from behind the bar and was yellin', "Git out, every last one of you." The man with the machete made a run at Charley. Liz gave him a yank one side and before Charley knew what had happened she was pulling him through the stinking latrines into a passage that led to a back door out into the street. "Don't you know no better'n to git in a fight over a goddam whore?" she was saying in his ear.

Once out in the street Charley wanted to go back to get his hat and coat. Liz wouldn't let him. "I'll get it for you in the mornin'," she said. They walked along the street together. "You're a damn good girl; I like you," said Charley. "Can't you raise ten dollars and make it all night?" "Jez, kid, I'm broke." "Well, I'll have to throw you out and do some more hustlin', I guess. There's only one feller in this world gets it for nothin' and you ain't him."

They had a good time together. They sat on the edge of the bed talking. She looked flushed and pretty in a fragile sort of way in her pink shimmy shirt. She showed him a snapshot of her steady who was second engineer on a tanker. "Ain't he handsome? I don't hustle when he's in town. He's that strong. He can crack a pecan with his biceps." She showed him the place on his arm where her steady could crack a pecan.

"Where you from?" asked Charley.

"What's that to you?"

"You're from up North; I can tell by the way you talk."

"Sure. I'm from Iowa, but I'll never go back there no more . . . It's a hell of life, bo, and don't you forget. 'Women of pleasure' my foot. I used to think I was a classy dame up home and then I woke up one morning and found I was nothing but a goddam whore."

"Ever been to New York?"

She shook her head. "It ain't such a bad life if you keep away from drink and the pimps," she said thoughtfully.

"I guess I'll shove off for New York right after Mardi Gras. I can't seem to find me a master in this man's town."

"Mardi Gras ain't so much if you're broke."

"Well, I came down here to see it and I guess I better see it."

It was dawn when he left her. She came downstairs with him. He kissed her and told her he'd give her the ten bucks if she got his hat and coat back for him and she said to come around to her place that evening about six, but not to go back to the "Tripoli" because that greaser was a bad egg and would be laying for him.

The streets of old stucco houses inset with lacy iron balconies were brimful of blue mist. A few mulatto women in bandanas were moving around in the courtyards. In the market old colored men were laying out fruit and green vegetables. When he got back to his flop the

Panama woman was out on the gallery outside his room holding out a banana and calling "Ven, Polly . . . Ven, Polly," in a little squeaky voice. The parrot sat on the edge of the tiled roof cocking a glassy eye at her and chuckling softly. "Me here all night," said the Panama woman with a tearful smile. "Polly no quiere come." Charley climbed up by the shutter and tried to grab the parrot but the parrot hitched away sideways up to the ridge of the roof and all Charley did was bring a tile down on his head. "No quiere come," said the Panama woman sadly. Charley grinned at her and went into his room, where he dropped on the bed and fell asleep.

During Mardi Gras Charley walked round town till his feet were sore. There were crowds everywhere and lights and floats and parades and bands and girls running round in fancy dress. He picked up plenty of girls but as soon as they found he was flat they dropped him. He was spending his money as slowly as he could. When he got hungry he'd drop into a bar and drink a glass of beer and eat as much free lunch as he dared.

The day after Mardi Gras the crowds began to thin out, and Charley didn't have any money for beer. He walked round feeling hungry and miserable; the smell of molasses and the absinthe smell from bars in the French Quarter in the heavy damp air made him feel sick. He didn't know what to do with himself. He didn't have the gumption to start off walking or hitchhiking again. He went to the Western Union and tried to wire Jim collect, but the guy said they wouldn't take a wire asking for money collect.

The Panama woman threw him out when he couldn't pay for another week in advance and there he was walking down Esplanade Avenue with Grassi's accordion on one arm and his little newspaper bundle of clothes under the other. He walked down the levee and sat down in a grassy place in the sun and thought for a long time. It was either throwing himself in the river or enlisting in the army. Then he suddenly thought of the accordion. An accordion was worth a lot of money. He left his bundle of clothes under some planks and walked around to all the hockshops he could find with the accordion, but they wouldn't give him more than fifteen bucks for it anywhere. By the time he'd been round to all the hockshops and musicstores it was dark and everything had closed. He stumbled along the pavement feeling sick and dopy from hunger. At the corner of Canal and Rampart he stopped. Singing was coming out of a saloon. He got the hunch to go in and play *Funiculi funicula* on the accordion. He might get some free lunch and a glass of beer out of it.

He'd hardly started playing and the bouncer had just vaulted across the bar to give him the bum's rush, when a tall man sprawled at a table beckoned to him.

"Brother, you come right there an' set down." It was a big man with a long broken nose and high cheekbones.

"Brother, you set down." The bouncer went back behind the bar. "Brother, you can't play that there accordeen no mor'n a rabbit. Ah'm nutten but a lowdown cracker from Okachobee City but if Ah couldn't play no better'n that . . . " Charley laughed. "I know I can't play it. That's all right." The Florida guy pulled out a big wad of bills. "Brother, do you know what you're going to do? You're going to sell me the goddam thing. . . . Ah'm nothin' but a lowdown cracker, but, by Jesus Christ . . . "

"Hey, Doc, be yourself. You don't want the damn thing." His friends tried to make him put his money back.

Doc swept his arm round with a gesture that shot three glasses onto the floor with a crash. "You turkey-buzzards talk in your turn. Brother, how much do you want for the accordeen?" The bouncer had come back and was standing threateningly over the table. "All right, Ben," said Doc. "It's all on your Uncle Henry . . . And let's have another round a that good rye whisky. Brother, how much do you want for it?"

"Fifty bucks," said Charley, thinking fast. Doc handed him out five tens. Charley swallowed a drink, put the accordion on the table and went off in a hurry. He was afraid if he hung round the cracker 'ud sober up and try to get the money back, and besides he wanted to eat.

Next day he got a steerage passage on the steamer *Momus* bound for New York. The river was higher than the city. It was funny standing on the stern of the steamboat and looking down on the roofs and streets and trolleycars of New Orleans. When the steamer pulled out from the wharf Charley began to feel good. He found the colored steward and got him to give him a berth in the deckhouse. When he put his newspaper package under the pillow he glanced down into the berth below. There lay Doc, fast asleep, all dressed up in a light gray suit and a straw hat with a burntout cigar sticking out of the corner of his mouth and the accordion beside him.

They were passing between the Eads Jetties and feeling the seawind in their faces and the first uneasy swell of the Gulf under their feet when Doc came lurching on deck. He recognized Charley and went up to him with a big hand held out. "Well, I'll be a sonofabitch if there ain't the musicmaker . . . That's a good accordeen, boy. Ah thought you'd imposed on me bein' only a poa country lad an' all that, But I'll be a sonofabitch if it ain't worth the money. Have a snifter on me?"

They went and sat on Doc's bunk and Doc broke out a bottle of Bacardi and they had some drinks and Charley told about how he'd been flat broke; if it wasn't for that fifty bucks he'd still be sitting on the levee and Doc said that if it wasn't for that fifty bucks he'd be riding firstclass.

1917

Walt Whitman

Three New Orleans Sketches

Peter Funk, Esq.

P E T E R F U N K , like all other illustrious personages who have become so well known, as no longer to need the titulary soubriquet of *Mister,* was born and brought up—no one knows where. At least the information we have on this point is exceedingly uncertain and contradictory. Without, therefore, descending into the particulars of his early training and history, or minutely tracing up the rationale of cause and effect, by showing that a youth of moral proclivity will, in time, run into that species of moral gum-elasticity which goes to constitute the blood and bones of individuals comprising his *genus,* we shall proceed at once, in *medias res,* as the boys say at college, and make known to you, gentle reader, that Peter Funk is a young gentleman "about town" who holds the highly responsible office of by-bidder in a Mock Auction—being engaged to said work by "the man who sells the watches."

You're a gentleman of leisure about New Orleans, may be, stranger, and lounging about Royal street. You hear the musical sound of the "human voice divine," crying out "fivenaff, five-n-aff—only going at twenty-five dollars and-n-a-ff for this elegant gold watch and chain, in prime running order, just sent in by a *gentleman leaving town,* and only five-n-aff! Did I hear you say six, sir?"

Perhaps you drop in, and if you are not careful how you look at the musical auctioneer he will accept of your look for a wink, and, according to the philosophy of the auction room, a wink passes for a bid, and you find yourself in the nominal possession of "an elegant gold watch and chain, in prime running order, just sent in to be sold by a gentleman leaving town," before you are well aware of what you are about. So take care how you look when you are in the patent auction shops. There stands the auctioneer in all the serious earnestness of a man begging for his life, and, with voice and looks and gestures, seems like one speaking sober truth, and "nothin' else." Only half a dozen individuals comprise his audience, and these half a dozen are Peter Funk and his *corps de reserve.* Peter looks somewhat stouter to-day than he was yesterday, and has exchanged his cloth coat and cap for a blanket coat and *chapeau blanc,* and his whiskers have shared the fate of "the last rose of summer"—that is to say, they have evaporated—dropped off: they are *non est inventus*—gone!

Yes, that's Funk and his five interesting associates in business—"companions of his toil, his feelings, and his fame"—Peter the 1st, Peter the 2d, Peter the 3d, Peter the 4th and Peter the 5th—he himself being no other than Peter the Great, or the Great Peter—"Peter Funk, Esq."

Now, stranger, take care what you're about. You're the only bona fide customer—if customer you choose to call yourself—that has entered the portals of the auction shop as yet, and Peter Funk Primus and Peter Funk Secundus have done all this bidding that makes the crier keep up such a hubbaboo. Well, you don't know of this fact and you think "a man's man for a' that," and you don't understand the secret of Peter Funk and his associates, or the service they're engaged in, and you only see a fine-*looking* watch, "just sent in to be sold by a gentleman leaving town," and going dog cheap. You nod your head, and straightway the countenance of the crier brightens up, and his voice grows even more vociferous than before. He's got a bid—a real bid—and the first and only one. He tacks on five dollars more, and now he's heard going it in fine style: "Thirty, thirty, thirty, thirty—only going at thirty dollars for a splendid elegant gold lever, with seventeen pairs of extra jewels, lately imported, and now must be sold!"

He cries on at this rate for perhaps ten minutes, occasionally casting a glance at the passers-by to see if any *greeneys* [green-horns] can be tolled in. Peter Funk takes the watch in his hand and examines it attentively, and with a very significant look, as though his judgment was perfectly satisfied, he says deliberately, "Thirty-five!"

"Against you, sir," cries Mr. Auctioneer, and forthwith sets off with unusual volubility, crying out *ore rotundo,* "thirty-five, thirty-five—only going at thirty-five!"

"Thirty-five dollars for such an elegant gold watch is certainly cheap as dirt–they ask eighty-five or ninety at the stores"; and as these thoughts revolve in your mind, you think you might as well make five-and-twenty dollars as well as not, as there are plenty of boys up in your county who would jump at the bargain–and you nod again, the auctioneer having in the meantime directed the whole force of his vocable artillery at you, and launched forth in such a rigamarole of praise of said time-piece that you couldn't well resist his very passionate appeal.

"Forty dollars!" is quickly caught up. "*Only* going at forty dollars!–forty! forty! forty! forty!" and now the crier turns to Peter, the interesting Peter, whose turn for serious deliberation has again come. He again examines the watch, turns it over and over again, and, as he hands it up to the crier, says, in a very low but decided tone of voice, "Forty-five!"

By this time one or two other loungers like yourself have dropped in, and monsieur crier applies himself with exceeding earnestness in lauding the watch, as never, sure, watch was lauded before, except perhaps at a patent auction. While you are revolving in your mind whether to go [up to] fifty, some other greeney from one of the upper parishes, or maybe from Mississippi, with his pockets full of money, cries out "Fifty, by God!" and you are relieved from what would have been a very dear bargain to you–the invoice price of said "elegant gold lever" having been only $17.50. They are "made to sell," and many are the green 'uns that are bit, by the persuasive speech of the auctioneer, and still more persuasive biddings of his interesting coadjutor in this pretty business, Peter Funk, Esq., the subject of our present "sketch."

I was pretty well acquainted with Funk before he went into the "auction and commission business"; we boarded a while together at the same house. Since his embarkation into the business of buying watches, we have grown offish with one another: he never knows me in the auction room, though we may be standing side by side; and, to tell the truth, I hardly know him half the time in the various disguises he assumes, for he scarcely ever dresses the same for two days in succession–being in cap, cloak and whiskers on one day, and the next *aliased* up in a white or green blanket. Some say he was from Old Kentuck, and others again aver he is a North Carolina Tennessean; while others allege him to have been a direct importation from the nethermost corner of Down East—having resided a year or two in Texas by way of a seasoning. Of this I can say nothing—but am of opinion that if ever Peter Funk received a "fotching up" according to old-fashioned New England Puritanism, he must have become amazingly warped in his morals ere he reached the latitude of Louisiana.

To sum up the character I have to give of Peter Funk, I shall simply say that he at present thrives well, and will make a business man of himself if he keeps on. He is one of those men who reverse the saying of Hamlet, that "conscience makes cowards of us all." Peter's conscience makes no coward of him—*argal*, Peter'll be rich one of these days. It's a bad thing to have

> "the native hut of resolution
> Thus sicklied o'er with the pale cast of thought."

and Peter takes none of these sickly thoughts, or any other consideration, "for the morrow," except it be what coat or what colored whiskers he shall put on.

Daggerdraw Bowieknife, Esq.

We do not say that our hero lives in New Orleans now, but he "used to did," and that's enough for a chap whose business it is to make "Sketches." He lived here once upon a time, and flourished extensively—went to the Legislature and to Congress, for aught we know—that is, the Congress of Texas, while that "lone star" was shining with bedimmed lustre in the political firmament.

Squire Bowieknife emigrated, some years ago, to a village in Mississippi from one of the Carolinas. He was a limb of the law, and by dint of an abundance of swagger, in a short time fought his way into notice. There are parts of Mississippi where a man may graduate into public favor, through the merits of gunpowder, with a rapidity that is astonishing. It requires a peculiar conformation and organization—a fitness of things, as it were—to constitute an individual who can thrive upon sharp steel and patent revolvers, but Bowieknife was the man, and "he went in with a rush."

He found his way to New Orleans, and now has gone to Texas, followed by the ghosts of no less than six hale, hearty men; at least, that were such before his shooting irons made daylight shine through them. Never did man stand more upon a point of honor than he did: he would cavil upon the hundredth part of a hair if he thought a bit of a fight was to be got out of his antagonist: and upon the most trifling misunderstanding in the world, he would attack you in a street fight, or "call you out" and shoot you down, as though your life were of no more value than a cur dog's. Oh, he was a brave fellow, and people were afraid of him, and we cannot wonder at it.

But it so happened, that the Hon. Daggerdraw Bowieknife was not, by any manner of means, so punctual in meeting his own little liabilities as he was in being first upon the ground to take part in the murderous duel—in other words, he was one of those "damned highminded, honorable, clever fellows," who would rather shoot a man than pay him what he owed him. There are such men in the world, and our friend was one of them: they pretend to be the very soul of honor, but an honest debt, such as an honest man would pay with entire punctuality, these sons of honor "pass by as the idle wind, which I regard not." One day, Daggerdraw sallied out from his office to take a walk into town. He was armed and equipped, though not "according to law," but he was, in common parlance, quite "loaded down to the guards" with fashionable killing tools. In each pantaloons pocket he carried a small loaded pistol: in his bosom, and within reach, was the handle of a large bowie-knife, weighing just one pound and a half, one of those murderous weapons more efficient than the Roman short sword, and equally serviceable at cutting or thrusting. Daggerdraw had done bloody deeds with it in both ways, as more than one individual in Mississippi had experienced to his sorrow. This said big butcher-knife had run the rounds of several street fights, and was the dearly beloved of its dreaded owner. Whether the personal prowess he displayed in its use was a violation of the laws of decency and humanity, and befitted him more for the society of desperadoes and professional cut-throats, is altogether another question. No man doubted the bull-dog courage of this disciple of Blackstone, but whether any of the sympathies of human nature, such as make man the being he is, had an abiding place in his ferocious heart, is not for us to say, though it may well be supposed there were none.

Yes, there he goes! and there is blood upon his shirt now, or at least there is revenge brooding in his thoughts, and ere long the life of some doomed one must pay the forfeit. He was not a bad-looking man either, being gentle enough in his dress and address, but

"There was a lurking devil in his sneer,
That raised emotions both of hate and fear."

Why is it that a false sense of honor requires men to face in deadly combat such as Daggerdraw? Perhaps they suppose, as Bob Acres says, in Sheridan's *The Rivals*, that honor follows them to the grave. We are in opinion with Bob's servant, that this is the very place one might make shift to do without it, and that the honor and applause, such as it is, whips over to the adversary. Very well: Squire, take your grand rounds, and as you walk the streets, feel secure that men are afraid of you, but take good care and don't get afraid of yourself. I've heard strange stories about you—how that you never sleep o' nights—that you pace the long gallery of your boardinghouse with restless and uneasy steps, and while others luxuriate in the blessings of "tired nature's sweet restorer," sleep is a stranger to your eyelids. I have heard that the lone and solemn hour of midnight is a terror to you, and that the ghosts of murdered Banquos will rise mentally to your vision, as a meet reward for your deeds of awful transgression, and your disregard of the injunction, "Thou shalt not kill."

Some men become noted, some are celebrated, and others, again, have the stamp of notoriety fixed to their names: such is the unenviable condition of him whom we have here sketched. He has made his mark through life, but it has been in the spirit of the pestilence and the destroyer.

Timothy Goujon, V. O. N. O.
(Vender of Oysters in New Orleans)

There is in all cities bordering nigh unto the sea, a certain species of fish ycleped oysters, very much desired by the dwellers in said cities, and very much sold by certain individuals, of rare peculiarities, called oystermen.

In this goodly city of New Orleans (albeit, not so very good either), there abounds a class of worthy citizens, named as above, and who exercise the office and administration of fishes of this nature, styled, as we have said, oysters. The daily duty of these individuals—free citizens of a remarkably free city—is to vend by retail the interior fleshy and somewhat savory substance of these shell-fish, as above alluded to. The outer crust, or envelope of these, being of a tough, unyielding and indigestible quality, is rejected and thrown aside as worthless, nothing being eaten by the children of men but the puffy contents thereof. To sell such, is the business and daily care of those called, in common language, oystermen—the French style them écaille.

It cannot have escaped the notice of the most casual observer of men and things, that the streets and well thronged thoroughfares abound in certain brick tenements, professedly devoted—not the buildings but the occupants—to the preparing and rendering fit for the mastication of all and sundry reputable citizens—at least those who possess the wherewith to pay for them—these said shell-fish, fished up by a pair of iron claws out of the briny deep. These tenements, bearing aloft the outward insignia of their rank and condition, are to be found in the crowded walks of the city—and he "who runs may read," and he who is hungry may pass in and be served, not only to his heart's content, but also to his stomach's, which is the best of the bargain. We ourselves have refreshed and regaled the "inner man," many times and oft by those luxuriating viands compounded by those disciples of the illustrious kitchener, paying our quota of current coin meanwhile, and going joyfully on our way. But of late we have ceased in our visitations to these temples—finding that a repletion of a stomach and a similar condition of the brain-pan were always in an inverse ratio the one to the other. When the stomach was full of luxury and good eating, the brain was empty—barrenness and desolation prevailing throughout "the dome of thought, the palace of the soul." In such an extremity, having ever been taught to respect mind rather than matter, we have preferred to become even as one of "Pharaoh's lean kine," in order to have use and exercise of said article of brain. Everybody remembers the story of the old Dutchman so happy and so contented, who said that "he chust eats and thrinks till he's full, and then he schmokes and schmokes, and thinks about notin at all."

'Tis not, therefore, to these Epicurean depots we refer, or to the proprietors thereof—not by any manner of means: they are well favored men, which, as Dogberry says, "is the gift of nature": they wear black coats and carry canes. These, in the strictness of speech, and the bounds of propriety, come not under the classification above alluded to. We refer to certain graceless *sans culottes*—no, not *sans culottes* either, literally, for that would be "most senseless and fit"—but in the political sense of the term: men, who, in the scale of the social thermometer, do not reach boiling point by any means. It was to this enterprising portion of the body politic that Timothy Goujon belonged. Long had he lived and labored in the cause of science, for he was a practical naturalist—perhaps you may say a *conchologist*—spending his days and his nights among shell-fish—he was a vendor of oysters.

Goujon made his advent in "this breathing world" in the city of Bordeaux or in some of the faubourgs thereof. His parents being grave and close-mouthed people—a national characteristic—very naturally placed Timothy, when he had come to years, at the occupation which he has followed through life—namely, a fisher and a vendor of oysters. Of the particulars of his crossing the Atlantic, and finding himself erect, like other "featherless bipeds," here upon the levee of New Orleans, we are sorry we have no well detailed account. Neither he nor his parents before him were able to exercise the art of chirography, and therefore, of the deeds of his early life—how many times with furious grasp upon the iron tongs he has dragged these unoffending fishes from their natal bed, or murderously thrust the knife into their bosoms, and torn them from their comfortable little homes—of these things we are not informed, and must therefore, with provoking brevity, remain as mute as this same commodity in which he so perseveringly deals.

We have heard that a year or two ago he involved himself in the rent of a small box of a corner shop, where his beautiful triangular lantern, covered with red worsted, and bearing the inviting inscription of "*Always Oysters, fryd, rost & in the shel*," hung out by night as a point of local attraction to the hungry and wayfaring, both of which varieties of worthies it is presumed every sizeable city contains. This speculation did not succeed, and Timothy sold out his stock in trade, including the beautiful red worsted emblem of gastronomy, and betook himself independently to the levee, like a gentleman, where he might breathe a purer air, and give exercise to his lungs, at the same time vending *viva voce* the inanimate quadrupeds which lay piled up with so much *sang froid* in his boat beside him.

Often, of a Sunday morning, we have heard the melodious, guttural voice of Timothy Goujon, in that place in the city of New Orleans where men and women do, at this especial hour of the week, "most congregate," namely, in the Market-place. They have we seen and heard the sentimental Goujon trill forth harmonious ditty in accents somewhat like the following, though it would require a mixture of the French horn and the bassoon to grunt out the strain with any degree of exactness, especially the chorus: "Ah-h-h-h-h-h-h-h-h à bonne marché – so cheep as navair vas – toutes frais – var fresh. Ah-h-h un véritable collection – jentlemens and plack folks. Ah-h-h come and puy de véritable poisson de la mer – de bonne huitres – Ah-h-h-h-h-h-h-!"

Adieu, Goujon, sell your oysters, and pocket your small gains, and live quietly and comfortably, *chaqu'un à son goût*, and *chaqu'un à son gré*.

1848

Robert Penn Warren

Mason City

T O G E T there you follow Highway 58, going northeast out of the city, and it is a good highway and new. Or was new, that day we went up it. You look up the highway and it is straight for miles, coming at you, with the black line down the center coming at and at you, black and slick and tarry-shining against the white of the slab, and the heat dazzles up from the white slab so that only the black line is clear, coming at you with the whine of the tires, and if you don't quit staring at that line and don't take a few deep breaths and slap yourself hard on the back of the neck you'll hypnotize yourself and you'll come to just at the moment when the right front wheel hooks over into the black dirt shoulder off the slab, and you'll try to jerk her back on but you can't because the slab is high like a curb, and maybe you'll try to reach to turn off the ignition just as she starts the dive. But you won't make it, of course. Then a nigger chopping cotton a mile away, he'll look up and see the little column of black smoke standing up above the vitriolic, arsenical green of the cotton rows, and up against the violent, metallic, throbbing blue of the sky, and he'll say, "Lawd God, hit's a-nudder one done done hit!" And the next nigger down the next row, he'll say, "Lawd God," and the first nigger will giggle, and the hoe will lift again and the blade will flash in the sun like a heliograph. Then a few days later the boys from the Highway Department will mark the spot with a little metal square on a metal rod stuck in the black dirt off the shoulder, the metal square painted white and on it in black a skull and crossbones. Later on love vine will climb up it, out of the weeds.

But if you wake up in time and don't hook your wheel off the slab, you'll go whipping on into the dazzle and now and then a car will come at you steady out of the dazzle and will pass you with a snatching sound as though God-Almighty had ripped a tin roof loose with his bare hands. Way off ahead of you, at the horizon where the cotton fields are blurred into the light, the slab will glitter and gleam like water, as though the road were flooded. You'll go whipping toward it, but it will always be ahead of you, that bright, flooded place, like a mirage. You'll go past the little white metal squares set on metal rods, with the skull and crossbones on them to mark the spot. For this is the country where the age of the internal combustion engine has come into its own. Where every boy is Barney Oldfield, and the girls wear organdy and batiste and eyelet embroidery and no panties on account of the climate and have smooth little faces to break your heart and when the wind of the car's speed lifts up their hair at the temples you see the sweet little beads of perspiration nestling there, and they sit low in the seat with their little spines crooked and their bent knees high toward the dashboard and not too close together for the cool, if you could call it that, from the hood ventilator. Where the smell of gasoline and burning brake bands and red-eye is sweeter than myrrh. Where the eight-cylinder jobs come roaring around the curves in the red hills and scatter the gravel like spray, and when they ever get down in the flat country and hit the new slab, God have mercy on the mariner.

On up Number 58, and the country breaks. The flat country and the big cotton fields are gone now, and the grove of live oaks way off yonder where the big house is, and the white-washed shacks, all just alike, set in a row by the cotton fields with the cotton growing up to the doorstep, where the pickaninny sits like a black Billiken and sucks its thumb and watches you go by. That's all left behind now. It is red hills now, not high, with blackberry bushes along the fence rows, and blackjack clumps in the bottoms and now and then a place where the second-growth pines stand close together if they haven't burned over for sheep grass, and if they burned over, there are the black stubs. The cotton patches cling to the hillsides, and the gullies cut across the cotton patches. The corn blades hang stiff and are streaked with yellow.

There were pine forests here a long time ago but they are gone. The bastards got in here and set up the mills and laid the narrow-gauge tracks and knocked together the company commissaries and paid a dollar a day and folks swarmed out of the brush for the dollar and folks came from God knows where riding in wagons with a chest of drawers and a bedstead canted together in the wagon bed, and five kids huddled down together and the old woman hunched on the wagon seat with a poke bonnet on her head and snuff on her gums and a young one hanging on her tit. The saws sang soprano and the clerk in the commissary passed out the blackstrap molasses and the sowbelly and wrote in his big book, and the Yankee dollar and Confederate dumbness collaborated to heal the wounds of four years of fratricidal strife, and all was merry as a marriage bell. Till, all of a sudden, there weren't any more pine trees. They stripped the mills. The narrow-gauge tracks got covered with grass. Folks tore down the commissaries for kindling wood. There wasn't any more dollar a day. The big boys were gone, with diamond rings on their fingers and broadcloth on their backs. But a good many of the folks stayed right on, and watched the gullies eat deeper into the red clay. And a good handful of those folks and their heirs and assigns stayed in Mason City, four thousand of them more or less.

You come in on Number 58 and pass the cotton gin and the power station and the fringe of nigger shacks and bump across the railroad track and down a street where there are a lot of little houses painted white one time, with the sad valentine lace of gingerbread work around the eaves of the veranda, and tin roofs, and where the leaves on the trees in the yards hang straight down in the heat, and above the mannerly whisper of your eighty-horsepower valve-in-head (or whatever it is) drifting at forty, you hear the July flies grinding away in the verdure.

That was the way it was the last time I saw Mason City, nearly three years ago, back in the summer of 1936. I was in the first car, the Cadillac, with the Boss and Mr. Duffy and the Boss's wife and son and Sugar-Boy. In the second car, which lacked our quiet elegance reminiscent of a cross between a hearse and an ocean liner but which still wouldn't make your cheeks burn with shame in the country-club parking lot, there were some reporters and a photographer and Sadie Burke, the Boss's secretary, to see they got there sober enough to do what they were supposed to do.

Sugar-Boy was driving the Cadillac, and it was a pleasure to watch him. Or it would have been if you could detach your imagination from the picture of what near a couple of tons of expensive mechanism looks like after it's turned turtle three times at eighty and could give your undivided attention to the exhibition of muscular co-ordination, satanic humor, and split-second timing which was Sugar-Boy's when he whipped around a hay wagon in the face of an oncoming gasoline truck and went through the rapidly diminishing aperture close enough to give the truck driver heart failure with one rear fender and wipe the snot off a mule's nose with the other. But the Boss loved it. He always sat up front with Sugar-Boy and looked at the speedometer and down the road and grinned to Sugar-Boy after they got through between the mule's nose and the gasoline truck. And Sugar-Boy's head would twitch, the way it always did when the words were piling up inside of him and couldn't get out, and then he'd start. "The b-b-b-b-b-" he would manage to get out and the saliva would spray from his lips like Flit from a Flit gun. "The b-b-b-b-bas-tud-he seen me c-c-o-" and here he'd spray the inside of the windshield-"c-c-com-ing." Sugar-Boy couldn't talk, but he could express himself when he got his foot on the accelerator. He wouldn't win any debating contests in high school, but then nobody would ever want to debate with Sugar-Boy. Not anybody who knew him and had seen him do tricks with the .38 Special which rode under his left armpit like a tumor.

No doubt you thought Sugar-Boy was a Negro, from his name. But he wasn't. He was Irish, from the wrong side of the tracks. He was about five-feet-two, and he was getting bald, though he wasn't more than twenty-seven or -eight years old, and he wore red ties and under the red tie and his shirt he wore a little Papist medal on a chain, and I always hoped to God it was St. Christopher and that St. Christopher was on the job. His name was O'Sheean, but they called him Sugar-Boy because he ate sugar. Every time he went to a restaurant he took all the cube sugar there was in the bowl. He went around with his pockets stuffed with sugar cubes, and when he took one out to pop into his mouth you saw little pieces of gray lint sticking to it, the kind of lint there always is loose in your pocket, and shreds of tobacco from cigarettes. He'd pop the cube in over the barricade of his twisted black little teeth, and then you'd see the thin little mystic Irish cheeks cave in as he sucked the sugar, so that he looked like an undernourished leprechaun.

The Boss was sitting in the front seat with Sugar-Boy and watching the speedometer, with his kid Tom up there with him. Tom was then about eighteen or nineteen – I forgot which – but you would have thought he was older. He wasn't so big, but he was built like a man and his head sat on his shoulders like a man's head without that gangly, craning look a kid's head has. He had been a high-school football hero and the fall before he had been the flashiest thing on the freshman team at State. He got his name in the papers because he was really good. He knew he was good. He knew he was the nuts, as you could tell from one look at his slick-skinned handsome brown face, with the jawbone working insolently and slow over a little piece of chewing gum and his blue eyes under half-lowered lids working insolently and slow over you, or the whole damned world. But that day when he was up in the front seat with Willie Stark, who was the Boss, I couldn't see his face. I remembered thinking his head, the shape and the way it was set on his shoulders, was just like his old man's head.

Mrs. Stark – Lucy Stark, the wife of the Boss – Tiny Duffy, and I were in the back seat – Lucy Stark between Tiny and me. It wasn't exactly a gay little gathering. The temperature didn't make for chitchat in the first place. In the second place, I was watching out for the hay wagons and gasoline trucks. In the third place, Duffy and Lucy Stark never were exactly chummy. So she sat between Duffy and me and gave herself to her thoughts. I reckon she had plenty to think about. For one thing, she could think about all that had happened since she was a girl teaching her first year in the school at Mason City and had married a red-faced and red-necked farm boy with big slow hands and a shock of dark brown hair coming down over his brow (you can look at the wedding picture which has been in the papers along with a thousand other pictures of Willie) and a look of dog-like devotion and wonder in his eyes when they fixed on her. She would have had a lot to think about as she sat in the hurtling Cadillac, for there had been a lot of changes.

We tooled down the street where the little one-time-white houses were, and hit the square. It was Saturday afternoon and the square was full of folks. The wagons and the crates were parked solid around the patch of grass roots in the middle of which stood the courthouse, a red-brick box, well weathered and needing paint, for it had been there since before the Civil War, with a little tower with a clock face on each side. On the second look you discovered that the clock faces weren't real. They were just painted on, and they all said five o'clock and not eight-seventeen the way those big painted watches in front of third-string jewelry stores used to. We eased into the ruck of folks come in to do their trading, and Sugar-Boy leaned on his horn, and his head twitched, and he said, "B-b-b-b-as-tuds," and the spit flew.

We pulled up in front of the drugstore, and the kid Tom got out and then the Boss, before Sugar-Boy could get around to the door. I got out and helped out Lucy Stark, who came up from the depths of heat and meditation long enough to say, "Thank you." She stood there on the pavement a second, touching her skirt into place around her hips, which had a little more beam on them than no doubt had been the case when she won the heart of Willie Stark, the farm boy.

Mr. Duffy debouched massively from the Cadillac, and we all entered the drugstore, the Boss holding the door open so Lucy Stark could go in and then following her, and the rest of us trailing in. There were a good many folks in the store, men in overalls lined up along the soda fountain, and women hanging around the counters where the junk and glory was, and kids hanging on skirts with one hand and clutching ice-cream cones with the other and staring out over their own wet noses at the world of men from eyes which resembled painted china marbles. The Boss just stood modestly back of the gang of customers at the soda fountain, with his hat in his hand and the damp hair hanging down over his forehead. He stood that way a minute maybe, and then one of the girls ladling up ice cream happened to see him, and got a look on her face as though her garter belt had busted in church, and dropped her ice-cream scoop, and headed for the back of the store with her hips pumping hell-for-leather under the lettuce-green smock.

Then a second later a little bald-headed fellow wearing a white coat which ought to have been in the week's wash came plunging through the crowd from the back of the store, waving his hand and bumping the customers and yelling, "It's Willie!" The fellow ran up to the Boss, and the Boss took a couple of steps to meet him, and the fellow with the white coat grabbed Willie's hand as though he were drowning. He didn't shake Willie's hand, not by ordinary standards. He just hung on to it and twitched all over and gargled the sacred syllables of *Willie*. Then, when the attack had passed, he turned to the crowd, which was ringing around at a polite distance and staring, and announced, "My God, folks, it's Willie!"

The remark was superfluous. One look at the faces rallied around and you knew that if any citizen over the age of three didn't know that the strong-set man standing there in the Palm Beach suit was Willie Stark, that citizen has a half-wit. In the first place, all he would have to do would be to life his eyes to the big picture high up there above the soda fountain, a picture about six times life size, which showed the same face, the big eyes, which in the picture had the suggestion of a sleepy and inward look (the eyes of the man in the Palm Beach suit didn't have that look now, but I've seen it), the pouches under the eyes and the jowls beginning to sag off, and the meaty lips, which didn't sag but if you looked close were laid one on top of the other like a couple of bricks, and the tousle of hair hanging down on the not very high squarish forehead. Under the picture was the legend: *My study is the heart of the people.* In quotations marks, and signed, *Willie Stark*. I had seen that picture in a thousand places, pool halls to palaces.

Somebody back in the crowd yelled, "Hi, Willie!" The Boss lifted his right hand and waved in acknowledgment to the unknown admirer. Then the Boss spied a fellow at the far end of the soda fountain, a tall, gaunt-shanked, malarial, leather-faced side of jerked venison, wearing jean pants and a brace of mustaches hanging off the kind of face you see in photographs of General Forrest's cavalrymen, and the Boss started toward him and put out his hand. Old Leather-Face didn't show. Maybe he shuffled one of his broken brogans on the tiles, and his Adam's apple jerked once or twice, and the eyes were watchful out of that face which resembled the seat of an old saddle left out in the weather, but when the Boss got close, his hand came up from the elbow, as though it didn't belong to Old Leather-Face but was operating on its own, and the Boss took it.

"How you making it, Malaciah?" the Boss asked.

The Adam's apple worked a couple of times, and the Boss shook the hand which was hanging out there in the air as if it didn't belong to anybody, and Old Leather-Face said, "We's grabblen."

"How's your boy?" the Boss asked.

"Ain't doen so good," Old Leather-Face allowed.

"Sick?"

"Naw," Old Leather-Face allowed, "jail."

"My God," the Boss said, "what they doing round here, putting good boys in jail?"

"He's a good boy," Old Leather-Face allowed. "Hit wuz a fahr fight, but he had a lettle bad luck."

"Huh?"

"Hit wuz fahr and squahr, but he had a lettle bad luck. He stobbed the feller and he died."

"Tough tiddy," the Boss said. Then: "Tried yet?"

"Not yit."

"Tough tiddy," the Boss said.

"I ain't complainen," Old Leather-Face said. "Hit wuz fit fahr and squahr."

"Glad to seen you," the Boss said. "Tell your boy to keep his tail over the dashboard."

"He ain't complainen," Old-Leather-Face said.

The Boss started to turn away to the rest of us who after a hundred miles in the dazzle were looking at that soda fountain as though it were a mirage, but Old Leather-Face said, "Willie."

"Huh?" the Boss answered.

"Yore pitcher," Old Leather-Face allowed, and jerked his head creakily toward the six-times-life-size photograph over the soda fountain. "Yore pitcher," he said, "hit don't do you no credit, Willie."

"Hell, no," the Boss said, studying the picture, cocking his head to one side and squinting at it, "but I was porely when they took it. I was like I'd had the cholera morbus. Get in there busting some sense into that Legislature, and it leaves a man worse'n the summer complaint."

"Git in thar and bust 'em, Willie!" somebody yelled from back in the crowd, which was thickening out now, for folks were trying to get in from the street.

"I'll bust 'em," Willie said, and turned around to the little man with the white coat. "Give us some cokes, Doc," he said, "for God's sake."

It looked as if Doc would have heart failure getting around to the other side of the soda fountain. The tail of that white coat was flat on the air behind him when he switched the corner and started clawing past the couple of girls in the lettuce-green smocks so he could do the drawing. He got the first one set up, and passed it to the Boss, who handed it to his wife. Then he started drawing the next one, and kept on saying, "It's on the house, Willie, it's on the house." The Boss took that one himself, and Doc kept on drawing them and saying, "It's on the house, Willie, it's on the house." He kept on drawing them till he got about five too many.

By that time folks were packed outside the door solid to the middle of the street. Faces were pressed up against the screen door, the way you do when you try to see through a screen into a dim room. Outside, they kept yelling, "Speech, Willie, speech!"

"My God," the Boss said, in the direction of Doc, who was hanging on to one of the nickel-plated spouts of the fountain and watching every drop of the coke go down the Boss's gullet. "My God," the Boss said. "I didn't come here to make a speech. I came here to go out and see my pappy."

"Speech, Willie, speech!" they were yelling out there.

The boss set his little glass on the marble.

"It's on the house," Doc uttered croakingly with what strength was left in him after the rapture.

"Thanks, Doc," the Boss said. He turned away to head toward the door, then looked back. "You better get back in here and sell a lot of aspirin, Doc," he said, "to make up for the charity."

Then he plowed out the door, and the crowd fell back, and we tailed after him.

Mr. Duffy stepped up beside the Boss and asked him was he going to make a speech, but the Boss didn't even look at him. He kept walking slow and steady right across the street into the crowd, as though the crowd hadn't been there. The red, long faces with the eyes in them watching like something wary and wild and watchful in a thicket fell back, and there wasn't a sound. The crowd creamed back from his passage, and we followed in his wake, all of us who had been in the Cadillac, and the others who had been in the second car. Then the crowd closed behind.

1946

Lyle Saxon

Gumbo Ya Ya Superstitions

Sickness

(Medicines, Applications, and Charms to Cure and Prevent)

ASTHMA

A charm (or fetish) to cure asthma is made of some of the victim's hair tied up in red flannel, which is then placed in a crack in the floor.

Medicine: Make a tea of the root of the wild plum cut from the sunrise side. Cut and boil two hours in an iron pot. Give two tablespoons three times daily.

Folk practices: Wearing a muskrat skin, fur side in, on the chest. Smoking jimson weed.

BACKACHE

Charm: Make nine knots in a tarred rope and tie it around your waist.—Mrs. A. Antony, 718½ Orleans Street.

Charm: Belt of snakeskin.

BEE STING

Apply seven different kinds of leaves to a bee sting.—Mrs. Josephine Fouchi.

BITES

For insect bits: Soak whole balsam apples in whiskey. Apply apple skin.

Charm for snakebite: If bitten near water, beat him to the water and dip the part bitten. That will remove the poison and the snake will die instead of you.—Mrs. C. Andry, 1947 N. Johnson Street.

Medicine for snakebite: The juice of plantain banana leaves every hour in doses of one teaspoonful, and the mashed leaves applied to the wound.—Raoul.

Charm: Cut open a black hen, and while she is still jumping hold her over the bite. When the chicken has stopped fluttering the poison will be gone.—Mrs. Davis, 2412 Sixth Street.

Charm: Have a snake doctor suck the bite.

Treatment: Burn a reed and let the smoke rise into the bite.

BLADDER

Feed roasted rat to a bed-wetter.—Vance Balthazar, Isle Breville.

Feeding fried rat to a person with a weak bladder will stop bed-wetting.—Mrs. W. Nicholas, 1979 Miro Street.

Feed parched pumpkin seeds with salt for bed-wetting.

BLEEDING

There is a secret verse in the Book Ezekiel which, if read, will stop bleeding.—Jack Penton, 1508 St. Charles Street.

BLINDNESS

To prevent—Charm: Pierce ears and wear earrings.—Mrs. Truseh.

Medication: infusion of parsley roots with pinch of alum.—Mrs. S. James, 1951 Johnson Street.

BLOOD *(Poor or Bad)*

Medicine: "Jack Vine tea is the best blood purify you can get. . . . We allus made tea out of it when we would be in the swamps."—Verise Brown.

Medicine: For bad blood, a handful of gum moss, thimbleful of anise seed, handful of corn shucks, rain water. Steep and take every morning.—Clorie Turner, 1467 Sere Street.

BOILS

Application: A poultice of catnip leaves for chigger boils, or flea boils. Or, an infusion of equal parts of sumac leaves, sage, and swamplily roots boiled down. Add a cup of lard to the strained infusion and boil until the water is out, and use the salve.

Application for ordinary boils: Poultice of mashed jimson weed or mashed elderberry leaves.

Or: Pounded okra blossoms and sugar will bring a boil to a head.—Katherine Hill, 638 Lafayette Street.

To draw a "rising" to a head, or draw festering splinters out, beat the skin of the tail of a 'possum and put sugar on it, and apply.—Bill Harris, Spring Creek.

BOWLEGS
Treatment (said to cure): Wipe the legs of child with a greasy towel every day.—Theresa Martin, 2318 Jackson Avenue.

BROKEN LIMBS
Treatment: Wrap in clay mud.—Mrs. O. Crowden, 1954 Johnson Street.

BURNS
Cajun treatment: If you burn your finger while lighting a cigarette, stick it quick behind your ear.

Charm for burns: Read the "fire passages" in the Bible. Those who know these passages never reveal them till death, for to do so would cause them to lose the power.—Bill Harris, Spring Creek.

CHILLS AND FEVER
Charm: Squeeze a frog to death in the hand.—Katherine Hill, 638 LaFayette Street, Baton Rouge.

Charm: Go toward the bed as if to get into it, but get under instead.

Medicine: Tea of L'Herbe Cabri (coatgrass).

COLDS, CROUP
Medicine (Cajun): Red wine in which a melted tallow candle has been mixed.—Mrs. Oscar Scott, Natchitoches.

Medicine: Mamou tea made with the beans or the roots. Also crapeau (toadgrass) tea.

Treatment for pleural complications: Mare's milk rubbed on the back of the neck will cure pleurisy.—Vance Balthazar, Isle Breville.

Medicine for croup: Powdered birdeye vine added to milk.—Lizzie Chandler.

Charm to prevent: Wear a dime and some salt in the heel of your shoe.

COLIC *(baby)*
Medicine: Chicken gizzard tea. Or catnip tea.

Charm (fetish): A string with nine knots in it worn around the waist until it rots off.

Ceremony with incantation: Say your prayers and turn the baby head down and heels up three times an hour.—Mrs. S. C. Douglas, 2010 St. Thomas Street.

CONSTIPATION
Medicine: "Ole missus useter give us Blue Mass Pills when we needed medicine. It sho did make us sick. We had to get sick to get well, ole missus said."—Rebecca Fletcher.

CORNS
Let a snail crawl across your toes.

CRAMPS *(in legs, in stomach)*
Charm (reptile fetish) for cramps in legs: An eel skin with nine knots tied in it worn around the leg.—Vance Balthazar.

Medicine for cramps in stomach: A tea of snake root.—J. Eccles, 710 Bourbon Street.

CUTS
Incantation to prevent bleeding and infection: Recite a verse from the Bible.—Jack Penton, 1508 St. Charles Street.

Application: Fat meat, garlic, and live cockroaches bound on.

DIABETES

Medicine: Instead of water, drink, for three months, tea made of boiled huckleberry leaves.

DIARRHEA

Medicine: Oakleaf tea.

DROPSY

Medicine: Tablespoon of the juice of elder sprouts three times a day until cured.—Albert Dupont, Houma.

EARACHE

Medicine: Pinch the head off a sowbug and drop the drop of blood you will find into the ear. You won't have earache again.—Mrs. Bill Harris, Spring Creek.

Medication: The blood of a live roach, tablespoon of hot water, pod of red pepper, three grains of sugar. Heat and mix with lard. Put on cotton and insert in ear.—Mrs. U. Lipinay, 2522 St. Anthony.

ERYSIPELAS

Application: Poultice of raw cranberries.

Application: Blood from the ear and tail of a horse. If a very bad case, more than one application will be necessary.

FAINTING

Treatment: Let the patient smell his left shoe. Rub his right hand.—E. Blanchard, 1920 Sixth Street.

FEVERS

Chinaberries strung and placed about the baby's neck will absorb and prevent fever.—Mr. and Mrs. J. C. Sanders, Spring Creek.

For a high fever: Obtain a pigeon which has never flown out of the cage, cut him open and lay him on the "mole" of the patient's head. The fresh blood of the pigeon will draw the fever.—Mrs. W. Nicholas, N. Miro Street.

For fever, wrap the head completely in leaves from the Palma Christi (castor oil plant).—Mrs. A. Barry, 2234 Feliciana Street.

"St. Jacob's quinine grows mos' everywhere, an' that's good for fevers."—Gracie Stafford.

To exorcise yellow fever: Place about two inches of water in a tub. Stand an axe head on its nose in the water and balance three black horsehairs and a white one on the edge of the axe. Sprinkle a small amount of red pepper on the horsehairs and carefully push the tub under the bed—the contents must not be disturbed. Then scatter a handful of corn meal in the form of a cross in front of the patient's bed and wet this cross thoroughly with rum made from molasses. Then repeat the following incantation (voodoo):

"Heru mande, heru mande, heru mande.
Tigli li papa.
Do se dan godo
Ah Tingonai ye!"

GOITER
Charm: Touch a dead person, then lay the hand on the goiter.

HAIR
To make it grow, cut off a piece on Good Friday and bury it.

HAY FEVER
Medicine: Tea of goldenrod roots.

HEADACHE
Charm (fetish): A string with nine knots in it hung around the neck will cure.—Mary Rachel, Isle Breville.

Charm: Rattles of a rattlesnake worn in the hatband and *back*. Wear them for twelve months and you will never have another headache.—Mr. and Mrs. Bill Harris, Spring Creek.

Wrap the head in the leaves of the Palm de Christi (castor oil plant).

HEART TROUBLE
Charm (fetish): Two nutmegs worn on a string about the neck until the string breaks and the nutmegs fall off.

HICCOUGHS

Charm: Look directly at the point of a knife blade. This will also cure sneezing.–Rev. E. D. Billoups, 318 Eve Street, Baton Rouge.

INDIGESTION

Eat sand and charcoal.

Make a tea of the inside skin of a chicken gizzard.

KIDNEY TROUBLE

An infusion of swamp-lily root should be used as drinking water. Crush half a cup of the root and steep in a quart of water.

LOCKJAW

"Tea made out of roaches is good for lockjaw. My maw give my brother one spoon and his jaws came unlocked. He ain't never had dat anymore."–Wilkinson Jones.

Medicine: A strong tea of chicken manure taken while hot.–Miss M. Reiss, 2534 Bourbon Street.

If roach tea does not bring relief to a lockjaw sufferer, mash up live roaches and make him eat them.

MALARIA

Medicine: A tea of blackjack vine.

Charm: Put a piece of nightshade in a pan under the middle of your bed. On the tenth day pick it up, turn your back to the east, and throw it over your right shoulder. Don't look back at it.

MATERNITY

To exorcise after-pains: Cross an axe and a hatchet under the bed and place a jar of water on the dresser.

The red thread attached to egg yolks is fed to young mothers to give them strength.

Turn the child's navel cord to the left to keep it from wetting the bed.–Henrietta Lewis.

Measure an undernourished child from neck to toes with a woolen string. Burn the string and feed the ashes to the child.–Henrietta Lewis.

When a baby has been cross and fretful for several nights, it is a sign that an evil person or a witch has been sucking at its breasts. (The sticky ooze from an infant's breasts is called witch's milk.) To keep the evil person from returning, stand a broom at the front door.–Mrs. A. Antony, 718½ Orleans Street.

MEASLES

Medicine: Shuck tea and sheep pills (dung) are widely employed.– Wilkinson Jones.

Boiled garfish with red peppers.

MUMPS

To exorcise: Make a cross on each side of the throat with lard and retrace with soot from the chimney.

Wrap a snake skin next to the face.

NERVOUSNESS

A piece of valerian root in the pillow will quiet nerves.

NOSEBLEED

To stop it, place a tight coral necklace about the neck. Or a chain of silk.

OVERHEATED BLOOD

Medicine: A strong infusion of cactus leaves in water.

Medicine to prevent babies from having hives: Catnip tea.

PNEUMONIA

Medicine: A strong tea of the roots of wild iris (pneumonia plant).

Application: Boil the hoofs of a pig until of the consistency of molasses and spread on the back and chest.

RASH

Charm: Rub on hair off a black cat's back.

Application: Three crushed oak buds.

Snake skin, raw flesh side next the skin.

RHEUMATISM

Apply: Rattlesnake oil; alligator fat, buzzard grease, worm oil or frog oil.

The Irish potato and buckeye are favorite charms.

Medicine: Fry a toad frog and a handful of red worms and feed to the sick person.–Victoria Boland, Houma.

RICKETS

Treatment: Wash the baby's legs in cow's milk.–Mrs. Regina, 2331 Allen Street.

RINGWORM

Application: The milk from fig trees.

SKIN BLEMISHES

Birthmarks will disappear if the newborn is fed a few drops of whatever caused the mark.

SMALLPOX

Strong black pepper tea. Let the tea stand one night before drinking.–Lizzie Chandler.

SORE THROAT

Tea made of dry dog manure.

Drink rabbit-track tea. One must find the trail and take up the tracks oneself.

Peeled prickly pear in water until the water is slimy. Drink the water.–Miss R. Page, 2510 Annette Street.

SORES

Application: Beat up mullein leaves and apply to old sores.

Years ago when children had sores on their heads the old folks would put tar caps on their heads.

A live frog, split, and applied to a cancerous sore, will effect a cure.

SPASMS

If a person has "spasms," pull his clothes off and burn them right away. He will quiet down.–Vance Balthazar.

Strip a child, burn his clothes, and give him two drops of beef gall.

SPRAINS

Favorite treatments are winding with snake skin or applying a piece of mud-dauber's nest mixed with vinegar.

STAMMERING

Make the child eat from the same dish as a little dog.

STIES AND SORE EYES

For sore eyes, take a rose and put it in a water glass and let it stand outside at night where the dew can fall on it. Before the sun rises, wipe your eyes with the dewy rose. Take the rose in and use it three times a day.–Miss I. Prude, 1917 Annette Street.

"When you get a sty, go to the cross-road and say: 'Sty, sty, leave my eye, and catch the first one who passes by.' It sho will leave."–Silas Spotfore.

STIFF NECK

Charm: "A very dirty dishrag stolen from a house unbeknownst to the occupants and wrapped about the afflicted one's neck will cure it."–Mrs. Blue, 2310 Bourbon Street.

STOMACH CRAMPS

Put a tub of water with stale bread under the bed, or a steel object under the pillow.–Henrietta Lewis.

Medicine: Tea of blackberry roots.

Make a fetish with ashes off the hearth sprinkled with salt and water and put in an old stocking. Place this on the stomach.–Ellen Mollett.

SUN PAIN

In the Delta country there is an affliction called sun pain, which the older people claim is peculiar to that section of the country. Sun pain is a periodic pain located at the back of the head. It grows and wanes with the sun's movements in the sky. To cure this, several remedies have been developed. One old man goes from door to door calling out, "Cure you sun pain!" He has little bottles of river water in which spiders' eggs have been placed. The user is directed to bathe his forehead with the water. Another cure is to bathe the forehead three times a day in a pan of river water, and when the sun goes down to throw the water toward it. In the most elaborate cure, the affected person must strip and seat himself in a tub of river water, facing toward the setting sun. Then a friend or relative stands behind him and dipping the hands into the water, passes the water first over the seated one's shoulders, then over the head in the form of a cross. When this is done, the pain leaves at sunset and never returns —Mrs. A. Antony, 718½ Orleans Street.

SUNSTROKE
Treatment: Tie a towel over the top of a glass of water; place glass upside down on patient's head and in a few minutes the water will boil. When it stops boiling, the patient is better.

SWEATS
For night sweats place a plan of water under the bed and the sweating will cease.–Laura Rochon, 2410 Conti Street.

TEETHING (CHARMS AND TEETHERS)
Swamp lily, dried, strung, placed around the child's neck.–Lizzie Chandler.

"Take crawfish, rub de chillune' teeth, will make them cut teeth easy."–Lindy Joseph, McDonoghville.

If baby is teething hard, let a dog kiss him in the mouth.

Put a hog's eye tooth on a string around the baby's neck (teether).

A necklace of alligator teeth (charm or teether).

To keep a teething baby from being sick, kill a rabbit and rub the child's gums with the warm brains.–Mrs. Bill Harris, Spring Creek.

Negro teether: A cow tooth, or a string of Jacob's Tears (a kind of seed).–Mrs. A. Antony, 718½ Orleans Street.

A necklace of eight vertebrae of the dog shark. (The dog shark is noted for large sharp fine teeth.)

THRUSH

A man who has never seen the father of the child may blow his breath in the baby's mouth. A letter written to such a one, giving the name and birth date of child, will be as effective. When the man reads the letter the thrash will be gone.

Rub the liver of a white dog in the child's mouth.

Rub inside of mouth with chicken manure.

Nine live sowbugs worn in a sack about the neck.

TOOTHACHE

Tie a garlic bag around the thumb.

Rub the gums with the bark or seed of a Prickly Ash (known on Pecan Island as the Toothache Tree), or insert some in the cavity.

TUBERCULOSIS

A dime, or copper wire worn around the ankle, will prevent.

Sea gum (a tarry solidified marsh ooze), mixed with grease and taken as well as applied by rubbing, is good for consumption.—Albert Dupont, Houma.

Alligator oil. Give daily. (An old woman, seeing that the dogs fed cracklings of alligator fat left a grease spot, where they slept, knew the oil was good.)—Mrs. A. Antony, 718½ Orleans Street.

An old woman once had a "vision," then made a medicine of cow manure and rain water for tuberculosis. It cured the tuberculosis.

TYPHOID

Bathe with a tea of peach leaves.

An aid in convalescence: Teaspoon of chimney soot (not stovepipe soot) steeped in a pint of water. Settle with a beaten egg, drink with sugar and cream three times daily.

"UNDERGROWTH" *(puniness)*

To make a stunted child grow, wipe the soles of his feet every day with an old dishrag.

To make him walk: Set him in the doorway and sweep his legs with a new broom.

VOMITING

Crush and steep peach tree leaves. Drink water slowly.

WARTS

Pass the affected part over a dead person.—Katherine Hill, 638 Lafayette Street, Baton Rouge.

Haydel and Reynold, wart curers of Old New Orleans, examined the growths, then told patient, if a man, to return with a rooster; if a woman, to bring a hen. When this was done, the wart disappeared.

WHOOPING COUGH

Urine and salt taken three times a day for three days.—Isaac Mahoney, Houma.

A Negro charm is to make the patient cough in the face of a catfish.

Have a blown horse breathe into the child's nostrils.—August Coxen, Schriever.

WORMS

Candy made from jimson weed and sugar.

Garlic mashed and put in milk, taken on a dark moon, will stop worms in kids.—Lindy Joseph, McDonoghville.

Tie garlic around neck to prevent.

WOUNDS AND POISONING

A tea of mashed roaches. Tablespoon every two hours.—Laura Jenkins, Hubbardville.

Smoke a wound made by a rusty nail with the fumes of burning woolen cloth or sugar.

MISCELLANEOUS CHARMS TO CURE OR PREVENT

To prevent poison ivy, wear metal on neck, arm, or leg. To stop nose-bleed, let the blood drop on a cross made of two matches. To cure sore throat, swallow a gold-colored bead. To prevent poisoning from snakebite, carry the tooth of the kind of snake to whose bite you may be exposed. Garlic and asafoetida placed around the neck in times of epidemic will make it immune. A remedy, if it is to do the most good, must be given without being asked for, and the recipient must not thank the giver.

1945

AUTHOR BIOGRAPHIES

Rumanian poet ANDREI CODRESCU makes his home in New Orleans, where he edits *Exquisite Corpse: A Journal of Letters and Life* and is a commentator for National Public Radio. Codrescu wrote his *first* autobiography at age 23: *The Life and Times of an Involuntary Genius.*

ANONYMOUS is, in fact, the chronicler of a 1699 Mississippi River expedition, ordered by the King of France with the aim of establishing a Louisiana colony. Our guide is slightly overzealous in his claim of discovering the river's mouth, as Hernando de Soto forged his way there in 1542.

WALKER PERCY never liked being called a Southern novelist, but it is hard to think of a writer with better paintings of the modern South than those in *The Moviegoer, The Last Gentleman, Love in the Ruins,* and *The Second Coming.* The psychiatrist-turned-novelist lived across Lake Pontchartrain in Covington, Louisiana, until his death in 1990.

Jazz legend LOUIS ARMSTRONG played his first horn in the Crescent City. His vivid recollections of growing up New Orleans–style were published in *Life* magazine in 1966.

New Orleans native ANNE RICE's string of best-selling, bayou-based novels include *Interview with a Vampire, The Vampire Lestat,* and *The Feast of All Saints.*

ZORA NEALE HURSTON's fiction depicts black life in the early-twentieth-century South. Her innovative, folklorish style paved the way for contemporary Southern writers such as Alice Walker and Toni Morrison. *Hoodoo* is from *Mules and Men.*

Editor, writer, and curmudgeon LAFCADIO HEARN contributed daily columns to the little-known New Orleans paper *The Item.* They are collected in *Creole Sketches.*

In the late 1960s, JOHN KENNEDY TOOLE's mother forced Walker Percy to read a manuscript that her son had written just before he took his life. Percy has been entranced—as have many since—by the hefty Don Quixote, Ignatius J. Reilly, and his French Quarter jaunts in *A Confederacy of Dunces*.

Naturalist and author JOHN JAMES AUDUBON visited New Orleans in 1821. His impressions of the city are collected in *Journal of John James Audubon*.

TENNESSEE WILLIAMS's haunting dramas include *Vieux Carré, A Streetcar Named Desire, Cat on a Hot Tin Roof,* and *The Glass Menagerie*. Many of his plays are set in New Orleans, where he lived throughout the 1940s.

Socialite/novelist TRUMAN CAPOTE was born in New Orleans and penned several stories about his hometown, the most acidic of which are found in *Music for Chameleons*.

WILLIAM THACKERAY's Southern exuberations are found in his 1856 narration of Mr. Roundabout's escapades, *The Roundabout Papers*.

Slightly hysterical historian M. DUMONT's chronicles of eighteenth-century New Orleans were gathered in the 1853 anthology *Historical Collections of Louisiana*.

ISHMAEL REED lives in Oakland but often writes about the South. His numerous novels and essays include *The Last Days of Louisiana Red, Shrovetide in New Orleans,* and *Mumbo Jumbo*.

WILLIAM FAULKNER, author of such modern classics as *The Sound and the Fury* and *As I Lay Dying,* quit his postmaster job and moved to New Orleans in 1924. There he met Sherwood Anderson and began con-centrating solely on writing, contributing regularly to Anderson's *Double Dealer* magazine. This excerpt is from *Absalom, Absalom!,* one of Faulkner's many stories and novels set in New Orleans.

ELLEN GILCHRIST's novels and stories are generally set in the South and include *Victory Over Japan, The Annunciation,* and *In the Land of Dreamy Dreams.*

In his ceaseless travels, MARK TWAIN, a.k.a. Samuel Clemens, visited New Orleans several times. He liked the food and people, but found the city's only real architecture to be its cemeteries. *Southern Sports* is from *Life on the Mississippi.*

Poet CARL SANDBURG's biography *Abraham Lincoln: The Prairie Years* traced young Abe's unusual journey down the Mississippi.

New Orleans native KATE CHOPIN's tales of the turn-of-the-century South are found in *The Awakening* and *The Complete Works.*

JOHN DOS PASSOS's account of a Mardi Gras road trip, originally a magazine article, is found in slightly different form in his 1930 novel, *The 42nd Parallel.*

On a visit to New Orleans, poet WALT WHITMAN contributed "Three New Orleans Sketches" to a local paper, *The Daily Crescent,* in 1848.

Poet and novelist ROBERT PENN WARREN was the United States' first Poet Laureate. *All the King's Men,* his thinly veiled description of the notorious Huey Long, stands as a classic of modern literature.

LYLE SAXON's hearty *Gumbo Ya Ya* was assembled for the Works Project Administration in 1945. It's now considered the classic New Orleans handbook of folklore, ghost stories, and magic potions.

CREDITS